IMPRESSIONS

IMPRESSIONS

Antal Kovács

ATHENA PRESS
LONDON

ISBN 1 84401 679 X

First Published 2006 by
ATHENA PRESS
Queen's House, 2 Holly Road
Twickenham TW1 4EG
United Kingdom

Printed for Athena Press

Chapter One

Robyn Hawthorne did not believe in mixing business with pleasure, but she made exceptions. David Swaab was one of them. Nature had given him that little bit extra; he was the darling of the Sydney 'in' set, and very popular with women in the know. David also happened to be one of the most successful film directors in Australia.

Robyn and David had spent the night together, and now it was seven in the morning. The bright light of the rising sun pierced through the venetian blind and made little blue patterns on the white sheets. Their two bodies were intertwined in bed, heaving and turning in soft focus, a shifting whirlpool of shade and colour. Suddenly it was all over. David fell back into the silk sheets as Robyn slipped out of bed and went to the bathroom.

Without her contact lenses she was almost blind. The bedroom, the flat, and the spectacular harbour view were just a blurred mess for her. Then she put her contact lenses in, and looked at the full-length bathroom mirror.

'My God, you're beautiful,' she said, then turned on the radio as she stepped into the shower. Robyn was happy. The world was a wonderful place, and David was the greatest lover in the universe. She stretched in the shower, flexing her muscles, and a feeling of satisfied tiredness came over her. She turned the tap sideways, and the icy cold water made her skin tingle. It was great to be alive.

When Robyn returned to the bedroom she found David doing up the zip of his jeans. He looked very serious, concentrating on getting dressed. His long hair was reminiscent of a bygone age. Though his clothes were up with the latest fashion, and his designer jewellery was positively of the future, David was an ageing hippie, shop-soiled and outdated. What the hell, thought Robyn. I *need* the bastard...

She turned to him with a broad smile. 'Do you want some breakfast, David?'

'No thanks – I should have left hours ago. I'm shooting this commercial in Dubbo.'

'What commercial?'

'Oh, just a piece of shit, really.'

David was still struggling with his zip as Robyn stepped up to him and kissed him on the lips.

'Cut it out, Robyn!'

'What's the hurry?'

'I'm sorry, I didn't mean it like that.'

'It's OK. I'll see you tonight.'

'I can't make it tonight, sorry.'

'OK – give me a call when you've got some time.'

'That's not what I meant. Honest, Robyn.'

'Now don't make it worse! What about the script?'

'It's not for me, Robyn. I'm sorry.'

'What's wrong with it?'

'Everything. The man's not even literate.'

'What does that mean?'

'He can't write.'

'But it's a great story, David,' said Robyn with a touch of desperation. 'He may not be a professor of literature, but…'

'Pity… I must go.'

'And what am I going to tell Ericson?'

'Tell him I can't make up my mind,' he said and kissed Robyn on the cheek. 'I'll call you soon.'

She grabbed David by the crotch of his designer jeans. It was an impulsive gesture, but she felt she had to do something. She hated being rejected, even by a piece of shit like David.

'You'd better, or I'll cut your balls off!' She smiled and let him go.

Robyn went back to the bathroom. She listened to some rubbish on the radio as she moved around the flat, but did not really take in any of the programme. Her good mood had deserted her. She was hoping that David would like the script. Without a name director she could not get it off the ground, and the project had been in development for six months.

I'll think of something, she told herself as she put on the kettle. That was the start of her morning routine. Living alone, she was used to looking after herself, and she did not have to think about what she was doing. She managed to get dressed, read the morning paper, have breakfast, and collect her files needed for the day all in one gloriously choreographed movement. Then something caught her attention on the early morning chat show. It was the Terry Robinson Show. Robyn hated it, but listened to it every morning, like half a million other people in Sydney.

Dr Malcolm Reid was the guest. He had been something of a celebrity all week on account of his appointment to the Chair of English Literature at Leichhardt University. The media picked up the story, and the public lapped it up. Pommy-bashing has always been an Australian pastime, and Terry Robinson was the most notorious Pommy-basher in Sydney. If ever there was a redneck, Terry Robinson was it. Everybody detested him in Australia, and his morning chat show had topped the ratings for years. Sipping her coffee, Robyn sat out on the balcony listening to the radio.

'Nobody needs reminding that Malcolm here has been hitting the headlines, but just in case there's somebody out there who hasn't read the papers,' Terry Robinson went on, 'Malcolm Reid is the new lecturer in English Literature at Leichhardt. He is an expert on experimental theatre, new media and the Literature of the Absurd – whatever that is...'

Terry Robinson paused for the expected reaction from his listeners. He was a professional. Nobody could take that away from him; even Robyn responded.

'Go on, Terry, wade into him! Who needs literature anyway? Absurd or otherwise.'

Malcolm said nothing.

Terry carried on. 'I've got your book here, Malcolm. *The Refuse Collection*. It says on the cover that you were born in 1966 – is that correct? You're a bit long in the tooth...'

'Not for a university appointment. But you're right. I was born in 1966, on the day that André Breton died. To the second.'

'And is that significant?'

'It was – for my mother and all her friends.'

'Why? Who is this Andrew Breton?'

'Well, you must be having me on, Terry. Everybody knows who André Breton was.'

'Terry doesn't, and he's not kidding you, mate,' said Robyn to the radio.

'I don't,' said Terry.

'I told you!' shouted Robyn triumphantly.

'He was surrealism himself,' explained Malcolm wearily. 'When he died, surrealism died.'

'So, how about your mother?'

'She was a surrealist painter. She was a member of the group undergoing a process of occultation...'

'And what's that?' interrupted Terry.

'It was Breton's idea. He wanted the movement to become a secret society.'

'Why the secrecy?'

'The surrealists started to dabble in magic and the occult, when they got bored of politics. They were keen on Celtic iconography when my mother visited their exhibition in Paris, *Perennité de l'Art gaulois*. That was in 1955. My mother has never been the same after that. She took to the hills in Wales with a group of dedicated followers of Breton and painted nothing but Celtic icons.'

'Fine, but what about the timing of your birth?'

'They thought it was an important sign, and I was brought up like a surrealist Buddha. That can confuse a child.'

'That makes you almost forty years old.'

'Yes.'

'That's a little old for a young professor, isn't it?'

'You should ask my employers. They think I am the right man, and I agree with them. I know that I'll be a tremendous success.'

'You're modest, too!'

'You think so? That's kind of you, Terry.'

'I'm reading the blurb on your book. Educated at St Paul's at Brook Green. A Levels at fifteen. St John's College, Oxford, at seventeen, and a First in English at twenty. Lecturer at twenty-two at Christ Church, Oxford. Then editor of *La Poubelle*, a Gagaist magazine. What on earth is Gaga?'

'A bit like Dada, but spelt differently.'

'Is that a joke, mate? I'll let that pass, Malcolm, but controversy follows you wherever you go.'

'I'm getting used to it.'

'And enjoying every minute of it.'

'I haven't got much choice, Terry. I am controversy personified. Scandal goes a long way back in my family. My grandmother was Annabelle Fryern and my grandfather, Morgan Courtenay-Marshall, the last of the Bloomsbury Set to scandalise England.'

'I've never heard of them, Malcolm.'

'Celebrated writers, Terry. The darlings of Bloomsbury...'

'Is this one of your Gaga jokes?'

'It's all for real, Terry. You could say I have a scandalous, but unquestionable literary pedigree.'

'Wasn't that Courtenay-Marshall a queer?'

'Well done, Terry!' Robyn laughed at the radio.

'Homosexual, yes; queer, no,' said Malcolm.

'I find all this hard to believe.'

'*You* find it hard, Terry? How do you think I felt when my mother told me who my grandparents were?'

'I don't know. Tell us.'

'It was a shock beyond belief.'

'But you got over it?'

'Yes, I got over it.'

'Back to the book, Malcolm. *The Refuse Collection* is a selection of your poems – is that correct?'

'Yes, that's correct.'

'It's just a load of rubbish, isn't it?'

'Nice one, Terry,' said Robyn as she finished her coffee. 'You've missed calling him a Pommy bastard.'

She looked out over the harbour. It was a glorious morning with the sun glaring from a dark blue sky. The ferries departing from Circular Quay looked like toy boats amongst the butterflies of sailing boats. There was heavy traffic on Harbour Bridge, as always. Robyn went inside, picked up a couple of files from her desk, a handful of scripts, and her black leather briefcase, still listening to the interview.

'But what's it all about?' asked Terry. 'It's just a big con, isn't it?'

'No. It's no con. If you count the morphemes—'

'Hold on, hold on…' interrupted Terry, 'what are those?'

'Let me put it another way. If you divide the number of words in *The Refuse Collection* by the purchase price, you'll find that the reader is getting excellent value for his money.'

'And what kind of literary criticism is that?'

'Loosely speaking, Structuralist.'

'Follow that, as they say,' said Terry uneasily. 'We'll be back after this short message.'

As the commercial jingle took over Robyn turned off her radio and picked up her telephone.

'It's me, Carol. I'm going to be twenty minutes late. See if you can get me a copy of a book by Malcolm Reid … *The Refuse Collection* … Right, see you.'

★

The radio studio was a dark place; a cold and inhospitable labyrinth of glass partitions and plastic-lined cubicles. Little flashing lights were reflected everywhere on the hard surfaces, but they lacked magic – the place felt like a mortuary. Shirt-sleeved engineers moved about like zombies, dressed for outside, their bronzed flesh came out in goose pimples, because the air conditioning was overdone, like everywhere else in Sydney.

There was silence while Terry Robinson played the commercials reel. He stared at Malcolm with undisguised hostility. Terry did not care much for his celebrity guests, and showed it.

Malcolm stared back at him. He did not care much for Terry either. He felt light-headed and he could not take anything seriously. He had been in Australia for over three weeks now; long enough to sleep off any jet lag, but he still felt odd; nothing seemed real, it was all surface without any substance.

Terry Robinson was real enough, though. He wore a light-weight, grey Terylene suit, a crumpled, off-white acrylic shirt, and a nylon tie with every colour of the rainbow on it. He was tall and fat, and had the kind of body that no clothes could ever fit. His face was rough and crude; irregular with mean, piggy eyes. He was a peasant, a yob and a redneck; and from the look on his face, he was proud of it.

What am I doing here? mused Malcolm, but before he could answer himself Terry Robinson interrupted his thoughts.

'Welcome back,' he sneered into the microphone. 'I am Terry Robinson and my celebrity guest is, er, Dr Malcolm Reid. We were talking about the Literature of the Absurd. Right, Malcolm, what is the Literature of the Absurd?'

If I told you, Terry, you wouldn't understand it; and you don't give a shit anyhow, thought Malcolm; but he said, 'It's a reflection on the human condition. Modern writers consider the human form of existence to be absurd. They believe that it can only be represented in art forms which are themselves absurd. Intellectuals used to think that man was a rational creature, living in a society with an orderly structure, governed by universal laws of an intelligible world. Clearly, this is not so...'

'Says who?'

'Well, take a look around you!'

'The world seems rational to me.'

'Then you won't like the Literature of the Absurd.'

'You're too right, mate!'

Malcolm looked up during the momentary pause. Terry's face turned red with anger as he glared back at Malcolm; sweat poured down his brow in spite of the freezing cold air conditioning. Malcolm realised that for Terry it was not a game. He meant it all.

'Why should I like it?'

'That, I cannot answer,' said Malcolm calmly. 'You can do as you like. There's no compulsion.'

'And do people like the Absurd?'

'*The Refuse Collection* sold out the first week of its publication. It went into four reprints... that's not bad for a joke.'

'I don't see the joke.'

'Because you think the world is normal. As I see it, we come from nothing, do nothing of worth, and go nowhere. That is funny. That is the joke. That's what *The Refuse Collection* is about.'

'But nothing makes sense in your book.'

'Exactly.'

'I want to know how you got this job, Malcolm. We've got enough weirdos in Aussie. Why import you?'

'There you are, you've found something absurd at last.'

11

'As a taxpayer, I'd like to know what you are going to teach to our young Australians.'

'You'll have to enrol, Terry, and you'll find out. Who knows, you may benefit from the experience.'

'Now, that's funny, Malcolm, really funny and absurd,' said Terry Robinson; but he was not laughing; he was staring at Malcolm with burning hate in his eyes.

Chapter Two

Malcolm was a little drunk. He was plied with drinks all day as he did the celebrity run of television, radio and newspaper interviews. He even managed to spend a couple of hours at the university. It was good news for them, as the university hadn't had so much publicity for ages. All the same, Malcolm was weary of all the media attention; but the dean assured him that he would be left in peace, eventually. Malcolm was not entirely convinced.

It was late in the evening. Malcolm had no idea where he was, or how he got there and why. The place was an upmarket art gallery in fashionable Paddington. The rooms were packed with Sydney's influential and beautiful people. It was a reception, the opening of an exhibition; but thankfully, there was no sign of the media. Only the very rich were invited.

Malcolm enjoyed the warm hubbub of humanity. He stood in a corner of the room and watched smartly dressed waiters rush about with champagne and trays of masterfully crafted canapés. All the women were glamorous; all the men looked lean, sunburnt and athletic. There was an air of open sensuality about the place.

Malcolm was happy with life as he took another glass of champagne. He observed the party discreetly. On the walls hung a collection of Impressionist watercolours, vaguely familiar, but he could not place the painter. Everything in sight commanded a telephone number price tag, but nobody seemed to be interested in the paintings. The people present were there to be seen; they were only interested in each other.

He was aware that the women were eyeing him, but he was used to that. His feeling of disorientation was still with him; he half expected that if he pinched himself he would find himself in a Soho wine bar, but before he could try the experiment, his musing was interrupted by the arrival of Paul McDonald.

'Hello, I'm Paul,' he said in a fruity English voice that sounded very out of place. 'I run the gallery.'

'Malcolm Reid,' said Malcolm as they shook hands.

'I know who you are. Let me show you around.'

He took Malcolm by the arm and ushered him around the room. McDonald was a gentleman – every inch. He was impeccably dressed in a Savile Row suit, and moved with the elegance of the successful.

'All the pictures in this room are by John Peter Russell,' he said with a touch of pride.

Malcolm had no idea who John Peter Russell was, but he was under the impression that he should know.

'He reminds me of an early Matisse,' said Malcolm.

McDonald's eyes lit up in recognition of a fellow connoisseur.

'That's not surprising. It was Russell who introduced the young Matisse to Impressionism. They painted together in Brittany,' said McDonald as he opened his catalogue at the appropriate page.

'There's a biography of Russell in your catalogue. He was a colourful character, Russell. Spent most of his life in Europe. He married Rodin's favourite model, Marianna Mattiocco. His best friends were Monet, Toulouse-Lautrec, van Gogh…'

'OK, OK, I get the picture.'

Ignoring the interruption, McDonald took two full glasses of champagne from the tray of a passing waiter, handed one to Malcolm, and carried on talking.

'Seriously, not many people know about John Peter Russell, but I think he is one of the best.'

'I believe you,' replied Malcolm as he took a closer look at one of the paintings.

'I'm telling you, he's the forgotten Impressionist. That's why these watercolours will go for five-figure sums. You wouldn't get a Matisse for that.'

'I know,' said Malcolm with a smile. 'Here you can get an Impressionist bargain. As good as a Matisse, but at a fraction of the price on account of being down under and slightly forgotten.'

'You can take the piss, but Russell was a great painter…'

'Do you have any work by contemporary artists?'

'No. I prefer them dead,' said McDonald only half joking.

'They are too much trouble alive. Anyhow, there's more satisfaction in nineteenth-century paintings.'

'And presumably more money.'

Robyn was talking to Philippa Penders. Gallery openings were not her normal form of socialising, but she was working on a film project about John Peter Russell. Philippa was a good friend, much older than Robyn, but still staggeringly beautiful. She wore an expensive dress from Paris. Her only piece of jewellery was a diamond necklace that must have cost a fortune, but everything about Philippa said class. She also happened to be a very heavy drinker. Holding a glass in her hand, she was busy talking to Robyn.

'It was a ghastly party. The food was dreadful and the men were boring. I couldn't wait to get away. Are you listening to me?'

'Uhum… Boring party, Philippa. I've heard you. Who's that gorgeous-looking man with Mac?'

Philippa had to stand on tiptoe to see, and she almost spilt her champagne.

'My God, you're subtle, Philippa,' said Robyn.

'Sorry. Couldn't see.'

'Well, who is he?'

'He's Malcolm Reid, a poet or something.'

'Oh, that's Malcolm Reid? He doesn't look forty. He's in good shape, physically, I mean.'

Robyn looked at Malcolm without bothering to hide her interest in him.

'He's just arrived from England. Didn't take you long to spot him,' said Philippa cattily.

'You should know me by now.'

'I do… He's invited to my party later tonight.'

'And me?'

'You're a shameless hussy, Robyn.'

Philippa drank her glass of champagne in one gulp. A waiter stood by patiently until she took another full glass from his tray. Philippa turned back to Robyn.

'Would you like to be introduced?'

'I thought you'd never ask.'

Philippa took Robyn's arm and led her towards Malcolm, but she stumbled, and almost fell over.

'My God, you're pissed again, Philippa.'

'Aren't I?' giggled Philippa. 'Perhaps it's best that I hang onto you. Lead on, Robyn.'

They made their way across the crowd, giggling like a pair of schoolgirls, but nobody in the room took any notice of them.

Malcolm and McDonald moved to another room, still looking at the watercolours. They were deep in conversation, when Philippa cut in on them.

'That's enough of art, Mac. How about some introductions?' she said breezily.

'Malcolm, I'd like you to meet a friend of mine,' said McDonald. 'Robyn Hawthorne... Malcolm Reid.'

As Robyn and Malcolm shook hands, McDonald stepped back to meet a new arrival. 'I'll see you around,' he said to Malcolm and smiled at the two women.

Robyn turned to Malcolm, completely ignoring Philippa. 'So, what have you bought?' she asked him.

'Oh, I haven't got round to that yet.'

'But you will. Mac can be very persuasive,' said Philippa, trying to be part of the group. To her disappointment, Malcolm was only interested in Robyn.

'Are you a collector?' he asked her.

'Heavens, no, not me! I'm involved with John Peter Russell in a completely different way.'

'He is dead,' Philippa butted in. 'I would've thought you had enough trouble with the living, Robyn.' But as she was ignored yet again she decided to move on. 'Must mingle... bye.'

'What did she mean?' asked Malcolm as Philippa moved out of earshot.

'Search me,' said Robyn. 'You mustn't mind her, Philippa's smashed most of the time.'

'Strange lady, but lovely.'

'You are supposed to be interested in me.'

'I am. So, what's your connection?'

'I'm making a movie about John Peter Russell.'

'So, he's quite famous then?'

'Not yet. But you're quite a celebrity yourself.'

'Not by design, I can assure you.'

'I heard you on the Terry Robinson Show this morning. He gave you a hard time, but you mustn't mind him. Terry hates art,' she explained, and added as an afterthought, 'and Poms.'

'He just hates – and it's not a pretty sight. Spending a morning with him is an experience I could have done without.'

'You gave as good as you got,' said Robyn as she raised her glass to Malcolm. 'Here's to you, Malcolm. Welcome to down under.'

'You're very kind,' replied Malcolm, raising his glass to her.

'What brought you here?' asked Robyn.

'It's a long story. Are you a good listener?'

'Try me, Doctor,' she said as she looked into his eyes.

He was embarrassed by her forward manner. She had a terrific figure, her very being exuded sex, she was young and desirable by anybody's standards; but Malcolm held back. He was used to making the first moves.

'Why?' he asked provocatively.

'Are you telling me to mind my own business?' Robyn made light of the hard edge in his voice. She was not going to be put down just like that. Not another rejection – not two on the same day.

'Exactly... mind your own bloody business,' said Malcolm, changing his voice back to a more sociable register.

A waiter stopped by them. Malcolm took a new glass and raised it to Robyn. 'And here's—'

'Looking at me, kid?' she interrupted.

'If you like,' laughed Malcolm appreciatively.

They were friends again.

'I like,' said Robyn smiling at him.

Malcolm said nothing; he just grinned at her. It was what he considered to be his enigmatic smile.

'You're not so much a poet,' she went on, 'more like a piss-artist.'

'And in the best English literary tradition,' he replied, as Philippa re-joined them. Malcolm used her arrival as a convenient excuse for retreat. In spite of all the teasing and smiles, he was scared of Robyn. His instinct told him to keep away from her.

'If you'll excuse me,' he said to them, merging into the crowd.

Robyn stared after him. Her eyes were full of anger as she turned towards Philippa. 'What are you squirming at?' she asked.

'Not doing so well, Robyn?'

'He's playing hard to get,' she said dismissively.

Malcolm drifted into another room. The conversation was a little louder, and there was a happy glow on every face he looked at. He knew he was drunk, but happily drunk; he felt relaxed as he took another glass of champagne. He glanced back towards Robyn and Philippa, but couldn't see them anywhere. He took their absence with a tinge of regret. Philippa intrigued him, though he had already forgotten how he came to meet her. He still remembered that he was invited to her party.

Malcolm could not make up his mind about Robyn. She was a beautiful creature. Every one of her gestures was divine, and he knew she would haunt him for ever. Her delicate hands, her refined profile, her silken hair, and her deep, deep eyes were enough to drive any man crazy with desire. He wanted her so much that it almost sobered him up. He was pleased by her approaches, but at the same time, the alarm bells of caution rang deep down in the pit of his stomach.

Malcolm made his way towards the lavatories. He put his glass on a tray and went into the gents. He pushed open one of the cubicle doors and, to his greatest horror, he saw a young man shooting up heroin as he sat on the lavatory seat.

The man glanced at Malcolm vacantly. There was no recognition in his eyes as he looked down again, and carried on concentrating on the needle. He was oblivious to everything else, including Malcolm. He existed in a world of his own.

'Sorry,' said Malcolm, shutting the door in embarrassment.

The man ignored him, but that fleeting glance of depravity etched itself onto Malcolm's mind: the young face with the body of an old man; the empty look staring out from dull, deep sunken eyes. The *waste*. Malcolm never saw anyone using a needle. He remembered films and television, but the real thing was more shocking than anything he had seen before.

He left the lavatories as fast as he could and hurried back to the safety of the art gallery. He felt a lot happier amongst the noisy crowd, and made his way over to Robyn. She was talking to Philippa and McDonald.

'So, it was that Malcolm Reid? How did you meet him, Mac?'

'I phoned him at the university…'

'Talk of the devil,' interrupted Philippa. 'Looks as if he's seen a ghost.'

Malcolm appeared shaky as he joined the group.

'Now, take it easy, Malcolm. I'd like you to last a little longer,' said Philippa as she handed Malcolm a drink.

McDonald looked at Philippa quizzically, and she smiled back at him obligingly.

'I'm having a party tonight. Remember?'

'So you are,' said McDonald. 'So you are.'

'I'm dying of thirst, Mac.'

'Then we must get you another drink, dear lady,' replied McDonald as he took her by the arm, and led her towards the bar.

Malcolm stepped closer to Robyn, and whispered into her ear. 'You won't believe this, but there was a guy in the lavatory, shooting up with a needle.'

'Really?' she asked, without being bothered.

'I'm quite shocked.'

'This is Sydney, mate,' said Robyn a little more sympathetically. 'And it looks as if you too could do with some sort of a fix. Drink up, and I'll get you another one.'

As Malcolm gulped his drink down Robyn took him to the nearest waiter.

'How about a stiff brandy for my friend?'

'Certainly, madam,' replied the waiter as he handed Malcolm a huge tumbler.

Malcolm took a swig. The liquor reached his toes, and he felt a lot better. Robyn watched him without a word. As Malcolm sipped his drink, he looked about the room and saw the same happy faces. People came, people went, but it was all as before. Then Malcolm spotted a young man dressed in a white suit and wearing a black tie, as if he had just stepped out of a gangster film.

He even had the dark, handsome good looks of somebody from the Mediterranean to match his outfit.

'Who is that?' asked Malcolm. 'That guy in the white suit?'

'That's Carlo. Carlo Bellini.'

'He looks like a hood.'

'There are no prizes for guessing that, Malcolm. Carlo is a pusher, to be precise, and he'll supply you with anything you like – as long as you can afford it.'

As Robyn was talking, the young man from the lavatories walked over to Carlo. He reached into his inside pocket, and handed over a wad of money. Without the slightest attempt at concealment Carlo gave him a sachet of heroin.

'That's him,' whispered Malcolm excitedly. 'The guy I saw in the lavatory.'

'Don't get so worked up about it.'

'They couldn't give a shit who sees them,' said Malcolm, shaking his head in disbelief.

'I told you, you're in Sydney now. You'll have to get used to it. Like… when in Rome.'

The reception was still in full swing when Robyn and Malcolm left the art gallery. It was dusk, and the lights inside threw golden yellow shafts onto the blue slate pavement; the setting sun covered everything in a deep shade of red. It was the kind of picture that one normally sees only on chocolate boxes.

Malcolm walked a little unsteadily, and Robyn did her best to keep him vertical. He insisted on hanging onto the cast-iron railings, which made her task a lot more difficult. Malcolm tried to tear off a jacaranda flower, and almost fell flat on his face. It made her laugh. He was happy to make Robyn laugh, for she was beautiful. They behaved like children, and they knew it, but it was a magical evening that they would both remember for ever.

'It's very nice around here,' said Malcolm.

'This is Paddo, mate. Of course it's nice, if you can afford it,' said Robyn. 'Your car, or mine?'

'I don't mind, whatever you like,' said Malcolm with a wide grin on his face.

'Where is your car?' asked Robyn, suspecting a joke of some kind.

Malcolm's car was a beaten-up old Jag, parked partially on the pavement. It had cost him fifty dollars, and it had a week's guarantee. It was a miracle that he made it to Paddington at all, but Malcolm liked driving wrecks.

'There it is,' pointed Malcolm. 'The Jag.'

'It's definitely my car then,' said Robyn.

'As you like.'

Robyn led him to her car, a brand new BMW convertible. She opened the passenger door for Malcolm and helped him in.

'I see what you mean,' said Malcolm. 'I hope you can drive it. This is not a lady's car, you know.'

'I'll ignore that, you Pommy bastard. Don't you become the male chauvinist pig with me.'

Robyn put her foot down hard on the accelerator, and the car shot forward like a graceful wild animal. With screeching tyres, she drove up the hill towards Rose Bay, disturbing the peace of the tree-lined street of freshly painted houses with stained-glass Art Deco windows and wrought-iron balconies.

Chapter Three

Philippa's parties were exclusive affairs. She selected her guests in a haphazard way. Money was not her criterion, as everyone she knew had money. To be invited to her house one had to have something extra, and being in the news helped. For a while, Malcolm expected every door to be open to him in Sydney as a matter of course. He was a member of the privileged elite in England, so why not Australia?

The house was a masterpiece of modern architecture, all stone and glass, built on a slope towards the harbour. The walls enclosed a couple of giant trees, which were there for centuries before the Europeans arrived in Australia. The lush, tropical vegetation was artfully terraced right down to the water's edge, where her husband, Ralph Penders, had his twelve-metre yacht moored. The grounds covered three acres, a luxury beyond belief in Rose Bay, where house prices were expressed in long-distance telephone numbers, and even a studio apartment was something to brag about.

It was a glamorous setting for a party. The evening sky was full of stars and the city lights in the background shimmered on the water below. A couple of ferries crossed the harbour with their fairy lights glittering on the water, a visual feast to entertain Philippa's guests.

They were spread out all over the place: some in the gardens, some down by the water, others on the patio, and a few were watching a blue video in the huge living room. A Filipino waiter moved about silently, serving drinks. There was the usual heavy drinking, some drug taking; the atmosphere was bored relaxation. Nobody passed joints around; Philippa's guests smoked individual joints in the best North Shore tradition, or snorted coke from a silver mirror.

Malcolm recognised a couple of people from the art gallery, but he was happy to be on his own. He sat in a deep, chrome-and-leather armchair by the patio door, and observed the others through a haze of alcohol. He had never drunk so much before in his whole life, but he was still able to function in a time–space continuum of his own. He still felt the same disorientation that he had all day; in fact, he'd had the same bizarre feeling since he landed in Sydney. There was no explanation for it, yet everything was different whilst appearing to be the same. The starlit sky above him was not the sky he was used to, but he could not tell why; he knew that the Southern Hemisphere would be different, and he expected to find the sun in the north, yet he could not foresee the effect it would have on him. Particularly when he was zonked out of his mind.

Malcolm soon got bored with looking at the sky. He turned towards the living room, and saw Robyn talking to David Swaab. It was obvious that they were having an argument, but Malcolm could not hear them through all the noise of the music and the general chatter. Their gestures were enough.

A feeling of jealousy came over him. There was something intimate about Robyn and that man. It's only body language, his mind screamed at him, trying to suppress his original gut reaction. Don't take any notice of it.

McDonald took David Swaab's arm and led him away. Robyn shook her head as if continuing the argument with an invisible person, then shrugged her shoulders, and walked over to Malcolm.

'A penny for your thoughts?' she asked him.

'Who was that guy?'

'Which guy?'

'The one you were arguing with.'

'Oh, David Swaab? How did you know I was arguing with him?'

'I know. I am very sensitive to moods.'

'Good on you, mate,' said Robyn flatly.

'What was it about?'

'Just business. We've been working on a project for some time now, but it's not getting anywhere.'

'You want to talk about it?'

'No. But I am intrigued by your power of observation. How do you do it?'

23

'It's like motorcycle maintenance the Zen way. You let it happen, and the force does it all for you.'

'Sure, then you sober up in the morning.'

'I know I'm drunk, but the real me is in control. Subconsciously. I can do anything I want.'

'Sure you can,' said Robyn smiling.

'You don't believe me, do you?'

'Oh, but I do.'

Malcolm looked for a prop, and picked up a cocktail cherry from an ashtray as Philippa drifted over, watching Malcolm's antics.

'Can you see that bowl?' he asked, pointing to a punchbowl on the sideboard some forty feet from where they were sitting.

'Sure, I can see it.'

'I'm going to throw this cherry into that bowl, overarm, with my eyes closed.'

Malcolm closed his eyes, bent backwards, and raised his arm like a cricket player bowling. He released the cherry with a jerky overarm action. It landed in the middle of the bowl with a plop. Malcolm grinned, looking very pleased with himself.

'Don't say anything.'

Philippa was delighted. She clapped her hands like a little girl at the circus.

'Go on, do it again!'

'I couldn't.'

'You must be able to do it again,' said Robyn, 'now that you've done it once.'

'It doesn't work like that.'

Malcolm was about to expand on his theory of the force, but suddenly the mood of the party changed; the music stopped, the chatter died away, and everybody looked towards the hall.

Ralph Penders stood there quietly, all six foot five and sixteen stone of him. Slowly, he walked into the living room, and turned towards the television set. He stopped the dirty video by hitting the pause button.

'Philippa?' he called in a powerful but controlled voice. Penders was in his late forties. He had a commanding presence as he towered over everybody else in the room.

Shaking with fear, Philippa looked at her husband, and walked towards him, still holding her glass in her hand. The others stood aside to let her through. She kissed Penders on the cheek as if in slow motion.

'Hi... I didn't expect you till Friday,' she said trying to diffuse the hostile feeling in the air.

Penders looked down at her without a word. She was agitated and nervous as she still held the tall, delicate glass in her hand. Her fingers turned white as they tightened around the glass. The ice cubes jangled in the glass as her hand shook, and the sound reverberated in the silent room.

'Get rid of them,' said Penders.

Philippa gasped as her fingers squeezed the glass even tighter, until it shattered. The glass and ice cubes hit the marble floor. It sounded like an explosion. The broken glass cut Philippa's palm, and there was blood trickling down her deathly white arm. She did not dare to utter a sound as Penders turned on his heels and walked out. He paused for a split second as he reached Robyn and Malcolm.

'Robyn Hawthorne?' he asked her casually.

'Yes, Mr Penders,' she said, pushing Malcolm forwards.

'And this is?' asked Penders.

'Malcolm Reid,' said Robyn.

'How are you, Malcolm? I've seen your Channel Six interview.'

'How do you do,' said Malcolm holding out his hand.

Penders ignored it. He just carried on walking.

'We must have a chat sometime. Goodnight.'

Penders disappeared before Malcolm had a chance to say anything. Within seconds the whole place emptied. Philippa stood in the middle of the deserted room. She looked down at her wounded hand, but did not feel the pain; it seemed as if her hand belonged to another person. Malcolm moved towards her, but Robyn dragged him out of the place.

'I just want to say goodnight,' he protested.

'That's not a good idea.'

'It's a question of good manners.'

'Forget that,' she said as she dragged him out of the house.

It was late. The traffic was light as Robyn drove through Woollahra. Malcolm sat in the passenger seat, looking out into the dark. He was in a silent mood and she was busy with her own thoughts. The stereo played a moody piece of jazz and the only other sound to be heard was the gentle swish of the tyres. The city was silent.

She drove along Circular Quay and headed for the North Shore. Malcolm looked down at the water. Myriad lights were reflected from the Harbour Bridge and the street lights. The shimmering glitter fitted the mood of the music, and it felt like a mystical experience to Malcolm. Ages seemed to have passed before he spoke.

'He must be stinking rich.'

'Who? Penders?'

'Who else?'

'All Philippa's friends are rich,' said Robyn, 'but her husband is in a class of his own.'

'Well, just how rich is that?'

'What does it matter after the first billion?'

'As much as that?'

'I should be flattered he remembered my name,' mused Robyn. 'I've only ever met him once before.'

'How come?'

'I used to work for one of his television stations. He owned five at the last count. I don't suppose he even knows what he owns.'

'Not a person to cross, I suppose.'

'Uh-huh,' she agreed.

They fell silent as they crossed the harbour. Malcolm watched the iron girders glide past in perfect rhythm with the music. At the back of his mind he remembered a radio play about a character whose only function in life was to paint the Harbour Bridge. It took seven years before the paint had to be replaced, and it took seven years to paint the bridge. No sooner did he finish one end of the bridge than he had to start at the other end. It was a most profound play. Now what was it called? wondered Malcolm as he looked up, half expecting the man to be up there with his paintbrush and bucket.

'*Arthur's Bridge*,' he said aloud, as he remembered.

'What?' asked Robyn.

'Nothing important,' he said. He did not feel like talking. He had completely forgotten what the play was about. The only image that stayed with him was this unfortunate creature being up there, alone, painting endlessly, whilst the rest of the world passed him by.

Robyn turned off the Cahill Expressway and drove towards Mossman. The streets were empty. It was that dead hour when everything stops. Malcolm spotted an all-night liquor store, lit up like a Christmas tree with neon lights. He turned to Robyn.

'Would you pull in there?' he asked her.

'I've got all the booze in the world at home.'

'Just pull in.'

The attendant left his glass box, and walked over to the car. He eyed them suspiciously, then addressed Malcolm over Robyn's head.

'What do you want, mate?' he asked.

'A bottle of Armagnac. Jeanneau, if you have it.'

'And what's that, mate?' he asked testily.

'It's just like cognac, but it comes from Condom.'

'You should try the all-night chemist for that,' suggested Robyn, with a grin on her face. Malcolm did not expect her to say something like that, and looked at her disapprovingly.

'Stop pissing me about,' said the attendant. 'What do you want?'

'I'll have a bottle of brandy,' said Malcolm.

'The Château Poolowanna's on special. Seventeen dollars ninety-nine for a bloody big bottle.'

'You talked me into it.'

The attendant waited with visible annoyance for Malcolm to produce the money, almost as if there had been a long line of customers all waiting to be served.

It took Malcolm a while, but eventually, he managed to find the right-looking notes and handed them over to the attendant. The man came back with a bottle of Château Poolowanna, and handed it to Malcolm.

Malcolm never found out what Château Poolowanna was like; by the time Robyn opened the bottle, he was fast asleep in an armchair. She put the glass down by his side and went into the kitchen to make a pot of black coffee.

She tried to wake him in vain. Malcolm was dead to the world. She put the coffee down next to the brandy, put on a record, and turned the sitting-room sofa into a spare bed. Listening to the gentle piece of bossa nova, she sat in the other armchair, sipping her coffee.

Malcolm looked like a sleeping angel. She watched him for a while, then tried to move him to his bed. He opened his eyes for a few seconds as Robyn struggled with his limp body, and tried to hug her. She slipped out of his clumsy embrace, and dumped him on the sofa.

A devilish thought struck her and she acted on impulse. Robyn took a silk ribbon holding her hair back, then opened Malcolm's zip and tied the ribbon in a neat bow to his limp willy. He was lost in the land of nod, and did not notice anything.

She covered him up with a rug, took off the CD, pulled the curtains closed, and went into the bedroom.

Chapter Four

A shaft of light shone through a gap left in the curtains, right onto Malcolm's face, and it woke him up. He opened his eyes, blinking and screwing up his face, then sat up, and looked down at his open zip. He was surprised to see a ribbon tied around his willy. How on earth did that get there? he thought as he untied the bow and put the silk ribbon into his pocket.

He addressed his willy with a smile. 'I don't know where you've been, but I'm glad you've won the first prize.'

He zipped up his trousers and looked about the place. He could not recognise anything in the room, and had no idea how he got there. He got up and pulled the curtains open. The light hit him like a wall; he stepped back involuntarily and rubbed his eyes. He looked out of the French windows leading to the balcony.

It was a breathtaking sight. He was on the twenty-second floor of a tower block, right over the harbour; even the Harbour Bridge was beneath him. All its six lanes were jam-packed with cars. A rusty train rattled across the bridge carrying commuters to the city. Malcolm could only imagine the noise; from his vantage point he could see everything, but hear nothing. It was a most disconcerting feeling.

Ferry boats criss-crossed the deep blue water, leaving V-shaped patterns of froth behind. There was not a single cloud in the sky; it was just like the day before, and the day before that. I could get bored with all this sun, he thought as he stepped out onto the balcony. He kept well away from the edge, as he suffered from vertigo. The sun was just over the Opera House and its rays glittered on the ceramic tiles. Malcolm disliked the building; just like a stack of saucers in a washing-up rack, he thought. He remembered not to say that to anybody. Although he had only been there for three weeks, he'd learned that Australians loved compliments about their country, but could not take any form of criticism.

'What am I doing here?' he asked himself out loud, 'and just where the hell am I?'

He went back into the sitting room. He spotted a note left for him on a side table. He picked it up and read it: '*Gone to work. Help your hangover to breakfast. Make sure you close the door properly. I'll call you soon, Robyn.*'

He did not have a hangover; all the same, he went into the kitchen. The percolator was left switched on, and there was the huge bottle of Château Poolowanna right beside it. Malcolm poured some black coffee into an earthenware mug, and laced it with the brandy. He took a couple of sips and walked back into the sitting room.

Slowly some recognition seeped into his brain. By the time he finished his coffee, he remembered most of the previous day, and particularly Robyn. He turned her note over and wrote on the back of it: '*Thanks for the breakfast. Make sure you call me. See you, Malcolm.*' He scribbled down his telephone number, and walked out of the apartment. He pulled the door behind him gently, listening for the latch to click.

Malcolm stepped out into the sunshine and walked towards the Harbour Bridge. He felt full of energy now, and awake enough to enjoy the glorious morning. He had nothing arranged for the next couple of days, and he was free to do as he pleased. Only one thing worried him; he knew he had left a car somewhere, a beaten-up old Jag, but he just could not remember where. 'Oh, it'll come to me,' he said, shrugging his shoulders, 'and if not, it only cost me fifty dollars.'

Malcolm always drove wrecks. It was an inverted form of snobbery, because he hated petrolheads who talked about twin cams, turbo chargers and stainless steel reinforced tyres; he also admitted to be being a useless driver. Everybody else was a Formula One World Champion – or so they thought. Malcolm got his kicks out of nursing along cars that should not function at all by the laws of physics, thermodynamics, statistical averages, or any other form of science. He had once bought a Morris Traveller for five pounds and drove it up and down the M4 in England for eight months, before it fell apart.

A taxi cruised by, and Malcolm stepped off the pavement to

stop it. The driver pulled up with screeching tyres.

'You want to watch that, mate,' said the driver. 'I could've killed you, stepping out like that... Where do you want to go?'

'Oh, just to the other side,' said Malcolm vaguely as he got into the taxi.

'The other side of what, mate?'

'The other side of the harbour.'

'I'll take you to Kings Cross.'

The driver took an instant dislike to Malcolm, and kept silent. It suited Malcolm; he was happy to be left alone with his thoughts. As they reached the Botanic Gardens, Malcolm leaned forward.

'Could you stop here, please,' he said on the spur of the moment.

'Sure, mate,' said the driver slamming his brakes on. 'Thanks for the warning.'

Malcolm ignored the sarcasm and paid his fare. He thought about it for a while, then left a generous tip. The driver was not impressed. He pulled out from the curb and joined the traffic without saying a word.

Malcolm walked into the gardens. The peace and serenity of the place surprised him. The lawns were immaculately mowed, the flower beds were tended with loving care; the gardens were a little paradise, right in the middle of all the concrete and glass of the city. A sign amused him: BOTANIC GARDENS. Anywhere else on earth they would be botanical, he thought. He loved collecting words and expressions; his mind was crammed full of useless information, as he proudly liked to say. Botanic is correct, he thought, just a little old-fashioned. Victorians had botanic societies. 'Botanical' came from America, where the longer form of any word is always preferred.

He must have wandered about the gardens for half an hour, when he came across the Gallery of Modern Art. It was a hideous building, more like a warehouse than an art gallery.

Malcolm reached into his pocket, pulled out the catalogue he'd picked up the night before, and walked into the building. The place was deceptively large inside, but there was hardly anybody about. The silence was oppressive. Malcolm drifted from room to room, but saw nothing of interest; there were no paintings by John Peter Russell. He even bought a catalogue, and thumbed through it, but found no mention of Russell. He was determined to see his paintings; he was not going to leave the place before finding at least one of them. He walked over to the information desk. A pretty young woman looked up at him with a stiff smile and lifeless eyes. Malcolm knew instantly that it was a waste of time asking her anything about art.

'I'm interested in an Australian painter, John Peter Russell. You don't seem to have anything by him.'

'Did you check the catalogue, sir?' she asked.

'I did. There is no mention of him. That's why I am asking you.'

'John Russell?' she asked.

'John Peter Russell.'

'He doesn't ring a bell,' she said, still smiling.

'He was a painter, not a bell-ringer,' quipped Malcolm, but his wit was wasted on her.

'If he's not in the catalogue, then we won't have anything by him.'

'You must have. He is the best known Australian Impressionist.'

'I've never heard of him, but I could look him up on the computer,' she said.

My God, we're getting there, *dumbo*, thought Malcolm, and said aloud, 'That's a great idea. Why don't you do that? John Peter Russell… two Ss and two Ls.'

She logged onto the database and keyed in 'John Peter Russell'. She was not an IT wizard, and screwed up her eyes in concentration. Suddenly her face lit up with genuine delight.

'Oh, here he is. "Peasants in a Field near Monte Cassino" and "Regatta in Sydney Harbour".'

'In which room?' asked Malcolm.

'They are in Canberra.'

'Thank you very much,' he said with heavy sarcasm.

'Hold on, we've got some drawings by him, but you will have to make an appointment. You've got to write a letter to the curator.'

'Can't I just talk to him?'

'She's on holiday.'

'She must have an assistant.'

'Yeah, the assistant curator is here.'

'Then can I see her?'

'He's busy.'

'How do you know?' asked Malcolm in exasperation. 'He may not be busy at all. You could try to contact him.'

'All right. I'll see if I can get hold of him,' she said, unperturbed as she dialled a number on the internal telephone. 'Information desk. Somebody here wants to see the John Russell drawings ... John Peter Russell ... All right, I'll send him up.'

The receptionist turned to Malcolm, smiling happily.

'Up the stairs, turn left, and it's the last door on the right... I think that's right...'

'Thanks for your help,' said Malcolm sarcastically. 'I appreciate all the trouble you've been to.'

'You're welcome,' she replied, not noticing the edge in his voice.

Malcolm walked up the stairs, and was met at the top by a middle-aged, balding little man.

'This way please. I'm the assistant curator.'

'Thank you.'

'We haven't got much room here; that's why we like people to make an appointment. But as you are here, I might as well show you what we have. It's not a lot, I'm afraid.'

He led Malcolm along the corridor and stopped at the last door. He opened it for Malcolm. They entered an enormous room, filled with paintings stacked against the walls in storage racks. At the far end of the room a young man was busy cleaning an old canvas. Malcolm recognised him.

It was the man he saw shooting up in the lavatories the night before. He looked up from his work and smiled at Malcolm, obviously not recognising him. Malcolm smiled back.

In the meantime, the assistant curator pulled out a portfolio from one of the storage racks, cleared some space on a table and dusted off the old portfolio.

'This is all we have by John Peter Russell. Most of his work is in private collections. Can you show me some identification?'

Malcolm took out his passport.

'Are you on holiday?'

'No. I'll be in Sydney for some time.'

'I need to have your address as well, sir.'

'Leichhardt University... I'm a lecturer there.'

'In Art?'

'English Literature.'

'Oh, yes, I've seen you on the telly. Very interesting interview... Well, if you don't mind, I'll leave you to it. I've got an appointment. Just leave it all here when you finish.'

As he left the room Malcolm opened the portfolio. There were about thirty small drawings, sketches and charcoal studies; each piece numbered and mounted on cartridge paper. They were wonderful pieces of work. When Malcolm finished looking at the drawings, he walked over to the young man at the far end of the room.

He watched him work for a while. The young man was cleaning a painting by a Dutch master. His hands were gentle and deft as he worked a swab of cotton wool over the surface of the canvas.

'Tricky work, restoration,' said Malcolm.

'Not really,' replied the young man in a cultured West London accent, 'but you've got to have patience.'

'You're from England, too?'

'I came out on a six-month contract nine years ago,' he said as he put down his cotton wool swab, and held out his hand. 'I'm Jamie de Selway.'

'Malcolm Reid,' said Malcolm. 'I'm a lecturer at the university.'

'Fine Arts?'

'English Lit... You seem to be the first person I've met in Sydney who doesn't know all about me.'

'Should I?'

'There was a lot of nonsense in the media about my appointment.'

'I've missed it, I'm sorry,' he said, carrying on with his work.

'I suppose you've got a job for life here,' said Malcolm

motioning towards the stacks of paintings.

'No, I've almost finished, and I've been here a lot longer than I planned.'

'I thought once you've finished restoring the last painting, you had to start all over again, like painting the Harbour Bridge.'

'Nothing like it, but you've got to have the right temperament to be a restorer. I never wanted to paint for myself; I'm much too hooked on technique.'

'But you must have your preferences.'

'Sure. I hated working on that Reynolds,' he said.

'Why?'

'It's not a Reynolds at all – it's a blatant fake.'

'It looks genuine enough to me,' said Malcolm after he had inspected the painting for some time.

'I suppose it does.'

'But how do you know it's a fake?'

Jamie stopped his work, picked up the painting, and pointed to the background.

'This is a very good illustration of anachronism,' said Jamie.

'I'm sorry...'

'It's a word you often hear from art historians, but mostly in the wrong context,' smiled Jamie. Seeing that it still meant nothing to Malcolm, he carried on. 'If you look carefully, you'll see a railway viaduct in the right-hand corner. Joshua Reynolds died in 1792. There were no railways then. They came a lot later.'

'And nobody has noticed that,' said Malcolm in amazement.

'Evidently not. Mind you, there are lots more worse Reynolds about. All genuine, and in respectable art galleries.'

'I don't understand. Do explain.'

'He let his apprentices do most of the work, and some of them weren't terribly good.'

'What do you think about John Peter Russell?'

Malcolm's question completely unsettled Jamie. He froze still for a second, then started to pack up his equipment.

'He's fine, if a little derivative.'

'I've just seen an exhibition of his watercolours,' said Malcolm.

'Were you at the opening last night?' asked Jamie.

'Yes, in Paddington,' replied Malcolm. 'I was with Robyn

Hawthorne. She's the producer who's making a film about Russell.'

'I know,' said Jamie as he looked at Malcolm again, but could not remember him. He turned away, and started to clean up.

'Look… it's been nice talking to you, but I must lock up now.'

'I was surprised that I couldn't find any of his work here,' went on Malcolm. 'John Peter Russell was from Sydney. I would've thought this was the obvious place for his paintings. Why aren't there any here? Why?'

'I wouldn't know. You'll have to ask the curator when she gets back… This way, please.'

Jamie ushered Malcolm towards the door. He seemed to be physically relieved once Malcolm was out of the room. Jamie locked the door carefully.

'I suppose this must be your lunch time,' said Malcolm.

'That's right.'

'What are you doing for lunch?'

'I've made a previous arrangement,' replied Jamie defensively. 'I'm meeting somebody already… bye.'

Jamie hurried along the corridor and ran down the steps two at the time. Malcolm followed him thoughtfully. He tried to figure out what had upset Jamie.

Chapter Five

Jamie could not have called at a worse time. It was getting on for one thirty, and Penders had still not managed to sort out his morning mail. He picked up the receiver while still reading a document spread out on his desk.

'I told you not to call me here, Jamie.'

'But it's very important, Mr Penders—'

'Don't tell me,' said Penders, stopping him in mid-sentence, 'I'll see you on the seven-fifteen ferry.'

'Can't I see you before that?'

'No, you can't. I'll see you on the ferry.'

'I'll be there, if that's what you want, Mr Penders.'

'That's what I want,' he said, and put the receiver back into its cradle. He swivelled around in his enormous chair, and looked out of the window, but he was not interested in the panoramic view of the city. What does Jamie want? He sounded frightened out of his wits, the poor bastard. Hell, I'll find out this evening, and I'll worry about it then, he thought as he turned back to his desk.

Penders had perfect recall and a photographic memory. It was easy for him to compartmentalise his thoughts; tackling each problem at a time of his choosing. It saved him a lot of trouble.

His headquarters were in the tallest building in Sydney, and his office and private penthouse at the very top. He was reputed to be the richest man in the Southern Hemisphere, and for a man of barely forty, it was a tremendous achievement.

Penders was born in Summer Hill, in the western suburbs of Sydney, but he considered himself to be a New Australian. His father, a Hungarian with a Romanian passport, had arrived down under in 1948.

Rudolf Pandúrkunszentmihályi was the name his father had given him. He became Ralph in school, as it saved him fighting his schoolmates every day. Penders came some time later, as it sounded better for an Australian. In any case, it was a lot easier to pronounce than the alternative.

The family traced its roots back to the thirteenth century to a small hamlet in eastern Hungary, Pandúrkunszentmihály. The Romanian border moved westwards in 1920 to comply with the Treaty of Trianon. Hungarians have a long-standing tradition of fighting world wars on the wrong side, and losing a lot of territory as a result; not that Penders cared much for Hungarian history. Making money was a lot more interesting.

His mental prowess set Penders apart from his classmates. He never bothered taking notes, and relied entirely on his memory. He was twelve when he started using carefully planted markers, key words or phrases to help him remember exactly what he wanted. He was able to command his memory at will. Penders learned how to live with his unusual talent, and how to control his mind without going mad. After leaving school, he trained to be an electrician, because his father thought that was the height of scientific achievement, and that was the limit of his dreams for his son.

Halfway through his apprenticeship, Penders was advised by one of his tutors to take up accountancy to make use of his rare talent. His father soon got used to the idea, and thought it one better than being an electrician. Penders worked hard, and rose above his father's wildest dreams. He left Western Suburbs Polytechnic as a fully qualified chartered accountant, and was headhunted by the Inland Revenue people. He worked for the government for five years. His father was very proud of him. It was a pity that he had not lived long enough to see his son arrive at the very top. It was after his father died that Penders' career really took off.

A Hungarian butcher enticed him to leave the safe government post, and go into the meat-packing business. Penders was willing to take a chance, and considering that Pataki offered him a six-figure salary, he could not refuse. His partner managed to get hold of the recipe for genuine Hungarian salami. (That was just another state secret that got away.)

Amongst connoisseurs, the Hungarian variety is recognised as being the best of all salamis. Even Italians copy it, and call it *typo ungherese* – a rare compliment indeed. Pataki's recipe was the real article; the carefully guarded secret lay in the exact proportions of pork, beef and donkey meat.

Pataki & Penders were doing fantastic business throughout New South Wales, and had to double production in the first month, then double it again. To finance their expanding business they borrowed a lot more money than was wise. Inevitably, they got into serious financial difficulties. Penders risked the lot on a gambler's hunch and learned how to succeed in business. His solution was to borrow from Peter to pay off Paul, and rob them both blind in the process.

In the end, Pataki had to go. Penders paid him off handsomely, and they parted amicably. Penders took over the abattoir. Later he bought a 100,000-hectare cattle ranch in the Northern Territory. Once Penders started buying, there was no stopping, but it had never got out of hand, as he retained complete control. Penders knew exactly what he had bought, what he paid for it and the exact amount of profit he made. He kept all the details in his head. Nothing was written down; and as far as the books were concerned, they were all masterpieces of creative accounting.

Penders was loyal to his friends, and looked after his family generously, but the media hated him. With his rapidly gained wealth and power, he was reputed to be a hard man. He was not bothered by the gossip in the papers; he just took what he wanted, and he wanted the lot – including newspapers and television stations.

He built a business empire of interlocking, cross-collateralised companies, constantly growing bigger by new acquisitions. Penders bought ailing companies and turned them into profitable concerns, then sold them, using the proceeds to buy yet more.

Philippa came with a rock musical in which Penders invested $20,000. The show almost had to close after five weeks. He took up all the shares for peanuts, sacked half the cast, brought in a new director, and became the sole owner of the longest-running show in town. Philippa was part of the package, a member of the cast who had to go, but she did not mind leaving the stage. Being married to Penders had its compensations.

There was not a single day that he had not bought or sold a

company, and when Jamie called, Penders was in the middle of an ambitious and complex takeover bid. He was determined to buy a Japanese coal-mining company, and the going was getting rough. He needed all his wits about him.

★

It was the evening rush hour, and Circular Quay was packed with shoppers and office workers heading for home. Ferries of all sizes departed by the minute to different parts of the harbour, dodging each other on the choppy waters.

Jamie stood by the gangway of the Watson's Bay ferry. He was a bundle of nerves, and kept on looking over his shoulders. Penders surprised him as he stepped out of the crowd unexpectedly, and Jamie almost jumped out of his skin.

'You're a bit nervous, Jamie,' said the big man.

'I'm sorry, but I just had to see you, Mr Penders,' replied Jamie. 'It's about—'

'In a minute, in a minute, Jamie,' Penders cut in.

He walked up the gangplank, and Jamie followed him. They were watched by Penders' minders, Doug and Tony. Doug was a lanky Australian with long blond hair. Tony was a stocky character with dark hair and an olive skin. They hid in the crowd, but managed to stay close to Penders for security, yet allowing him complete privacy. Jamie looked at them with concern.

'Don't let them bother you,' said Penders. 'They are with me.'

'I know.'

As the ferry left Circular Quay, the sun set behind a tall office building. Its dying rays cast a warm, magical glow over the city. The street lights were switched on and shone brightly against the darkening sky. Penders took in the beauty of the scene. As the ferry rounded the Opera House, the Harbour Bridge lights came on to complete the picture. Penders watched the riot of deep red colours for a while, then turned towards Jamie.

'Right, Jamie,' he said. 'Tell me all about it.'

'I was working in the restoration room, when this guy came in, snooping around the place.'

'What do you mean, snooping?'

'He turned up without an appointment and asked for the Russell portfolio, but he was really after me.'

'And how do you know that?'

'He hardly looked at Russell's drawings. He flipped through the portfolio in a couple of minutes. I'm telling you, he was more interested in me than anything else.'

'Are you sure?'

'That's the impression I got.'

'All right. Who is he?'

'He said his name was Malcolm Reid, a lecturer at the university.'

'Oh, yes,' said Penders thoughtfully, 'but what did he want?'

'I don't know. He asked a lot of questions about Russell. I'm really worried, Mr Penders.'

'There's nothing to worry about.'

'He was at the reception last night, but I can't remember him. He said he was with Robyn Hawthorne, the film producer. I think you know her, Mr Penders.'

'Yes, I know her. Don't worry about it, Jamie, but if this Malcolm Reid approaches you again, try to find out what he's after.'

'But, it's just—'

'No buts, Jamie. Find out what he wants!'

'I'm sorry.'

'There is nothing to be sorry about. You did the right thing, Jamie. Now, just take it easy,' said Penders, and walked away.

Penders leant on the railings, and looked out into the fast fading light over the Botanic Gardens. This time, the beauty of the evening was completely lost on him. He was deep in thought wondering what to do about Malcolm Reid.

★

Penders was an early starter; he liked to be in his office by seven, because he treasured the couple of extra hours it gave him. By nine he had completed most of the day's business.

He picked up one of the many telephones on his desk.

'Doug?'

'Yes, Mr Penders?'

'Is Tony with you?'

'Yes, Mr Penders.'

'I want to talk to you both, right now.'

'Yes, Mr Penders.

Doug and Tony arrived in the office almost instantly. Penders nodded at them, but did not waste any time on preliminaries.

'I've got a little job for you,' said Penders as he handed them a folder with some background information, contact details and the photographs of Robyn and Malcolm.

'I want to know what these two are up to, especially when they are together.'

'Yes, Mr Penders. Video or audio surveillance?'

'I don't need to see them, but I want to know what they say.'

'Is there a budget on this?' asked Tony.

'Spend what you need. I have to know what these two are up to. I'd like a report on any contact between them. As soon as you can.'

'What about your personal security?' asked Doug.

'Don't worry about me. I'll get Paul and George to look after me while you're on this job. You just keep a close tab on these two.'

'*Yes, Mr Penders,*' they said in unison as they left.

Chapter Six

Malcolm had had a good day. He found his car, and took a year lease on an apartment in Redfern, not the most desirable part of Sydney, but the university was only a five-minute walk away. The flat was perfect, the rent was reasonable, and Malcolm was pleased with himself. He drove back to his hotel and checked out. There was a note left for him by Robyn – an invitation for dinner.

He moved into his new apartment, and celebrated the occasion with a bottle of Domaine Dey-Dey, a local bubbly. He fell asleep in the armchair, and woke up at two in the morning. He went to bed properly, and did not wake till ten the following day. He slept well, soundly and deeply, but felt more tired in the morning than the whole day before. He took a cold shower to wake himself up.

★

Robyn left early for work. She had a crisis on hand. One of the actors had gone down with hepatitis in the bi-weekly soap opera she produced. There was a script conference at eight thirty, but she was not bothered, they would cope somehow; she was more concerned with the lack of progress on the script about John Peter Russell.

Doug watched her as she drove out of the underground car park, and turned round the corner. Doug walked into the building and took the lift to the twenty-second floor. He entered Robyn's apartment by using a duplicate key. When he was satisfied that there was nobody about, he went about his business, planting microphones in the living room, kitchen, bedroom, bathroom, and even one on the balcony. Doug seemed to know exactly what he was doing, and the whole operation took him only a couple of minutes. He took the lift down into the foyer and walked out into the street. Fifty metres from the front door, he stopped by an old Datsun car and got into it.

He opened the glove compartment and switched on an MP3 mini-chip recorder the size of a matchbox. A green light came on, but the machine remained static. Doug picked up a small earpiece and dialled a telephone number on his mobile. It rang four times before Robyn's answering machine switched itself on.

'*This is a recorded Robyn Hawthorne. I'll get back to you as soon as I can. Please leave your name and number after the bleep.*'

He listened to Robyn's voice, adjusted the sound level, then switched off his mobile. Robyn's answering machine instantly cut off. Doug closed the glove compartment. He got out of the car and locked it; then he walked down the street.

Tony waited for him around the corner, sitting in a battered Holden station wagon.

'Right, mate,' said Doug as he got into the car. 'She's all wired up. Let's go to Redfern.'

Tony drove off without saying a word.

★

Malcolm was ten minutes early, and Robyn was late. They met in the foyer of her apartment block. He carried a large bunch of flowers and two bottles of wine; she was struggling with her briefcase and a large brown paper bag from the delicatessen.

Robyn showed Malcolm into her flat, still a little out of breath.

'Just make yourself at home,' she said, 'but first things first. How about a drink?'

She motioned towards the cocktail cabinet. He made up his mind to drink as little as possible without being too obvious.

'I'll have a large G and T,' she said.

Malcolm fixed the drinks, and made hers a stiff alcoholic one. He poured himself nothing but tonic water. Robyn dashed about the place. She was good at getting a meal ready in no time at all.

'Lemon and ice?'

'Yes, please. You'll find some ice in the fridge, in the freezer box at the top.'

Robyn unpacked the contents of the brown paper bag. It was full of delicatessen food, all ready to eat. She laid the table with the starter, placed some fruit in a large crystal bowl, replenished the cheese board, and then followed Malcolm into the kitchen.

She threw a couple of thick fillets of steak under the grill, mixed a bowl of salad and went back to the sitting room.

Malcolm struggled getting the ice cubes out of the aluminium tray; when he returned to the sitting room, the table was laid and Robyn was listening to her answering machine. She looked up at him as he handed her a tall glass.

'Sit yourself down,' she said as she took a sip. 'Heavens, Malcolm – your hand slipped or something? You're trying to get me drunk, aren't you?'

'Sorry. I'll get you some more tonic.'

'It's OK. I'll nurse this one along. I just want to see who's been after me... a working girl never stops, you know.'

She stabbed a button on the answering machine and listened to it while sipping her drink slowly.

'It's Greg Ericson, Robyn. Give me a call. You know what it's all about. The sooner the better.'

There were a couple more messages that meant nothing to Malcolm. It was all about her work and Robyn made a few notes in her personal organiser. Malcolm watched her from his armchair, sipping his tonic. She was aware of him watching and showed enough leg to keep him interested. She switched off the answering machine and walked over to the dining table.

'How do you like your steak, Malcolm?' she asked.

'Practically raw.'

'I was hoping you'd say that. That's what makes men so randy, lots of red meat. I'll just slip into something more seductive. You can open the wine.'

She went into the bedroom as Malcolm opened both bottles.

'And put something on the stereo,' she yelled through the open bedroom door. 'Something suitably romantic.'

Malcolm fingered along her CDs stacked by the bookshelves until he came to a CD of Stan Getz playing bossa nova. He put it on.

Robyn returned wearing a tight-fitting silk dress. She looked very sexy and she knew it.

'I love Latin music. I'm glad you put that on,' she said.

'I like jazz in any shape, but bebop in particular,' he said.

'It's the rhythm,' she said. 'I should know all about that, for a lapsed Catholic! Protestants have the pill and we have rhythm.'

Everything she said was full of sexual innuendo, and Malcolm was embarrassed by it. It also confused him, and he started wondering what exactly she wanted from him.

'I love the flowers. Thank you,' she said. 'I'd better put them into water before they wilt.'

Robyn left the room for a few seconds with the flowers and returned carrying a large cut crystal vase with the flowers. She placed the vase in the middle of the table.

'Let's start; the steaks will be ready in a minute.'

They ate the starter without a word. Avocado pears stuffed with a smoked salmon and caviar filling in a soured cream sauce. He tucked into the food, but his main interest was still Robyn. He kept on staring at her décolletage and she made a point of leaning forward as much as she could.

'But we're not drinking,' she said, 'and you've brought such excellent wine. Hunter Valley red, the best in Aussie.'

'Sorry,' he said as he poured the wine. 'I didn't think it would go with the starter.'

'Oh, but it does!'

They took a sip, and agreed that it went well with the avocado pears. They drank and ate merrily. She looked radiant in the candlelight, and he felt like making love to her. Never mind the food, though the steaks were excellent. They finished the wine with the steaks, and she brought in a bottle of vintage port with the cheese and salad. Malcolm was getting drunk fast. He tried hard not to give in, but she plied him with drink and he could not resist her.

'Cheers, Malcolm,' she said.

'Cheers. I have a feeling of déjà vu about all this,' said Malcolm.

'Naturally. You've been here before, don't you remember?'

'I half remember. I can only remember the morning after.'

'The morning after what?' she teased him.

'The morning after the night I stayed here,' he said defensively as he reached into his pocket and produced the ribbon he found tied to his willy. 'I found this, but I have no idea how I acquired it.

I can't remember anything about it...'

'You've forgotten it already? That sort of puts me in a spot. You spent the night here, and you don't know anything. You don't expect me to believe that...'

'I'm telling you the truth,' said Malcolm. 'I can't remember a thing between leaving that party in Rose Bay and waking up here, in your armchair. Honestly. I presume this ribbon is yours?'

'Could be.'

'Honestly, I can't remember a thing,' he repeated.

'And doesn't that worry you?'

'Should it?'

'You're asking the wrong question, Malcolm.'

'Well, what's the right one?'

'You should ask, did we or didn't we?'

'All right, did we?'

Robyn said nothing as she cleared away the plates.

'Well, did we?' he asked again.

'I'm not telling you,' she said.

'Why not?'

'Would you like some brandy with the coffee?'

'No, thanks. I'd better take it easy; I'm drunk enough already. Come on, Robyn, what happened the other night?'

'I'll tell you when I feel the time is right. Shall we talk about something else?'

'As you wish,' said Malcolm sullenly. 'Like what, for instance?'

'Like you, for instance.'

'All right. What do you want to know?'

'Why did you come to Sydney?'

'Why does anybody come to Sydney?'

'You're being flippant and it doesn't suit you. Why Sydney?'

'Teaching English Literature appealed to me.'

'But why here, in Sydney?'

'They asked me to come. I was headhunted. I didn't have to fill out an application form. All I had to say was yes.'

'I'm not convinced.'

'Well, it's never just one thing. Every time one makes a decision it's based on a combination of factors...'

'Like? Name me one.'

'How about a wet February in London?'

'That's a good one, but the South of France is closer to London.'

'Exactly.'

'So being eighteen thousand kilometres away is a plus?'

'Definitely.'

'You must have been upset about something. What was it?'

'Do you really want to know?'

'Yes,' replied Robyn quietly.

'My mother. We've had too many rows. The last one was really ugly, and I don't want to see her again.'

'Yeah, Sydney's far enough, I suppose. What was the argument about, if that's not too personal?'

'It is personal, far too personal, but I'll tell you. It was about my father. That's what we argued about.'

'I thought as much. You see, I've done some research about you. Tell me, how come your surname is Reid?'

'My mother was brought up by her stepmother, and she was a Reid. I got used to being a Reid, but I wanted to know who my father was. She refused to tell me; she fobbed me off with some stupid excuse, saying she'd tell me when the time was right, but I don't care anymore. I hope it's the Dalai Lama.'

Malcolm fell silent. Robyn hugged him gently, and gave him a glass of brandy. He drank it in a single gulp, and held out his glass for her to fill it up again. She did.

'I'm going to put the coffee on,' she said and went out into the kitchen. She took her time getting back, and Malcolm was composed again as he smiled at her.

'How about you? Tell me something about yourself!'

'We've had enough of families for one night,' she said. 'I ran away from mine just like you did, but for other reasons.'

'I'm sure my mother's worse than yours.'

'I wouldn't bet on that. My mother's in a class of her own.'

'But you're not going to tell me about her.'

'No. Perhaps another time.'

Malcolm couldn't keep his eyes off her body. He wanted to get into bed with her right away. Talking about families was the last thing he wanted to do. He walked over to her and made a clumsy attempt at trying to kiss her. Robyn pushed him away. He pulled back from her, blushing.

'Sorry… take it as a compliment,' he said.

Robyn had to stop herself from laughing. She wished she could have had a dollar for every time some man who made a pass at her used that excuse. She kept a straight face as she drank her coffee.

Malcolm just wanted to get up and go, but he couldn't think of an excuse. He drank his coffee in silence, then turned to Robyn and asked, 'All right, why did you ask me to come here?'

'I don't like the way you said that.'

'Come on – why me?'

'Why you what? What do you mean?'

'I'm not a complete idiot. I know when I am being picked up. Why did you pick me up?'

'All right. You're not just a pretty face, Malcolm. You can figure out things for yourself. You think I've got a hidden agenda?'

'Yes. What is it?'

It was all going wrong, Robyn reflected. He'd been putty in her hands, and now he had become difficult all of a sudden. She realised that she may have overdone the seduction act, but it used to work in the past. Perhaps Englishmen were different.

Limey bastard, she thought, but said nothing.

'You haven't answered me,' he insisted.

'All right, all right… I want you to help me with a film script. How about starting as friends, and see what happens? You say I picked you up, but you didn't run away screaming in horror, did you?'

'No, I was willing, I admit that.'

'Good,' she said sulkily.

'Friends?' he asked.

'Friends,' she said, 'but nothing else. OK?'

'OK,' he said. 'Now tell me about this script.'

'I'm working on a project based on the life of John Peter Russell, the painter, but I told you that already.'

'Yes. You told me. How can I help? I've never written a film script in my life; in fact I don't think I've ever seen one.'

'It doesn't matter. You can write it the way you like,' she said as she handed him a script.

Malcolm flipped through the pages, looking at the layout and form. He read a few sentences, then handed it back to her.

'Well, it's written.'

'It's not good enough,' she said.

'I wouldn't know about that. I don't know what a good script is like. It's not something I could help you with.'

'You've been to the cinema. You've seen films.'

'Yes, I've been to the cinema. And I've seen space rockets, but that doesn't make me a rocket scientist.'

'Look, just read this script and tell me what you think of it...'

'I can tell you that right now. It's rubbish.'

'You can tell – just like that?'

'I think so.'

'How?'

'A single sentence is enough; the man can't write.'

'How do you know it's a man?'

'Isn't it?'

'Yes, it's a man. Why don't you read it all the way through, and give me an honest opinion.'

'I don't need to read any more. It stinks, and you know it too.'

'OK. It stinks. Won't you please read the research notes at least? It's a terrific story. Russell was a terrific guy. He was rich, talented and handsome. He married the most beautiful woman in Paris – Marianna Mattiocco. He carried her off to a fairy-tale castle that he built for her on Belle-Ile...'

'In Brittany?'

'Yes, an island off the Brittany coast. Their love affair was the most terrific thing imaginable. They had friends like van Gogh, Toulouse-Lautrec and Rodin. Marianna was the model for Rodin's world-famous statue, "France". She was the kind of lady to inspire an entire nation. It would make a terrific movie.'

'You've used "terrific" four times in your pitch... That must be his favourite word.'

'Whose?'

'The man who wrote that script. He used it nine times in eleven sentences.'

'Stop pissing about, Malcolm. Are you going to help me or not?'

'All right. I'll help.'

'Terrific,' she said, smiling at him. 'I'll give you all the material I have on Russell.'

Robyn left the room and returned carrying a heavy shopping bag containing the script – all four drafts of it – plus the research notes and the galley proofs of Russell's biography. Malcolm took the bag from her.

'I'll read it all, and I'll let you know.'

She opened the front door for him and kissed him gently on the cheek. 'Thanks, Malcolm. And thank you for the flowers…'

'There's a condition,' he said, standing in the door.

'What?'

'You must tell me what happened that night.'

'Nothing happened.'

'We didn't, then?'

'No, we didn't, and we're not going to, either – until you write that script for me.'

She pushed him out of the door and sent him on his way. That was not the way Malcolm thought the evening would end, but he was happy as he got into the lift. He concluded that she probably liked him, and he was looking forward to spending some time with her. He was interested in John Peter Russell anyhow. He had three weeks to spare before term started – why not write the script?

Chapter Seven

As usual, Penders was in his office at the crack of dawn. He was listening to an MP3 mini-chip player. Malcolm's voice was saying: 'You must tell me what happened that night.'

'Nothing happened,' replied Robyn's voice.

'We didn't, then?'

'No, we didn't, and we're not going to, either – until you write that script for me.'

That was the end of the recording. Penders smiled to himself as he switched off the player and put it away in a drawer of his desk.

★

It took Malcolm all morning to sort out the material on Russell. There were four different scripts. He started with the last draft in order to save some time, but that was a mistake because the script made very little sense. He suspected that screenplays were not meant to stand on their own as pieces of literature, but Malcolm expected them to be coherent, if nothing else. Following the surrealist thinking of his upbringing, he read the third draft next. That was marginally better; the second draft was a further improvement, but the first draft was the best of the four. But even that was complete rubbish, the kind of nonsense they used to make in Hollywood in the Thirties. Not that Malcolm was an expert on the genre, but he had sometimes switched the television on the wrong channel in the middle of the day. The scripts were for those kind of films; all the stock characters associated with Bohemian artists in Paris living in attic studios overlooking the rooftops and the Eiffel Tower on the skyline. All their beautiful model mistresses outfitted by the best couturiers in town. Champagne parties at the Moulin Rouge and the Folies Bergères. All squeaky clean, antiseptic and deodorised.

The galley proofs were just as useless. The book was the perfect example of how not to write a biography: all trivia and conjecture, seasoned with name-dropping. 'Had Russell visited the Exposition Universelle he would have been impressed by the Tour Eiffel, one of the finest examples of architecture in iron, built by Gustave Eiffel for the 1889 Paris Exhibition,' Malcolm read aloud, laughing. 'Well, did he or didn't he? I'd like to know!' he screamed as he put the galley proofs down. The research notes for the biography looked a lot more helpful, as they were written in chronological order. He jotted down the important dates and names:

1858. Born 16th June. Father: John Russell, managing director of a foundry in Darlinghurst. Mother: Charlotte Ann Nicholl, daughter of William Grimsell Nicholl, the famous sculptor. Both parents are descended from respectable English families. The Russells claim aristocratic connections to the Bedfords in England.

1870. John Peter is sent to the Goulburn boarding school at Carrorrigang. Excels at games, boxing in particular.

1874. He is packed off to the South Seas on a holiday as a sixteenth birthday present. He is a strong young man, physically fit and over six foot tall. Sows his wild oats in Tahiti, like many other Europeans.

1875. John Peter sails to England. Apprenticed at Roby's of Lincoln to become an engineer.

1879. Qualifies as an engineer, but wants to become a painter. Returns to Australia hoping to show at the International Exhibition, but the hanging committee rejects his paintings.

His father dies on 1st December at 1 Bell Terrace, Acton, London, during a holiday in England.

1879. John Peter winds up his father's estate. His inheritance is £50,000, invested at 6% p.a. It produces a yearly income of £3,000.

1880. John Peter sets up a studio in Sydney. It is intended as a business venture, but it loses money heavily. John Peter sends his subscription to the Slade School of Art in London.

1881. Sails on board SS *Liverpool*. Meets Tom Roberts, who studies at the Royal College of Art in London. He becomes famous later for his landscapes of New South Wales.

1882. John Peter goes on an eighteen-month sailing trip

round the world, painting seascapes in oil on the way.

1883. Walking holiday in Spain with his brother, Percy, also Tom Roberts and William Maloney, an Australian medical student.

1884. Spring painting holiday in Cornwall. Enters English amateur boxing championships. Becomes champion at light-heavyweight. Moves to Paris. Rents apartment at 73 boulevard de Clichy. Dodge MacKnight sponsors him to the Atelier Cormon. MacKnight is a young American painter and a student at the studio. Fellow pupils are: Henri Toulouse-Lautrec, Louis Anquetin, Julian Rabache, Eugene Carrière, Emile Bernard and A S Hartrick from Scotland. Harry Bates, a sculptor from London, introduces John Peter to Marianna Mattiocco, the most beautiful woman in Paris. Her nickname is 'the Golden Gates of Hell'.

1885. Russell and Marianna fall in love at first sight, and she moves in with him. They set up house at 1 impasse Hélène.

1886. Vincent van Gogh joins the Atelier Cormon, and becomes a good friend. Vincent spends a lot of time with Russell and Marianna in their home, as he finds it difficult to make friends.

1886. Russell and Marianna go on a painting holiday to Brittany. They meet Paul Gauguin at Pont-Aven, and take an instant dislike to him. They consider him to be a poseur. Later, they move on to Belle-Ile, an unspoilt island off the Brittany coast. Russell meets Claude Monet, and invites him to his home at Goulphar. They paint together and he is exposed to Monet's revolutionary ideas on colour.

1887. Russell buys land on Belle-Ile, and starts to build a house near Goulphar. Painting holiday with Marianna to Moret-sur-Loing on the mainland. They stay with the Sisleys.

1888. John Peter marries Marianna at the Hôtel de Ville, Paris. Witnesses: Julian Rabache, William Dodge MacKnight, Moret Achille Cesbron and Henri Bisbing. They move to Belle-Ile. Russell completes building his home, the Château de l'Anglais.

1889. Russell exhibits with Impressionists at the Café des Arts.

1891. Painting holiday in South of France.

1896. Sarah Bernhardt buys the old fort on the north end of Belle-Ile. Russell detests her.

1897. A young Henri Matisse and Russell paint together. Russell gives him a present of two drawings by van Gogh.

1900. Russell buys the Villa Mequillet in Neuilly for the family, and they settle down in Paris.

1908. Marianna dies of cancer on 30th March. She is buried on Belle-Ile. Russell disperses his children to various boarding schools, and rents a villa on Lago di Orta not far from Lago Maggiore.

1909. John Peter sells his castle on Belle-Ile for £4,000 after he had spent £45,000 building it.

1911. Russell meets Caroline de Witt Merrill, a school friend of his daughter, Jeanne. Caroline is almost totally deaf.

1912. Russell marries Caroline de Witt Merrill, and buys a new property, in Neuilly, 56 rue Borghese, Paris 14.

1914. Caroline gives birth to Russell's sixth son, Hereward. War breaks out. Russell buys an apartment for Jeanne in Paris; hires a studio for his paintings, then leaves for London, because his five sons by Marianna are all fighting the war in the British Army.

1918. The war is over, and all the Russells survive it.

1921. Russell leaves Genoa for Australia to start a new life.

1922. Russell rents a fisherman's cottage at 22 Pacific Street, Watson's Bay, Sydney.

1928. Russell finishes terracing the gardens and the waterfront marina. Starts building a boat.

1930. Russell starts on interior decoration of the cottage, but dies on 22nd April while sailing his new boat alone. Caroline is on a visit to Europe.

Malcolm was pleased with his work; he managed to reduce the life of Russell to a manageable entity in the best tradition of the Literature of the Absurd. There it was, on just two pages: the essential Russell. All Malcolm needed was a new angle on Impressionist painters living in Paris during the belle époque. He thought Impressionism would inspire him and decided to do some research. It was not long before he was ready to write a treatment, in his own unique style.

J P R, A FILM TREATMENT BY MALCOLM REID.

Story:

RED/HUE/C/SUNDAY. Russell is the ultimate amateur in the most complimentary meaning of the word. He is born in Sydney into a respected and prosperous colonial family; naturally, with a silver spoon in his mouth. His father is a wealthy businessman and he sends Russell to be schooled at Goulburn, which is one of the top establishments in New South Wales.

ORANGE/LIGHT–DARK/D/MONDAY. Russell excels at sports and grows into a six-foot-tall athlete. He returns to Sydney and takes up sailing as a hobby. At sixteen he visits Japan and the Pacific Islands on board a trading schooner, and starts to collect Japanese prints well before any other artist in Europe. He loses his virginity to a Polynesian princess. He becomes an expert player of sexual athletics. He returns to Sydney as a man of the world.

YELLOW/COLD–WARM/E/TUESDAY. Russell decides he wants to be a painter and studies at the Slade School of Art, London. He meets John Ruskin, who is a professor of aesthetics. They get involved in a heated argument about Ruskin's disastrous marriage and his pathetic attack on Whistler. They end up fighting, and Russell knocks the impotent windbag to the ground.

He leaves the art college and goes around the world on a sailing trip, painting seascapes along the way. Later, he goes on a walking and painting holiday to Spain, accompanied by his younger brother, Percy. Also in the party are: Tom Roberts, a fellow Australian painter who studied at the Royal College of Art in London; and William Maloney, a young medical student from Sydney.

In 1884 Russell becomes the boxing champion of Great Britain, fighting as light-heavyweight. He moves to Paris and works alongside Vincent van Gogh and Toulouse-Lautrec at the Atelier Cormon.

GREEN/COMPLEMENTARY/F/WEDNESDAY. In 1885 Russell meets the most beautiful artists' model in

Paris, Marianna Mattiocco. They fall in love and she moves in with him. A year later, they go on a holiday in Brittany and meet Paul Gauguin in Pont-Aven. From there, they move on to Belle-Ile and set up house in Goulphar, where he meets Claude Monet and they paint together. From Monet he learns the basics of Impressionism and starts to paint accordingly. The young lovers live an idyllic existence on their own paradise island. He builds a castle for his fairy princess on the top of the granite cliffs overlooking the rugged Atlantic coast, and also builds a wonderful sailing yacht. They spend the winters in Paris, and in 1889 Russell exhibits with the Impressionists at the Café des Arts. He is a founding member of the Impressionist group of painters and exhibits with them. However, he thinks of himself as a dilettante who paints for a hobby. Russell does not sell any of his work, because he does not want to compete with his friends in the marketplace, even though his work is considered to be as good as his friends'.

During this period, Marianna gives birth to a daughter and five boys. The family alternates living between Belle-Ile and Paris and leads a busy social life. Most of their friends are artists – all household names today – and Marianna and Russell are the life and soul of any party. In 1897 the young Henri Matisse, just out of art school, turns up on Russell's doorstep on Belle-Ile. They strike up a friendship and paint together. Russell teaches Matisse about colour. Just as Monet tutored him, Russell helps the young painter, thus bridging Impressionism with fauvism.

BLUE/SIMULTANEOUS/G/THURSDAY. Then it all goes wrong. Marianna dies of cancer, and she is buried on her beloved Belle-Ile. Russell is completely devastated by her untimely death and in a moment of impulsive madness burns all his paintings of her. He swears to give up painting for ever, and sells the house on Belle-Ile. He moves to Paris. In 1911 Russell meets Caroline de Witt Merrill, a school friend of his daughter, Jeanne. She is almost totally deaf. Unexpectedly, Russell and 'Felize' (his nickname for Caroline) fall in love, in spite of their age difference; she is twenty-two, he is fifty-three. For him, it is not the burning passion that he had for Marianna but a gentle love for a dear companion. They get married in 1912 and Russell takes up painting again, but only in watercolours. Felize gives birth to a son, Hereward.

DARK BLUE/SATURATION/A/FRIDAY. In 1914 war breaks out. Russell stores all his paintings in Paris and leaves them in the charge of his daughter, Jeanne. Russell, Felize and Hereward spend the war years in London, because Russell's five sons from Marianna are all soldiers, fighting the war for England. The war ends in 1918 and all the Russells survive it.

VIOLET/EXTENSION/B/SATURDAY. Russell, Felize and Hereward start a new life in Sydney. He buys a fisherman's cottage with its own private frontage on the harbour. He renovates the cottage and starts building a new sailing boat. Caroline returns to Europe to visit her mother while Russell makes the maiden voyage of his boat. He has a massive heart attack and dies as he sails into the sunset.

Screenwriter's Statement:

The screenplay reflects the revolutionary and groundbreaking rules of Impressionism. Seven is the magic number: there are seven primary colours, seven different contrasts, seven notes in an octave, and seven days in a week. The narrative unfolds using a seven-act structure.

The Seven Primary Colours:

Red, Orange, Yellow, Green, Blue, Dark Blue, Violet

The Seven Kinds of Colour Contrast:

Contrast of Hue
Light–Dark Contrast
Cold–Warm Contrast
Complementary Contrast
Simultaneous Contrast
Contrast of Saturation
Contrast of Extension

The Seven Notes in an Octave:

C, D, E, F, G, A, B

The Seven Days of the Week:

Sunday, Monday, Tuesday, Wednesday, Thursday, Friday, Saturday

The screenplay incorporates all the elements of Impressionism. The screenplay uses words in the same way as the Impressionist painters applied their colours to their canvas. In this system there are seven primary emotions, and they are never mixed or blended. Emotions are used in their pure form, and their juxtaposition against each other provides incessant tension. Seven kinds of emotions are contrasted, and they provide constant twists and turns to the narrative. The mood is set for each scene according to the chromatic scale of music, and the timescale is set to the seven days of the week.

The vibrating attack on the intellect by unprocessed concepts creates an impression of reality. The rhythmical contrast of pure emotions drives the narrative forward and produces the feeling of observing the world through the prism of the Impressionists.

Malcolm telephoned Robyn and told her that he had finished the film treatment. They decided to meet that evening at a floating restaurant in Rose Bay. Robyn was paying on her expense account. The place was ludicrously overpriced but it had a reputation for excellent seafood. It was packed out with people showing off their jewels. Robyn and Malcolm sat on deck, overlooking the water. They had the best table. As Robyn was one of the regulars, the waiters made a fuss serving her. They completely ignored Malcolm.

They were at the coffee stage, having finished off two enormous John Dories. Robyn was sipping her brandy as she read through the treatment. He looked out of the window, waiting for her response. The restaurant was decorated with coloured light bulbs, their reflections shimmering and dancing on the water like a pearl necklace. In the distance, a hydrofoil cut across the harbour, all lit up by the dramatic afterglow of the setting sun. Malcolm could not get bored with Sydney Harbour; it offered a different picture every time he looked at it, each more staggeringly beautiful than the last.

Tony sat at a small table between the kitchen door and the lavatories. He had acquired a hearing aid, and kept on adjusting it as he listened to the conversation between Robyn and Malcolm.

Doug sat in his second-hand Holden parked just outside the restaurant. He, too, could hear every word on his mobile as he recorded the sound on a small MP3 mini-chip machine.

'I'll tell you,' said Malcolm. 'Whoever threw the research notes together hasn't got a clue. The story has been completely missed.'

Robyn nodded in agreement as she put down the last page. She turned to Malcolm, smiling happily.

'This is the most unusual treatment I've read.'

'I'm glad you like it.'

'I never knew Russell had a fight with Ruskin.'

'He didn't,' said Malcolm smiling, 'but he could have. It is feasible, and the timescale is right for it.'

'But why do you want to put that in?'

'I never miss a chance of putting the boot into John Ruskin. It's personal. He stands for everything I hate: a constipated hypocrite, an impotent old windbag who could not perform. Poor Effie…'

'And who is she?'

'Euphemia Gray,' said Malcolm. 'His wife, who ran away with John Everett Millais.'

'The painter?'

'Exactly. Millais did not faint at the sight of Effie's pubic hair.'

'Come off it, Malcolm! Who's interested in all that?'

'I am.'

'All right,' said Robyn. 'But I can't see how this fits into our story. This has nothing to do with Russell.'

'I'll make it fit, don't you worry, and I am also going to get the Whistler story in. Just you wait.'

'You mean the infamous court case? The one he won, and got a farthing in compensation?'

'That's the one: "Nocturne in Black and Gold". Ruskin accused Whistler of throwing a pot of paint at the canvas. I love that painting. Criticising it only goes to show that Ruskin was a pompous idiot with no appreciation of art.'

'I've never seen it,' said Robyn.

'It's a fireworks party over the Chelsea skyline. It's a magnificent work in every respect.'

'I take your word for it, but I'm not too sure about this seven-act structure of yours.'

'I'll make it work, don't you worry.'

'How?'

'That's my secret. I've swatted up on scriptwriting and installed the latest Final Draft on my computer. I'm raring to go.'

'Good – so you're going to write me that script?'

'I said I would.'

'That's terrific! It's the best news I've had for months,' said Robyn, without meaning it.

'Sure?'

'Sure, I'm sure. I'm really excited, Malcolm. To your script,' she said, raising her glass of brandy. 'I just hope this rule of seven will pan out for you.'

Malcolm lifted his glass as he smiled at her.

'It will, it will, you don't have to worry about that. Well, that was the good news.'

'Don't tell me there's bad news as well...'

'They always come in pairs,' smiled Malcolm.

'OK, OK. Hit me with the bad news. What is it?'

'There are some conditions, and you'll have to agree to them in advance, otherwise there is no script.'

'That goes without saying,' she said.

'I won't accept a time limit. It will take as long as it takes, and you won't get to see a single page until I've finished it all.'

'I'm not sure I like that,' said Robyn.

'Take it or leave it. I won't negotiate on that. I had a dreadful experience once, and I don't collaborate with anybody. I work alone, or I don't work at all.'

'OK. What about payment?' asked Robyn.

'Just pay me double the going rate.'

'Why double?'

'Because you're desperate and I'm brilliant.'

'Right – double the writers' guild minimum.'

'No, Robyn. Double the going rate.'

Malcolm took a piece of paper from his pocket and handed it over to her.

'I wrote the figure down for you. Call me greedy if you like, but I am doing this for the money.'

'You are greedy,' said Robyn. 'Very greedy indeed.'

'Is that a yes or a no?'

'It's a yes, I suppose, but you're holding a gun at my head.'

'It's business. Nothing personal.'

'All right, I'll get a contract drawn up.'

They drank their coffees in silence. The waiter came, and filled up their cups again. They ordered more brandy, then more coffee.

'Now that we're going to work together, tell me something about yourself,' he said.

'There's not a lot to tell.'

'Tell me, I'm really interested. I'd like to know.'

'I'm an only child, and I've been spoilt rotten by my father. Even though I am Australian through and through, my father is English. He came here on holiday and fell in love with the outback. He stayed on in Aussie, and married a nice Irish girl from Sydney.'

'Roman Catholic?'

'Naturally. Father was converted, and I was brought up in a convent school. My parents lived apart. He was off into the bush, looking for uranium, and she stayed in Sydney with her family. When my father visited us, he used to bring me very expensive presents, the sort of presents he couldn't really afford.'

'That's normal.'

'Well, it got up my mother's nose. They are divorced now. He runs a uranium mine somewhere in Western Australia. I see him once a year, and he still spoils me with expensive presents that he still cannot afford. Well, that's it in a nutshell.'

'I wouldn't have thought you were a convent girl.'

'Exactly. They are the rebellious ones, Malcolm, the convent girls. Ask any psychiatrist.'

'I'll take your word for that. How did you get into television?'

'That's a long story.'

'We've got all night.'

'Well, I was good at languages: French, Italian and Spanish. I got a scholarship to the Sorbonne, and I was in Paris when an Australian production company was filming there. They put an ad in the papers, and I ended up interpreting for them.'

'Just like that?'

'Just like that. I kept in touch with a couple of guys on the crew, and when I came back to Sydney, they got me a job with a company making commercials. You know how it is – one job leads to the next, and before you know it, you're a producer.'

'Sounds exciting, Robyn.'

'Not really. I never had any ambition, I just wanted to enjoy myself, and I've been walking through open doors all my life. I was always lucky to be at the right place at the right time. The rest is just hard work, and I always managed to hire others to do that.'

'How did you come across John Peter Russell?'

'Mac is a good friend of mine.'

'You mean Paul McDonald?'

'Yes. He's an authority on Australian watercolours, and you could say that he discovered Russell.'

'You mean rediscovered?'

'If you like. The guy who wrote the biography is also a

friend… do you want to meet him?'

'No. Definitely not!' protested Malcolm.

'The project fell into place by itself. I managed to screw some development money out of Channel Three. I didn't expect to go into four drafts, though… But you're going to write me a masterpiece, aren't you?'

'Well, it will be different.'

'That's what worries me.'

'Oh, you'll be happy,' he said, smiling.

'By the way,' she said. 'I have a condition, too.'

'And what's that?'

'This is strictly business, Malcolm. Don't get any funny ideas. I never mix business with pleasure. You'll have to respect that.'

Chapter Eight

Penders spent most of his time in his office, making money. Sitting at his desk, he had everything in one place to run his business. A bank of television monitors showed all the constantly changing quotations from the stock exchanges in Sydney, Melbourne, Perth, Tokyo, Singapore, London and New York. He also watched the dozen television channels he owned – simultaneously – as well as dictating letters and conducting telephone conversations, often three at a time. Penders knew how to select the important elements of the data on display and to respond only to what was absolutely necessary. He concentrated on listening to an MP3 mini-chip player.

It was Robyn's voice: 'This is strictly business, Malcolm. Don't get any funny ideas. I never mix business with pleasure…'

The intercom interrupted Penders. He hit the pause button.

'Yes, Susie, what is it?'

'Greg Ericson is here to see you, sir.'

'Send him in.'

The door opened, and Ericson walked in. His stride was full of confidence, and he sat down without being offered a chair.

'I was going to say sit down, Greg, but you've done that already.'

Ericson was in his late thirties and had started going to fat. There was a small bald patch on the top of his head, which he tried to cover by combing his hair over it, without much success. He had soft blond hair and pink skin, just like a baby. He was a smart dresser, and used a most distinctive perfume for men. Ericson considered himself to be God's gift to women. He was the studio head of Channel Three that year.

'I'm sorry to drag you over,' said Penders, 'but it's a delicate matter. I don't want it to develop into something big – which it isn't, if you know what I mean?'

'Yes, I do,' replied Ericson, without having the foggiest idea what Penders was going on about. 'I understand what you mean exactly. No sweat, Ralph.'

'How is Robyn's project coming along?'

'I haven't had the script from her, but I know she's finished it. David Swaab read it, and he said it stinks.'

'David always says that. He likes rewriting scripts. How much have we spent on it so far, Greg?'

'Oh, I don't know off hand. Peanuts... Thirty thousand...'

'I wouldn't call that peanuts, Greg.'

'Sorry.'

'OK. Never mind the money. I have a feeling that Robyn will ask you for more. Promise it to her, but give her nothing.'

'So you don't want to go with her movie?'

'Who knows, Greg? Who knows? Just promise her the money.'

'Whatever you say, Ralph,' said Ericson with a knowing smile.

Penders ignored his familiarity and reached into a drawer. He wished Ericson would stop calling him Ralph, but he would pay for that, eventually. Penders made a mental note of it.

He handed Ericson a file.

'I'd like Robyn to have this. It relates to her project. John Peter Russell kept a diary. She may find a new twist or something in there. Who knows? Did you know that Russell offered a collection of his paintings to the Gallery of Modern Art in 1921?'

'Did he?'

'It's the sort of thing that could interest her.'

'Sure, Ralph. I'm seeing her this afternoon and I'll give it to her. If you don't mind me asking, where did you come across this?' Ericson asked, opening the file.

Penders minded, but he replied in an even voice.

'My wife collects Russell's paintings. She likes his work and bought his correspondence at an auction as a job lot. The diaries were amongst them. Now, this is not public knowledge, Greg, and I'd like to keep it that way.'

'No sweat, Ralph. I know what you mean.'

★

Robyn put off seeing Greg Ericson because she had spent all the development money and had nothing to show for it. But she had been in worse situations before. She decided to tackle him in a positive frame of mind; at least she had a new treatment to show him.

She sat opposite Ericson in his enormous office at Channel Three, smiling at him.

'You've been playing hard to get, Robyn,' he said.

'Just busy, Greg,' she said.

'When can I have the script?'

'To tell you the truth, Greg, you wouldn't want to read it. I've got to the fourth draft already, but don't want to show it to you.'

'You showed it to David Swaab.'

'The little shit told you. Never mind... I've got a new writer, Greg. He's brilliant. I'll show you his treatment,' she said as she handed it over. 'You'll love it. It's a completely different approach, and it's going to be a great movie.'

Ericson flipped through the treatment.

'*Read it*, Greg,' insisted Robyn.

'All right. And I've got something for you to read.'

Ericson handed her the file containing Russell's diaries. She opened it with great interest.

'I read yours, you read mine,' he said, beaming, believing he had said something really witty.

'No, Greg. It's "I'll show you mine, if you show me yours". That's what they normally say.'

'And you've always been pedantic,' he said as he started to read Malcolm's treatment.

Robyn's face lit up as she glanced through the photocopied diaries. She went from page to page with a wider and wider grin on her face. When Ericson turned to her, she was reluctant to put the file down.

'It's different,' said Greg, 'but is there a script in all this?'

'There is, Greg, there is. Take my word for that... Where did you get hold of this?' she asked, holding up the file.

'Does it matter?'

'Not really – not unless I have to pay for it.'

'No, it's on the house. If you must know, Philippa Penders has the originals. She picked them up at an auction, but she wants to keep it a secret.'

'The cow! She's supposed to be a friend.'

'Now, you're not going to say anything.'

'No, I won't. Promise.'

'I mean it, Robyn.'

'And I promise… Oh, there is one other thing: I've run out of money. I'll need a top-up, Greg.'

'How much?'

'Thirty K,' said Robyn trying to sound casual, but her voice had a tinge of desperation to it.

'No way.'

'I'll settle for twenty.'

'We'll see.'

'Oh, come on, Greg.'

'We'll see, like the blind man said.'

'Is that a yes, or just a positive maybe?'

'I'll try to get you some money, I promise. You just push on with the script.'

'I've always said you were human, Greg.'

★

Malcolm could not get used to Sydney: the oven-hot pavements and the blinding light outside, and the dark, freezing cold, air-conditioned interiors confused him. It was either too hot or too cold. He dressed for summer and spent the day shivering.

It was Malcolm's first visit to the 729 Club, the watering hole of Sydney's television folk. He was told that in the past there were only three television stations in Sydney: Channel Seven, Channel Two and Channel Nine – hence 729. Looking through the windows of the club one could see the ABC buildings, or Channel Two.

Robyn arrived five minutes after Malcolm.

'I'm sorry I'm late, but I've got a lot on. It was good of you to meet me here, Malcolm.'

'My time is your time. Do you want a drink?'

'Something soft – orange.'

Malcolm got her an orange juice as she spread out some papers on the low coffee table.

'I'd like you to sign this contract, Malcolm.'

'Now? I can't see a sausage.'

'Just sign it. I didn't ask you to read it.'

'I don't need a contract, Robyn. I trust you.'

'I know that,' she said wearily as she explained. 'You don't need it, but I do. To get more money out of Channel Three, I need to show them a contract between you and me. Your signature makes it my property, and in turn, Channel Three's property.'

'Anything you say. Where do I sign?'

'Here,' said Robyn, handing him her fountain pen, 'and here… and here.'

Robyn looked over his shoulder as he signed the papers. They were sitting on low chairs so she could not help brushing against his body. He took advantage of her and kissed her behind her left ear. She moved away from him, but she did not really mind him. She enjoyed the feel of his lips on her neck, but still protested.

'Don't, Malcolm. Stop messing about.'

'Well, what's wrong with that?'

'Strictly business, remember?'

'I'll never understand women,' he sighed.

Robyn said nothing; she collected the documents from the table, and put them into her briefcase.

'I thought you liked me,' said Malcolm.

'I'll like you a lot better if you write me that script.'

'I have a feeling of being used,' he sulked.

'You're getting paid for it, so stop complaining. How's it coming along?'

'I'm stuck. I'll have to do some more research. I want to know a lot more about Russell.'

'I thought it was all there,' she said.

'No. I need to know what kind of person he was.'

'Do you? Then I'd better let you have this.'

She handed Malcolm the file. He opened it, but could not make much sense of it in the darkness.

'What is it?'

'The diaries of John Peter Russell.'

'You're having me on!'

'I'm serious. His diaries should tell you something new about him. Incidentally, he offered a collection of his paintings to the Gallery of Modern Art.'

'Did he? When?'

'In 1921, but the trustees didn't think much of Impressionism, and turned his offer down. I wonder what happened to the paintings.'

'So do I. It's getting curiouser and curiouser,' said Malcolm, 'but it all makes sense. They have nothing from him. I know; I've been to the gallery. They have a couple of drawings, but that's all. I sensed an air of hostility towards Russell the moment I set foot in there. No wonder they won't show his paintings. They don't have any, because they refused to have them in 1921. That must be an embarrassment to them today.'

Malcolm was excited about the diaries and could hardly wait to get home. He left Robyn, and drove home like a madman. He put the answerphone on, and opened the folder. It contained photocopies of half a dozen different diaries. The first one started in 1874 and was probably copied from mould-made paper. The last began in 1921 and was originally written in an exercise book. Malcolm started to read from the end. He always began reading from the end. It was his surrealist upbringing.

20th August 1921, Genoa.

Another diary, when I promised never again. Here I am at sixty-three, setting out on a new adventure. With a wife of forty and a son of seven to keep me company. I'm helping Sandro with his sheep farm, but that's not the real reason. That's just an excuse. I've had enough of Europe. That war changed everything. We thought we could just pick up our lives where we left off. Wrong. Saw the war through with the family in one piece. That's an achievement. I'm proud of my children, but they bore me. They are far too conventional, after all that I taught them. Perhaps it's me who is bored, but why am I expected to keep up a childish curiosity about the world for ever? I must go now; Felize and Hereward are pestering me to look at the sunset.

21st August 1921, Naples.

The bay is magnificent. Hereward doesn't understand the saying 'To see Naples and die'. He wants to see Naples and live. How refreshing. I don't feel like painting on this trip. I don't feel like painting, full stop. Felize and Hereward are good for me, but it's not the same. But I am not going to open up old wounds. I'm done with all that. I've got to be good to them, because they love me so much. Dear old Felize, deaf as a doorpost, but a heart of gold. It's touching how patient and good-natured she is. I must thank my lucky stars that she married me. And I like Hereward, too.

23rd August 1921, Athens.

Went ashore and visited the Acropolis. The place is falling apart. Hereward thinks it needs a roof. He may be right at that. We had an expensive but indifferent meal. Greeks shouldn't attempt French cooking. I am still obsessed with the past, but paint I must. That is my life. If I stop painting I'll die. My hand still obeys my mind, but there is more to art than craft. Rodin taught me that, the old goat. He had nothing but lust in mind; he still managed to produce works of art. I need a new source of inspiration, and I am going home to find it. I need something to do to numb the pain, and to stop the mind from thinking. I have something to offer to Australia and I should have made this move a long time ago. It may have made all the difference. No more ifs and buts, and whys and whens. Time is running out for me and I must use it well. Nothing else matters, but new discoveries, invention and creation.

24th August 1921, Port Said.

It was a mistake to travel at this time of year. The Mediterranean is as calm as a millpond. Not even a suggestion of a breeze. The boat is like a floating oven. I dread to think what the Red Sea is going to be like. Hereward is full of energy, and dashes about the place. I get tired just looking at him. Felize cannot stand the heat either, but she suffers it with a smile on her face. I don't know how she does it. I am too hot to think. Not a time for formulating ideas.

29th August 1921, Indian Ocean.

It took five days to cross the Red Sea. It was as bad as I imagined, but both Felize and Hereward enjoyed the experience. The Red Sea is not like a proper sea, anyhow. Give me the oceans any time. I love the open sea and I hated that dusty sewer. I am happiest when I am sailing in my boat. Just me and the open sea. I must live by the sea, and paint the sea. I am going to paint the Hawkesbury. Not Sydney Harbour, beautiful though it is. I must paint the creeks, forests and seascapes unknown to the European eye. Nothing in oil, though.

10th September 1921, Fremantle.

At last, we set foot on Australian land. The first time for Felize and Hereward. They have never seen gum trees and kangaroos, or heard the kookaburra laugh. They were very excited, and I got maudlin about it. I am still an Australian; no amount of time spent in foreign lands can change that. It's going to be a long summer for all of us. Having left Europe in an August heatwave, summer is just beginning here. It is a surprise for Hereward.

14th September 1921, Port Adelaide.

Sailing past the Great Australian Bight never fails to impress me. Felize and Hereward had never seen anything like it. It's the scale of it that's so imposing. It confuses the sense of perspective completely.

16th September 1921, Melbourne.

I've never liked Melbourne, and I still don't.

18th September 1921, Sydney.

Apart from Sandro, only Percy came to see us arrive. I haven't seen Percy since before the war. He looks a lot older than I expected. He apologised for Edith not coming to see us arrive, but she'd organised a little party to welcome us all. Percy and Felize got on well. The customs behaved badly. The most unhelpful bunch of miserable layabouts I ever met. They opened every crate we had. They had to fumigate everything to kill foreign bugs, and insisted on keeping the paintings in quarantine. I suppose it shows that Australia is a real democracy – here they couldn't care less who you are. They are equally rude to everybody. I don't know what sort of welcome I expected, but I am a little disappointed. Coming home meant a lot, but Sydney is different from the way I remembered it. I expected some changes, but nothing like this. It has all changed for the worse.

21st September 1921, Sydney.

Edith's little family gathering was a disaster. She hasn't changed much, apart from getting fatter and older. I could never stand her, even when we were children. I wonder if she really is my sister, but Felize thought she was just like me, apart from the beard and moustache. Edith went to a lot of trouble getting all the Russells in one place, and all for my benefit. They have been kind to Felize. She thinks I have a wonderful family, but I know they don't like her. It doesn't matter as long as she is happy. They have always been a snooty lot, even Percy. I should have remembered. It is amazing how the mind gets dulled with distance and the passage of time.

2nd October 1921, Sydney.

Met up with the old clan. Bill Maloney has long stopped practising medicine. He is quite a name in politics now. Tom Roberts has made it to the top, which I had always expected. He is a father figure to younger Australian painters. Percy played host to the get-together, and we talked a lot about our walking tour of Spain. That was in 1883, almost forty years ago. How we have changed! We didn't have one single argument, not a raised voice – what happened to all that passion? Percy is building Victorian villas all over the North Shore. Tom has lost his desire for experiment, and he is happy with his pastoral landscapes, all fossilised around the turn of the century. Expressionism, fauvism, Purism, cubism, Vorticism, Orphism, Futurism are just so many words to them. We talked a lot about the innkeeper's daughter at

Lac Cazeau, and toasted the loss of her virtue. Incidentally, they all claim the honour of being first, when I remember distinctly that it was I. I didn't argue the point. She fell for me, and me only. I doubt if the other three even as much as kissed her. Most disappointing evening. I was glad to get back to Felize. At least she is a good listener.

9th October 1921, Sydney.

At long last, the customs have released the paintings. I called in to see the curator at the Gallery of Modern Art. Couldn't even get to see him. They wanted me to write a letter. I did, then tore it up. They've even lost the samurai sword I donated them in 1874. I am not going to get worked up over it. It is the Australian public I want to help.

19th November 1921, Sydney.

Sandro is going off the idea of sheep farming. He doesn't fancy all the hard work, now that he has visited a handful of stations in the bush. He is talking about going to New Zealand to grow apples. Bill Maloney suggested that I should exhibit my oils from Europe. I'm not sure it is a good idea. I intend to go forward, and I am more determined than ever to paint on the Hawkesbury.

22nd December 1921, Sydney.

Had a letter from the trustees. They would like to refuse the offer of my collection, but don't seem to know how. Sandro is definitely going to New Zealand. We are going to spend Christmas in Sydney. Edith insisted that we should have lunch with her, seeing that Felize hasn't got a proper home yet. What's the point of getting a proper home if we are all going to New Zealand? I am certainly not looking forward to Christmas day, but both Felize and Hereward are getting excited already. I must go along with all the merriment.

6th July 1922, 22 Pacific Street, Watson's Bay.

We are back from New Zealand. Sandro is settled in his orchard. We celebrated Hereward's tenth birthday in our new home. It was a gloriously sunny day, and a lovely party, even though Edith made some snide remarks about Felize. Thankfully she cannot hear all that well. Perhaps that's the secret of her happiness. Hereward enjoyed the fireworks, but it alarmed the neighbours. But they are good sports, all joined in the fun and drank us dry, even though all I had was French wine, and not their idea of a gargle.

18th September 1922, 22 Pacific Street, Watson's Bay.

We are settling in. Felize seems to cope, in spite of our limited finances. I have started laying out the gardens, but I have no idea when I'll get round to digging the marina. I have a couple of ideas for the kind of boat I want to build, but that'll have to wait a bit. First things first. The trustees turned down my offer. I can't say that I don't mind, because I do. I consider it to be their loss. It is the ordinary Australian I feel sorry for.

16th June 1928, 22 Pacific Street, Watson's Bay.

My seventieth birthday. Felize organised a surprise party, and all my remaining friends turned up. Seeing them together, I noticed how we are all getting old. I realise that I have not touched this diary for six years. Since then, I finished the garden, the marina is ready, and so is the boat. Hereward is a great help. I couldn't have managed it without his help. He is exceptionally strong for a boy of sixteen. I remember being a little giant myself at that age, but he has overtaken me in strength. It won't be long before I sail up the Hawkesbury, but I promised Felize that I'd decorate the interior of the cottage first. She waited long enough for it and I must finish it by the time she gets back from visiting her mother.

That was the last entry in the exercise book. Malcolm put the diary down with tears in his eyes.

Chapter Nine

Suddenly Malcolm had too much on his hands. He had sufficient information to begin on the film script, but he did not feel like writing. He thought he still needed to know more about Russell, or even better, to find out what happened to the collection of his paintings the trustees refused in 1922.

He looked at his watch. It was ten past five. The day just flew by. Malcolm fixed himself a stiff drink while trying to decide where to begin. After the third large gin and tonic he realised that it was too late to do anything else but write.

He switched on his word processor, took a deep breath and began. He went on hitting the keyboard without stopping for half an hour, then got stuck. He realised that before he could continue he had to find the paintings Russell offered to the Gallery of Modern Art. It was too late in the day to contact them, but first thing in the morning he would start the detective work. He picked up the Russell diaries again. This time, he started at the beginning.

19th June 1874, SS *Narrabeen* at sea.

My first day at sea without seeing land. Left Sydney two days ago. We are heading for New Caledonia. I have six months to go wherever I please, do whatever I like. It was my birthday present, but I think Father wants to see the back of me. He knows that I support the strikers, and I should have kept my mouth shut about the strike, but I had to tell him he was wrong to lock the men out. I was sixteen on the sixteenth. Had a lovely party and lots of presents. Mother gave me this diary. I promised to write in it every day, but I've broken that promise already. I wish they hadn't all come down to see me off. I didn't mind Agnes, but Edith was full of envy. And why did they bring baby Percy? Our families embarrass us all, but Father is more pompous than anybody else I know. I don't really know him. Being the eldest son, he expects me to do exactly what he did when he was young. Now that I am sixteen, he thinks I should be his best friend! He gave me a long list of places to visit, things to do, how to keep out of trouble etc., but I think getting into trouble is the best part of travel. All his stories about the South Seas are about getting into trouble: shipwreck, cannibals, smugglers and dusky maidens. He laid it on thick about the big chief's daughter. It could be embarrassing to meet my half-brothers in Honolulu!

21st June 1874, SS *Narrabeen* at sea.

We sailed past Lord Howe's Island, but kept away from the rocks. The captain pointed out the site of a couple of famous shipwrecks, but I could only see the rocks and the spray. If he was having me on, he kept a straight face. He is good at poker, but so am I. We've been playing cards every night, and I've made a few bob. I don't think the others like it very much, me winning, but being six-foot-two tall has its advantages.

22nd June 1874, SS *Narrabeen* at sea.

Started to sketch the ocean. I must thank Grandfather Nicholl for his box of watercolours. They are very good paints, even using them with salt water. He had them sent from London specially. I've been trying out different washes, but it's not easy to get it right. I want it to look simple and effortless. That is probably the most difficult thing to do, but I shall persevere. I thought the other sailors would think it sissy to paint, but they seem to be impressed. The ocean is fantastic; it changes every minute. I'll have to learn to paint very fast.

23rd June 1874, Noumea, New Caledonia.

My first landfall. They are all French here, apart from the natives. Picked up extra cargo, a grand piano, so we are going to sail to Espiritu Santo in the New Hebrides. It will add on another four, five days to the journey. I tried to sketch the men loading the piano, but gave up, laughing. Never saw so many idiots, all yelling and shoving. Everybody knew how to do it, but nobody was pulling at the ropes. Even I was tempted to offer my opinion, but the captain stopped me. He watched it all with a straight face, and kept out of it. Wise man.

25th June 1874, SS *Narrabeen* at sea.

Tried out another way of painting. Wet the paper completely, then kept on turning it around after each colour. They blend and wash into each other, but I cannot control the finished effect. The sea was playing up all day. We could be in for some rough weather.

29th July 1874, Espiritu Santo, New Hebrides.

We had a rough passage and I've been sick as a dingo. I didn't expect to be seasick, not after all the sailing I've done in Sydney Harbour and up the Hawkesbury. The swell was fifty, sixty foot, and I didn't realise what a fragile craft our schooner is. It looked impressive docked at Darlinghurst, but it was dwarfed by the waves. I thought we'd lose the aft rigging, but it held. The captain was never perturbed. Perhaps I'm not as good a sailor as I thought. We are anchored off the harbour. They are trying to lower the grand piano into a cutter hardly bigger than the piano itself. We are going to weigh anchor as soon as we get rid of the piano. The captain has lost enough time due to the storm already. It is a shame; I would have liked to walk about the place, though it looks a little bleak.

2nd August 1874, Suva, Viti Levu, Fiji.

Approached the island from the south-west with caution. The captain tells me there are over 800 islands in the Fiji group. Suva has a difficult harbour on account of the numerous little reefs. Must say, the captain handled it well. I was sorry to leave the SS *Narrabeen*, as they were all very kind to me, even though I took thirty pounds off them playing poker. They all assure me that I'll be unlucky in love. We shall see. My cousin Lionel met me. He was the only white man about, luckily. I wouldn't have recognised him, even though we met five years back when he visited Sydney. He is the son of Uncle Robert. For some reason the family never talk about him. I wonder if news of the feud between my father and Uncle Peter has reached Fiji.

3rd August 1874, Ra, Viti Levu, Fiji.

I feel shattered after yesterday's journey from Suva to Ra, where Uncle Robert lives. Lionel told me how well business was. Uncle Robert has made a fortune in sandalwood, and he has a contract to build a private railway for a sugar company. They brought in four hundred Indians from Mysore to do the work. The house pleasantly surprised me. It has all the luxuries one wouldn't expect in the middle of the jungle. Uncle Robert laid on some excellent tucker for my benefit. Fiji is the place to make money. The natives are constantly at war with each other. Deserters from the navy are flogging rum and muskets to them. It's all good business. Uncle Robert says he keeps on the right side of the law, but I wish he'd say it without grinning so much. I like him a lot. He thinks my father and Uncle Peter are humourless bores, and I agree with him. Not that I said anything to him; I don't want him to think that I'm sucking up to him. I think he did the right thing not to get involved with the ironworks. Apparently the strike is solid in Sydney.

5th August 1874, Ra, Viti Levu, Fiji.

I've spent the day painting. I had two bodyguards with me, Fijians with flintlocks, which would have done more harm to them than to any attackers; but they looked very fierce. My painting is improving. If only I could manage to paint what I intend. Learning is a long process, I suppose. Lionel is following me around. I wish he'd leave me alone. He must be starved for company, and he wants to go to Sydney. He is not interested in making money.

6th August 1874, Ra, Viti Levu, Fiji.

Painted the house today. I've managed to catch the shifting clouds in the sky. There is a feel of movement and speed about them. It's my best painting so far. Lionel let me into a secret; my father has a mistress. She lives in the Hôtel Modern, not far from the ironworks, up the hill towards Kings Cross. He followed my father and saw her. She is very young and beautiful, but wears rouge. I'm not sure Lionel should have told me about her. He is three years older than myself, but behaves like a child. I don't know what to make of his story. I made Lionel swear he'll never tell anybody else. I am the first person he told about it he says, but I don't believe him. I think he's just sucking up to me.

7th August 1874, Ra, Viti Levu, Fiji.

I've shown my painting to Uncle Robert. He was very kind about it, but he thinks IT IS NOT FINISHED! He asked me to let him have it, after I've finished it.

9th August 1874, Ra, Viti Levu, Fiji.

I let him have it. I FINISHED IT FOR GOOD. It's all stiff and lifeless, but he loves it. We drank a lot of champagne in the evening, and Uncle Robert talked a lot about the family. Robert Russell, my grandfather, was the first in Australia. He came from Scotland, and was an engineer by trade. He owned a foundry in Kirkcaldy with his brother, but they went bankrupt. Grandfather Robert started a foundry in Hobart Town in Van Diemen's Land, but the business was not a great success, and life was hard. Grandfather thought of moving on. Uncle Robert was the eldest of nine children. He went to Sydney to find out about business opportunities there. Sydney was a boom town without the convict problems of Hobart. They moved to Sydney, and set up the present works at Queen's Place, Darlinghurst. There was a lot of acrimony before the brothers sorted out who should run the business: it was Peter, the second eldest. Robert moved to New Zealand, then to Fiji. My father, John, was the third eldest. He took to the South Seas and became a trader. He was to marry a Hawaiian princess (so there is something to that story after all), when Peter asked him to return to Sydney. He was a brilliant engineer, but useless as a businessman. Peter and John ran the works together, but my father kept on having rows with his elder brother, and forced him out of the business. Peter was given an allowance, and went to live in London. According to Uncle Robert, it was Peter's English wife who made them quarrel so much. She was the cause of most of the trouble. He says that what she needed was a dozen children to sort her out, but she couldn't have any. She kept dogs and cats instead. Uncle Robert was unhappy about my father taking over the business; he reckons it should have been himself, but he is getting a fair allowance. It seems my father managed to turn the business around, and it is a profitable concern. Uncle Robert grudgingly admits to that, but if the strike carries on, there may be no business left to quarrel about. I should have found all this boring, but I think it's interesting. Quarrelling is a Russell family tradition. I don't feel so bad about not liking Edith, and I certainly won't go into business with Percy.

14th August 1874, Suva, Viti Levu, Fiji.

I've said my goodbyes to Uncle Robert and Cousin Lionel. They cannot say I rushed off in a hurry, but I don't think I could have stayed longer without falling out with them. I've found a French sloop, *La Mouette*, which is Tahiti-bound. I'm not sure that I fancy risking the journey on board her – she has the most peculiar rigging; usually there is a gaff-topsail and a forestay sail, but I cannot make any sense of this one. My father used to tell me that there are three ways of doing anything: the right way, the wrong way, and the French way. I can now see what he meant.

17th August 1874, *La Mouette* at sea.

I've decided to take a risk. The fare is very reasonable, if we ever get to Tahiti. I have no confidence in the crew. They don't like me, and it's reciprocal. I don't think they have been to France, ever, apart from the captain. Him in particular I mistrust. He's picked up some Australian expressions, and he is showing them off for my benefit. I think he's 'cranky', to use an Australian expression. We are hopping from island to island. They are collecting copra, vanilla, and mother-of-pearl from the smaller islands, where other ships don't normally call. I have no idea why the French and English so dislike each other. But in any case, I am

Australian, and I don't understand why they are giving me such a hard time. I started painting again.

19th August 1874, Buca Bay, Vanua Levu, Fiji.

We only dropped anchor for a couple of hours. There is a war in progress. The Fijians are armed to the teeth. The captain is involved in gunrunning, or something shady. We delivered a couple of crates, but collected nothing. It took a lot of bantering before all sides were happy, and we cast off. One of the crew has taken a positive dislike to me. He is at least three inches taller than I am, and every time he comes near me he swears at me in a language I cannot understand.

20th August 1874, Taveuni, Fiji.

Went ashore for a walk while the crew was loading with copra. Watched divers fishing for trocas shells. They go down to three fathoms, and stay under for a couple of minutes. They look half dead when they resurface, and spend hours recuperating between each dive. They are puny little fellows, not built for physical exertion. It is amazing what amount of suffering people will endure to make a living. They seemed happy enough when I approached them. Made a few sketches of the divers. They were impressed. I offered them some of my drawings, but they refused in panic.

22nd August 1874, Lakemba, Fiji.

Dropped anchor late evening. Crew went ashore for 'a root', as the captain informed me. When I pretended I didn't understand him he elaborated in broken English. Phrases like 'tit-happy' roll off his tongue in profusion. If he weren't so vile, I suppose he could almost be comical. Later, I tried a watercolour by the light of the moon. I won't know how successful it's going to be till tomorrow. The light was magical, but there is something hostile about this place – I can feel the presence of dead souls. I am not normally superstitious, but I'll be glad when we leave. The crew came back at midnight. I had an argument with the nasty one. He reminds me of a cock with a sore throat; his voice is shrill and he has a hooked nose. I'll have to watch him. Monsieur Cocorico had one jar too many, he could hardly stand straight. I walked away from him; one doesn't argue with a drunk.

23rd August 1874, *La Mouette* at sea.

I must paint by moonlight again. I am very pleased with the result. I've managed to capture that haunted feel of the island. The captain tells me the inhabitants are cannibals. They ate the last missionary, but did not like him. Tasted too much of whisky! Perhaps that was meant as a joke.

24th August 1874, Vatoa, Fiji.

Monsieur Cocorico tried to pick a fight with me after we'd dropped anchor. Luckily, I brought my boxing gloves with me from Sydney and a couple of spare ones. The captain was game, and we went ashore to box. The crew was thankful for an opportunity to bet on something new. Monsieur Cocorico was a lot stronger than I thought. He surprised me with a right hook, but he had no boxing craft, and I managed to keep him at length with left jabs, and picked him off as I pleased. He has a sore jaw now to go with his sore throat. I don't think I'll have any more trouble from him. Vatoa is a beautiful island. I've painted the reef. The swell is tremendous. I watched the Fijians coming back from fishing. Their skill is amazing; how they manage to bring in their fragile katta marams is a miracle. They paddle like madmen as they approach the reef, then using the power of the swell, they guide their craft through even the tiniest of openings in the reef. The waters are absolutely still inside the reef. Kattamaram means 'tied together wood' in their native tongue, and that's exactly what their canoes are. They look rickety, but I'd like to try them one day.

25th August 1874, *La Mouette* at sea.

We've left Fiji behind us, and are heading for Tonga, the Friendly Islands. I've got a black eye to match my bruised nose. It came up quite nicely. The crew keeps its distance from me as I paint on deck. I am still trying different ways. For watercolours one has to work very fast. The first line must be right. It's no good going over, trying to rework it. I like a wet paper and thick, undiluted paint. Each painting is an improvement on the previous one. I cannot wait to show them to Grandfather Nicholl.

27th August 1874, Nuku'alofa, Tongatapu.

I've left the *Mouette*. I never liked the boat, because the crew was the scum of the earth. This place looks friendly enough; it's an independent kingdom, right in the middle of nowhere. The king is Taufa'ahau Tupou, otherwise known as King George I. His kingdom is a democracy of sorts. I've learned this from the Reverend Roger Whitherspoon, a follower of the Wesleyan Church. He met me at the quay and kindly offered me accommodation. I couldn't very well refuse, though I tried. He kept on looking at my nose, but thank the Lord (now I've started to write the way he speaks), the swelling has gone down, and the black eye is barely perceptible. He didn't ask me anything about my face, so I told him nothing. He suspects I'm a lot younger than I look. I told him I was nineteen.

9th September 1874, SS *Mary Anne* at sea.

I'm Tahiti-bound in a square-rigged brig. A much better way to travel. I have a large cabin of my own, and I set up my easel inside it as I intend to paint at night again. The food is good. A nice change from Mrs Whitherspoon's cooking. I wasn't happy staying with them, there was too much Bible-thumping for my liking. Religion has never seemed important to me. Mustn't stay with men of the cloth again, however persuasive they may be. He never allowed me a moment to myself, and I have a nasty suspicion I know why. The Tongans may be Christians, but they are not called 'friendly' for their smiles. Some of the girls were very beautiful, and I felt the odd twitch in the loin. Reverend Whitherspoon made sure that I could do nothing about it.

Chapter Ten

Malcolm spent the morning at the Gallery of Modern Art. He went through everything in the reference library, but there was no sign of Russell's correspondence. He was checking the index cards for the second time when Jamie de Selway walked into the room.

'Hello, fancy seeing you again.'

'I hope you can help me,' said Malcolm as they shook hands.

'Sure. What would you like to know?'

'Anything – and everything – about J P Russell.'

'I know,' said Jamie. 'You told me last time you were here.'

'Did you know that he offered a collection of his paintings to this place in 1921?'

'No. I've never heard about that.'

'There must be some record of it somewhere here. He exchanged letters with the trustees, but I can't find them anywhere.'

'Oh, you wouldn't. Not here.'

'Well, where?'

'I'm not sure if it's possible.'

'Come on, just a peep. I won't tell anybody.'

'I suppose it's all right… Come with me.'

Jamie led the way along the corridor, and opened the door to a dark and cramped storage room. A couple of naked lights hung from the ceiling, but the forty-watt bulbs had no chance of illuminating the place. They stumbled along in silence until Jamie reached a line of rusting steel filing cabinets. He pulled out a couple of drawers before he found what he was looking for. It was a wooden tray of index cards. He flipped through them as Malcolm looked on expectantly.

'Let's see,' said Jamie. 'It must be here somewhere. Oh, yes, there is a file of correspondence. JPR/SSC 24 Z.'

'Good. Good man, Jamie.'

Jamie pushed in the heavy metal drawer, and moved along the

line of filing cabinets. Malcolm followed him excitedly. Jamie pulled out another drawer, and went through the dusty old files. Malcolm watched over his shoulder, hardly able to contain himself. Eventually, he pulled out a very thin file, and opened it.

'It's all been transferred to microfilm. August 24th, 1963, it says.'

'I see,' said Malcolm. 'How about the microfilm? I can't take the suspense, Jamie!'

'They are kept in the room we've come from.'

They walked all the way back. Malcolm was practically running, and Jamie had a job keeping up with him. It took a while before Jamie found the microfilm, and a lot longer to get the projector working. Eventually, Jamie wound on the roll of microfilm, but could not find the missing letters.

'They are not here,' said Jamie.

'They must be. Let me try,' said Malcolm.

Jamie stepped aside, and Malcolm wound through the roll of film. Between the 22nd and 25th of August there were just two pages marked 'DELETED'.

'There you are,' he said proudly.

'What do you mean?' asked Jamie.

'Russell had a battle with them. They hid the letters trying to save face. It's the same the world over. The basement of the Royal Academy is packed with masterpieces. The narrowness of the academic mind is beyond belief,' ranted Malcolm. 'I just hope they didn't destroy them.'

'Calm down, I'll see if I can find them. Where can I contact you?'

'Well, at the university, but I'll be home for the next couple of weeks. I'll give you both my numbers.'

Malcolm scribbled a couple of telephone numbers on a piece of paper, and handed it to Jamie.

'I'd be most grateful, but frankly, I don't hold out much hope that you'll find anything.'

'I'll call you, either way,' said Jamie as he folded up the paper and put it into his pocket.

Malcolm's next port of call was the Paddington Gallery. It was empty but for a couple of tourists. They were not well dressed enough to buy anything, and were left to their own devices. They drifted from room to room, clutching their nine-dollar catalogues close to their chests, guarding them as if they were made of gold.

McDonald was talking to Penders in his private office as Malcolm walked into the gallery. Penders noticed him through the two-way mirror.

'You've got a visitor, Mac, but I don't want to see him,' he said. 'I'll talk to you later.'

'All right, as you wish,' said McDonald as he showed Penders out the side door. 'It was nice to talk to you, Mr Penders.'

McDonald closed the door behind Penders, and went to meet Malcolm. He smiled as he held out his hand.

'Hello, Malcolm. Nice to see you again. Robyn tells me you're writing a script on JPR.'

'Trying to,' replied Malcolm as they shook hands. 'I'm stuck with my research. I thought you might help.'

'Sure. I had to do some homework myself to prepare a catalogue on JPR. You're welcome to that.'

'That's very kind of you.'

'Come into the office. I'll see if I can lay my hands on it.'

He showed Malcolm into his office. While he was looking for the documents, he kept an eye on the gallery through the two-way mirror.

'Oh, here we are,' he said proudly as he handed Malcolm half a dozen sheets of paper.

Malcolm skimmed through the notes.

'This relates to what you had on show. What about his oils?'

'JPR left his oil paintings in France in the care of his daughter. She bequeathed the lot to the Louvre. Rodin's silver bust of Marianna was amongst the collection. There was a lot of acrimony over the remaining oils, in the best Russell family tradition. They are all in private collections, apart from the oils of Marianna.'

'What happened to those?' asked Malcolm.

'Destroyed. Russell was so upset after her death that he couldn't even look at them. He burnt over a hundred pictures on a bonfire. They were his best work. I told you, painters can be a real pain in the butt. Russell abandoned oils after that altogether, and only painted watercolours.'

'Where do you get his watercolours from?'

'I can only get his Australian work. Fortunately, nobody is collecting JPR seriously, apart from Philippa Penders. I can remember a couple of them changing hands through my gallery.'

'And taking a handsome commission,' said Malcolm cattily.

'That's what I'm in business for. Admission fees and flogging catalogues wouldn't even pay the rent.'

'What do you know about Russell's oil paintings?'

'Not a lot. I couldn't afford to find out. Michel Boisset in Paris has compiled a catalogue, but it was far too expensive for me. Here's the address,' he said as he gave Malcolm a piece of paper. 'You can keep all that if you like.'

'Thanks. I'll get them photocopied and let you have them back. By the way, did you know that Russell offered a collection of his paintings to the Gallery of Modern Art in 1921?'

'No,' he replied. 'And what happened to them?'

'The trustees turned down his offer. Nobody knows what happened to the collection. That's what I'd like to find out.'

'Wouldn't we all?'

Malcolm liked being a detective. Next, he visited the *Sydney Correspondent*. The editor had not forgotten his interview for the paper. Unfortunately, they had little on John Peter Russell. Malcolm ploughed through a pile of newspapers, yellow and brittle with age, checking the obituary columns. He jotted down what little there was into a notebook, and left the newspaper library.

He called Philippa Penders on his mobile. His luck was in. She took his call.

'It's Malcolm Reid. I was at your party.'

'I know who you are, Malcolm. I haven't forgotten you. Now, what can I do for you?'

'I was told you're collecting John Peter Russell's paintings…'

'Who told you about the diaries?' cut in Philippa.

'Nobody,' replied Malcolm.

'It doesn't matter now,' sighed Philippa wearily. 'I suppose you want to see them?'

'Well, yes, if you can spare the time?'

'I can,' she said as she put down the telephone.

A wall of hot air hit Malcolm as he stepped out into the street. It was another scorching afternoon. There was not a single cloud on the horizon, and the sky was a dark shade of indigo.

Malcolm got in his beaten-up Jag, and wound all the windows down. It still felt like being in an oven. He only half remembered where Philippa lived, but he could always find a place, once he had been there. Alas, his navigational skills let him down in the Southern Hemisphere. He still felt as disorientated as on the first day; the sun shining up north confused him. He headed for Rose Bay, but soon lost his way. He was wondering why Philippa mentioned the diaries. He remembered clearly that he had said nothing about them. How does she know I've got them? he wondered, as he drove along street after street, each looking exactly the same as the one before. He drove through Rose Bay a couple of times before he turned into a familiar-looking street that led down towards the water's edge. It looked like the one he was searching for; he recognised it in spite of the shimmering heat haze over the tarmac, even though the last time he had been there, it was two in the morning. He pulled up outside Penders' luxurious house. His car looked positively out of place.

Philippa had a sublime beauty: exquisitely fragile, delicately fey, eternal, and – above all – unattainable. She had been aware of her effect on men from an early age, and found it difficult to understand. She believed herself to be normal, but nobody treated her normally. Philippa was worshipped for reasons unbeknown to her. Men thought she could solve their problems just by her very presence. Eventually, she learned how to cope with this image others formed of her; she said little, and let others make all the moves. It was a giant fraud, but if others invested her with divine powers, who was she to argue with them? At times she even fantasised about being ugly. Perhaps then she could have had a personality of her own, but being beautiful was less of a problem, and she accepted it philosophically; she may have been imprisoned by her looks, but it was a comfortable prison.

Malcolm stared at her, admiring her beauty like millions of others before him. He was completely lost for words. There was a bandage on her right hand. She followed Malcolm's eyes and touched the wound, almost subconsciously.

'Would you like something to drink?' she asked him to break the silence. 'Tea? Coffee? Something else?'

'Oh, nothing. I don't want to take up your time.'

'I have all the time in the world, Malcolm.'

'Then I wouldn't mind a nice cup of tea.'

A Filipino houseboy appeared almost as if by magic, and waited patiently for Philippa's command.

'We'll have some tea, Sam. Bring it to the summerhouse.'

The houseboy bowed silently, and disappeared into thin air. Philippa turned to Malcolm.

'I hear from Robyn that you're writing a script about JPR.'

'I've started writing it, but I'm still at the research stage.'

'I'll show you what I have,' she said as she took Malcolm by the arm. 'Come, I keep the paintings in the summerhouse.'

They walked through the beautifully kept garden. A Filipino gardener smiled at them as they walked past him. He was on his knees digging amongst the bushes.

'I couldn't help noticing, but all your servants have come from the Philippines,' observed Malcolm.

'Blame Ralph for that. It's his sense of humour. *Me is Philippa, they am good-fellow-Filipinos-belong-me,*' she said in Pidgin English. 'They are all wonderful people and I've come to like them a lot.'

The summerhouse was light and spacious. Here, the customary chill of air conditioning was replaced by a pleasant breeze blowing off the water. On the walls hung twenty or so watercolours by Russell, seascapes of Sydney Harbour from a similar vantage point near where they stood. Malcolm did not have to ask why; he remembered that Watson's Bay was just round the corner.

'I've been collecting JPR's work for some years,' she said. 'I'm probably Mac's best customer.'

Malcolm walked round looking at the paintings. They were all masterfully executed, but lacked passion. All the same, he was impressed by Russell's professionalism. Standing only centimetres away from his work, Malcolm felt he knew the man intimately. Knowing how Russell's life ended, the paintings took on a fresh poignancy, and were extremely sad. Adjoining the summerhouse, there was a small studio. Malcolm walked towards its door.

'Oh, there's nothing in there,' said Philippa.

'What do you mean, nothing?'

'It's nothing but a hobby – it wouldn't interest you,' she protested.

'May I?' he insisted.

'Well, if you must,' she replied with a sigh.

Philippa's work was rough and primitive, but she had a good sense of perspective and movement. They were also harbour views. She had a rich sense of colour; all primary shades reminiscent of the lush tropical flowers in the garden. Malcolm was impressed. He did not expect her to be capable of so much originality. She was Penders' little trinket, a china doll to be admired from afar; yet these were powerful paintings, pulsating with energy. It made no sense.

'They are wonderful,' he said.

The houseboy came with the tea.

'Sit,' said Philippa pointing to a comfortable cane armchair. 'We shall have tea on the terrace.'

'It's certainly a nice day for it,' said Malcolm.

She looked at him quizzically, and he felt like a complete idiot. Nobody discussed the weather in Sydney, not in midsummer.

'Milk?' she asked.

'Yes, please.'

'Strong?'

'Oh, as it comes,' said Malcolm.

She handed him a cup of perfect English tea, half Darjeeling, half Earl Grey. Malcolm took it for granted that it would be just right, and it was.

'You must tell me something about yourself,' he asked Philippa.

'Like what, for example?'

'Anything. I know practically nothing about you. Other than that you're Ralph Penders' wife.'

She smiled at his honesty.

'That's how most people know me,' she said, 'but I don't mind. I am happy to be Ralph's wife. Anyhow, I did nothing spectacular myself before I married him.'

'I thought you were an actress.'

'I had a couple of months on the fringe. I was Velvet Ripple.'

'Who, what?'

'Velvet Ripple. It was a good show: *The Procurement of Velvet Ripple*. I played the title role before Ralph took the show over and recast it. I was wrong for the part, anyhow. He replaced me with a big-busted, loud-mouthed, red-haired tart. The show took off and Ralph made a fortune. He was right, as always; I never felt easy in the part.'

'Why?'

'Because the show was all about the Australian male's idea of the perfect "root".'

'Wash your mouth out!' said Malcolm. 'You're not to speak like that. You shatter all my illusions.'

'Don't you start on that, Malcolm. My interest in you is strictly maternal,' she teased him.

'I hope not. I hate my mother.'

'That's a horrible thing to say!'

'But it's true, honestly. I hate her, deeply and passionately. It's all on record.'

'I don't want you to have the wrong impression about me,' she said. 'I'm just an ordinary woman. All I ever wanted was to have kids, and cook for my husband.'

'Pull the other one, Philippa,' he said brutally.

She fell silent suddenly. Malcolm looked up at her and she was on the verge of crying. He had no idea that it would upset her.

'I'm sorry, Philippa.'

'It's all right,' she said. 'How are you to know what upsets me and what doesn't?'

'But what did I say wrong?'

'Nothing. It's just that Ralph won't let me have any children.'

'Then leave him,' he said passionately.

'That's easier said than done... But I thought you wanted to know something about JPR, and not me.'

'Indeed. I'm all ears,' he said quietly.

'Who told you about the diaries?' she asked.

'You did,' he replied. 'Robyn gave me a set of photocopies, but she never told me where they came from, and I didn't ask.'

'Then why did you phone me?'

'Paul McDonald said that you collected Russell's watercolours. That's why I called you. I wanted to see them, and now I have.'

'Do you like his work?'

'Yes, very much.'

'They are very sad, aren't they?'

'Yes,' replied Malcolm, 'very sad.'

'I'll show you his letters. Come!'

She walked back into the summerhouse. Russell's letters and diaries were kept in a small filing cabinet by the door. Philippa pulled out the top drawer.

'I'm afraid they are in a mess. I've never had the time to sort his letters into any sort of order. I just dipped into it any old how. Help yourself,' she said. 'I've got a few things to do in the house. Take your time. You'll find the diaries in the lower drawers.'

'Thank you.'

Malcolm browsed through the letters. He had never expected to see so many letters. He skimmed through them, looking for anything dated 1921 or from the Gallery of Modern Art. Half an hour later, he had finished checking, but there was no sign of the correspondence relating to the Russell Collection, as Malcolm started to refer to the paintings in his mind. He took out the diaries. There were nine of them, bound in different shapes and sizes, all written in Russell's immaculate copperplate handwriting. The earlier volumes were neat and spacious, the later ones more hurried and crammed for space. The last one was just an exercise book.

Malcolm felt the presence of Russell again. He held the diaries reverently in his hands, and turned the pages as if he were performing a ceremony, then sat in the cane armchair on the terrace.

He said goodbye to Philippa when she returned. Malcolm wanted to get back home and read the rest of Russell's diaries.

Chapter Eleven

14th September 1874, Papeete, Tahiti, Iles du Vent.

Installed myself in a rented house, just off the market square. Papeete is a delightful little town. There is a constant breeze, thanks to the Trade Winds. The temperature is just right, around 80° all year round. I spend most of my time by the market square, the centre of all life in Papeete, day and night. It is a peaceful and relaxed place; nobody hurries, they all have time on their hands. I set up my easel in the shade of a giant tree with large, deep green leaves, and I was left in peace. A couple of girls have peeped over my shoulder, but when I looked at them, they ran away, laughing. I believe the prostitutes also frequent the market square, but I haven't seen any of them.

16th September 1874, Papeete.

I've become the focal point of the young girls in town. They parade up and down the market square, looking at me, giggling. I don't mind. I've been painting the market and I am reasonably happy with the results, but painting people is not easy. I must find a model to paint.

19th September 1874, Papeete.

I've found my model. Her name is Bea. She is fifteen and comes from the family of a chief. I've found lots of chiefs here. There are almost as many chiefs as there are gods on the island. In Tahitian mythology there are over three hundred different gods. Bea told me about the god Oro, who fell in love with a beautiful girl, a mortal. Their love affair gave birth to countless lovely children, and thus the long line of Areoi chiefs originated. She is descended from them, or in a roundabout way, from the mighty Oro himself. At least, I think that's what she said. Communication is a bit of a problem. Tahitians speak a curious mixture of French and English called 'Beach-la-Mar'. Bea speaks it well, unlike her chaperone, who is probably the ugliest woman I've come across in my entire life. It seems that Bea has taken a liking to me; she charges next to nothing for modelling. Other members of her family drop in from time to time to inspect how the painting is progressing. Not very well. They all think it's marvellous, but I think they are more impressed by the act of painting itself, than the result. They are a little scared of me, and dare not touch anything that belongs to me. It's tabu, as Bea says.

20th September 1874, Papeete.

Bea and I became lovers. It was inevitable. As far as she was concerned, it was a natural thing. I used to have notions of love and marriage connected to the act of coupling. It means different things in different cultures. Being an Areoi partly explains her attitude. They are all demigods of love and fertility. She chose me, because she wanted me, she said. It was a tremendous experience for me. We spent the night together coupling endlessly. She has no sense of shame in any way. My gold pendant fascinated her. It is the Bedford crest, a goat. We are related to the Bedfords, but I don't believe any of it. It's the typical colonial pretension that my father suffers from. We even have the Bedford crest above the door and on the dinner service. I don't mind wearing it around my neck, though; I've got so used to it that I would feel naked without it. Bea also wears a pendant, carved out of mother-of-pearl – a figure of an obscene god with an enormous phallus. She compares mine with that of the amulet in a fit of giggles, saying 'tiki' in her native tongue. I should feel flattered, but I don't know what 'tiki' means – the pendant or what I have that she admires so much. If I say 'tiki', she just collapses in a heap of laughter. I used to think a lot about how it would happen for the first time. I had a few wrestling matches with the sisters of my Goulburn school friends, but I've never thought losing my virginity would be like this.

24th September 1874, SS *Caledonia* at sea.

My departure from Tahiti was a little sudden. I would have liked to stay a lot longer, but my affair with Bea completely exhausted me. The *Caledonia*'s arrival in port was the perfect excuse. It is a four-masted brig with an iron hull. We've been making excellent progress since leaving Papeete. Bea came to see me off. She told me an old Tahitian proverb: 'The coral grows, palms shoot up, but man moves on.' I shall never forget her. Her soul has entered my body, my skin tingles with her very being if I only think of her. Her firm breasts, her agile body and the smell of her hair will haunt me for ever. She had the weirdest beliefs about the soul and afterlife. They believe that when they are asleep their souls leave their bodies, only to return as they awake. Death is just a longer form of sleep, though the body decays, the soul lives on for ever in a spirit world, where the gods are. Only unhappy and vengeful souls stay in our world. They become evil spirits and demons. The afterworld caters for every kind; there is one for happy people, and another for the miserable ones. Pigs go to a separate heaven of their own. I shall always think of Tahiti as a little paradise on earth, but I am moving on without regret. Bea was the perfect 'couplette', but I cannot imagine being married to her.

12th October 1874, London, Christmas Island.

We had an uneventful, but comfortable passage. I got on with my painting. The nude sketches of Bea are very stiff and lifeless; no amount of reworking can bring them alive. I must learn to draw properly. We dropped anchor off Cook Island, and took a cutter to the quay at London. We shall be here for a week while loading with copra and guano. An odd combination. The island is covered with docile birds: petrels, shearwaters, terns, boobies, noddies, and tropicbirds. They refuse to move as one walks amongst their noisy colonies. Captain Cook discovered the island in 1777, on Christmas Day. It is the largest atoll in Oceania. The island is the work of tiny corals. The captain went into great detail explaining the process, but I was not much interested. The food is excellent – mostly fish. I've even learnt the native tongue for it: 'te ika'.

29th September 1874, SS *Caledonia* at sea.

Weighed anchor during the night. We are bound for the Sandwich Islands. I'm going to try and draw some of the sailors. The captain gave me permission, but I find it difficult to draw the human figure. There must be a way to do it, but I cannot get the hang of it. I must seek expert tuition.

2nd October 1874, SS *Caledonia* at sea.

I've reworked Bea's pictures and they were the worse for it. I've destroyed them all apart from one. I really miss her.

16th October 1874, Honolulu, Oahu, Sandwich Islands.

Dropped anchor at noon. For the past two days we have been sailing by the islands: Hawaii first, with its twin cone-shaped volcanoes; Kahoolawe and Lanai are much smaller islands, with Maui right behind them, then Molokai, and Oahu last. From our vantage point they looked like a single island. It was good to see mountains again. I've left the *Caledonia*, as it is going to the Marshall Islands. I've had enough of island hopping and have decided to go to Japan instead.

18th October 1874, Honolulu.

Found a hotel by the royal palace. I had an introduction to Queen Liliuokalani, but she didn't have much to say. She is a giant of a woman, all quivering flesh. She was gracious enough, but I could feel she had other things on her mind. I've made more of an impression on 'Tautana', one of her many nieces, and she has invited me to see surf riding, whatever that is.

19th October 1874, Honolulu.

Surf riding is an ancient sport of the native kings. Young men of royal blood swim out to sea on a flat board, defying the surf. Paddling on their boards, they wait till a suitable wave comes, then ride it ashore over the boiling surf. It looks great sport. I tried, but failed miserably. I had my first pineapple, a fruit native to the island with aphrodisiac qualities. Tautana is as much a sport as Bea, but a more experienced 'couplette'. I've been warned about the pox, but she is the healthiest specimen of womanhood I've met. She says she's fifteen, but I reckon she must be at least nineteen. We explored our bodies at leisure, and she was suitably impressed. From what I've seen of the native men, they are not that well hung. I could enjoy a holiday here.

22nd October 1874, Honolulu.

Tautana introduced me to some of her sisters. I don't think their meaning of brother and sister is the same as ours; it just about covers every member of a very large family. Tautana and her sisters spent the night in my hotel bedroom playing all sorts of games. I am very tired, too tired even to write.

28th October 1874, SS *Edithnne Louise* at sea.

My first voyage on a steamer. We carry two auxiliary masts with square rigging, but do not seem to use the sails at all. The noise is quite disturbing, and so is the constant vibration of the ship. I've been shown around by the captain, and introduced to the engineer. Apparently, all engineers are Scots; this one is from Glasgow, and I couldn't understand a word he said. The engine room was an experience. I was impressed by the power of steam. There is something magical about the rhythm of the engine, the steam puffing and hissing from the cylinder, driving the crankshaft. It is the way of the future; the days of sailing are numbered, they all tell me. The captain is an old sea dog. French by birth, but English by habit. He asked me to mess with him and a few other first-class passengers. I agreed, because I'd like to practise my French. The food is excellent. We carry a small farmyard of animals for fresh meat, and all the garlic in the South Seas. I've had my first taste of 'absinthe'; it is all the rage in Europe, the captain says, but I don't really like it. He mixed a 'tremblement de terre' for me, which is half cognac and half absinthe, but I prefer the fine Bordeaux wines served with each meal.

30th October 1874, SS *Edithnne Louise* at sea.

The captain showed me his collection of pornographic daguerreo-types. How they can excite anybody escapes me. All the women are just tired old whores; the poses are more sad than alluring; and as for the orgies, they lack imagination. He also has some very interesting erotic prints from Japan, and I found those produced a twinge in the loin. He gave me an address in Yokohama where one can buy them. He also recommended a couple of tea houses where the geisha girls are supposed to be beautiful, though I don't think much of his taste in women. I have set up my easel in my cabin, and intend to do some work. The captain and his cronies don't really interest me. They prefer talking English; I cannot even practise my French with them.

31st October 1874, SS *Edithnne Louise* at sea.

The sea became a monster all of a sudden. We are pitching and rolling all over, and I find it difficult to keep upright, let alone paint.

13th November 1874, Tokyo.

It was a dreadful voyage, and made up for all the pleasant sailing in the South Seas. Tokyo Bay is a magnificent sight. Mount Fuji towers over the landscape. The harbour is crowded with sailing ships. Their masts are like a forest growing out of the sea. Spent the day shopping for warm clothes; it is winter here. Getting clothes to fit me is a problem as the Japanese must be all around five foot in height. Other than that, they have the latest European fashions. Found a good hotel, and got down to some long-neglected letter writing.

14th November 1874, Tokyo.

Took the train to Yokohama. It is the first railway line in Japan. It took an hour to travel the twenty-nine kilometres. I am being stared at wherever I go, on account of my height. Very few Japanese speak English, and to get about is a bit of a business, but they seem to be polite enough. I found the printers' place without much trouble, and bought twenty-four prints, not all of them pornographic. I watched them work. One of them speaks English, and told me that they use woodblocks made of cherry. The images are cut into the wood across the grain, in order to produce a fine line. There is a different woodblock for each colour, and they register perfectly. The prints are made colour by colour, and they can produce hundreds of prints from one set of blocks. I watched a new printing block being made. The initial drawing is done on rice paper, which is glued to the woodblock upside down, which gets reversed when printed. I was impressed by the drawings, their simplicity and flowing movement. When I got back to my hotel I destroyed most of my watercolours. I kept about a dozen, because I shall only keep and show my very best.

17th November 1874, Tokyo.

Met my artist friend from Yokohama, and he showed me around Tokyo. The emperor Meiji decided on a complete Westernisation of Japan, and here the American influence is as important as the European one. I met some samurai friends of my guide. They were suspicious of me at first, because they disapprove of all the changes. I'm told that the samurai ruled Japan for close on five hundred years in a feudal system. The shogun was the ultimate warlord. I was given two ancient samurai swords, and their generosity overwhelmed me. The swords are genuine works of art, made of the best tempered steel and sharp as razors.

18th November 1874, Tokyo.

Visited a traditional Japanese theatre in the kabuki style. I am told there is even an older tradition, the noh; but having seen kabuki, their comic opera, I have no desire to see noh, a serious drama. The din they make is unbearable to the European ear. My friend from Yokohama went into great detail to explain the plot. He needn't have bothered. All the same, it was an interesting evening. One of the actresses took a fancy to me, and I spent the night with her. She washed me from head to toe, cleaned my ears, rubbed me down with scented oils, and massaged me. We tried every possible position imaginable. She made coupling into a work of art, every move of hers was controlled, cultured; rolling on the mat with her was a strange ceremony. Completely humourless; not that I am complaining.

22nd November 1874, Tokyo.

I shall never understand the Japanese mind. I sat through a tea ceremony. They tell me it's a thing of infinite beauty, but I wasn't impressed. I also watched a potter working, using ancient methods going back to the fifth century, but that didn't impress me either. He had a hole on the wheel, put a small stick inside it and got it turning around, then put the stick down and threw a handful of clay onto the wheel; by the time he started to shape the clay, the wheel stopped. In went the stick, the ceremony was repeated time after time. They have had over fifteen hundred years to invent a more efficient way, like a spindle to turn the wheel by foot, but nobody thought of that. Booked my passage back to Sydney. It's a pity that I shall miss Christmas with the family, but at least I am going back to some warm weather. I cannot say that I enjoy the winter here. I thought of painting here, but I'm discouraged by my ignorance. I must go to art school. Watching my friend from Yokohama painting with a bamboo brush makes me envious of his skill. He showed me how to hold the brush, and how to paint with one single movement from the shoulder. I made a complete mess of it. On the other hand, he only knows three designs. He paints the same ones every time. He should get it right after fifteen years; it's just like another ceremony.

Chapter Twelve

Jamie had to wait for two days to see Penders. He was out of town on some urgent business, somewhere in West Australia, and could not be contacted. When they met in Taronga Park Zoo, Jamie was a bag of nerves. He could not understand why Penders had always chosen such odd places to meet. There they were, half past ten in the morning, feeding the cockatoos, under the surveillance of Doug. And why Penders needed minders was another mystery that Jamie never understood.

Jamie found the setting disconcerting. The incessant chatter of the birds had a surrealistic air about it. They screeched, with cries of, 'Have you got a biscuit, mate?', 'Hello, sailor!', 'Who's a pretty boy, then?', 'Give us a kiss, mate!' They were getting on Jamie's nerves. Penders was amused by the birds, and thought it was a great joke.

'You're not bothered by the birds?' he smiled at Jamie.

'They're a bit noisy, Mr Penders.'

'Ignore them… And what else did Malcolm Reid want to know?'

'Nothing else,' replied Jamie. 'He was looking for the letter about JPR's paintings. The ones he offered to the gallery in 1921.'

'Hmm… very interesting,' said Penders.

'He is trouble. I think he's going to cause trouble,' said Jamie, almost shouting over the noise of the birds. 'Can we move away from them, Mr Penders?'

'Sure. Calm down, Jamie.'

Penders moved away from the cage.

'He is trouble,' went on Jamie. 'I know it.'

'Let me worry about that. Does he trust you?'

'He has no reason not to. We get on well together and I think he likes me. I'm just worried—'

'Stop worrying, Jamie,' Penders cut in. 'Call him tomorrow and arrange to see him.'

'See him about what?'

'About the letter.'

'What letter?'

'About Russell's letter,' said Penders. 'For an intelligent young man, you can be incredibly thick at times. I'll get the text to you this afternoon. You'll just have to burn the midnight oil, Jamie.'

★

A giant red parakeet was screeching its head off, but nobody could hear it through the loud music. The Parakeet Club was named after the bird. The gilded cage took a central position, hanging above the dance floor, but nobody danced in the club. It was a wine bar where people went to be seen; not that one could see a lot in the pitch dark. The walls were black, some odd objects were picked out by spotlights: hand-operated sewing machines dipped in luminous yellow paint, children's tricycle wheels in blue, and an assortment of kitchenware in all the colours of the rainbow. Large-chested waitresses dashed about, wearing tight-fitting bunny costumes and serving Black Velvet, the 'in' drink in Sydney – Guinness and Australian champagne, mostly Seppelt's Great Western.

The wine bar was a popular watering hole for the smart set, mostly advertising and media people, sneaking out for an afternoon with the new talent in the office – just the place to find David Swaab.

He had just concluded a lucrative deal for a series of koala bear commercials to promote the latest whatever; he had already forgotten the product, but it was a terrific deal, he told Robyn.

'You were supposed to call me,' he lied.

'No,' said Robyn. 'You promised to call me.'

'It was the other way round, but what does it matter now? What about this Pommy friend of yours?'

'Which Pommy? I have lots of Pommy friends.'

'I hear it's serious.'

Robyn blushed without intending to.

'Me, serious? You must be joking, mate.'

'He is very decorative, but too old for you, I reckon.'

'I am more interested in his mind.'

'That's a likely story!' He laughed smuttily.

'He's writing a script for me,'

'Is he now?'

There was envy and jealousy in his casual question. Robyn got home with the message without having to try too hard.

'Yes, that's right,' she said.

'I'd like to see it,' he said.

So would I, thought Robyn, but she said confidently, 'All in good time, David. All in good time.'

'What are you doing this afternoon?' he asked.

'Why? Fancy a bit of heavy breathing?'

'I'd like to show you my one-eyed snake.'

'You've always been a sweet-talking bastard, David, but no thanks. I'm not in the mood.'

Malcolm was expecting Robyn to pay him a visit. He was looking forward to it. He laid in a good supply of booze, and hoovered the flat for the first time since he had moved in. He even made the bed – just in case. To kill time, he read more of the Russell diaries.

Penders sent the text of the letter with Tony. He looked the least likely person to visit an art gallery, but he did not hang about, just delivered the brown paper envelope and left. The assistant curator looked at him with suspicion, but had the good manners not to ask Jamie about him.

Jamie had to wait till the place was closed before he could start writing the letter. He pulled the dark curtains to, set up a small slide projector, and placed a sample of Albert Fairburn's writing into it; he was the curator of the gallery when Russell offered his collection of paintings to the state. Jamie tried to copy the neat handwriting. After a couple of trial pages he managed to reproduce the exact style.

He took an old sheet of paper with the arms and logo of the Gallery of Modern Art, and began. He had to get it right for the first time as he only had a single sheet of paper from the 1920s. At least the paper was authentic. He copied the text without comprehending its meaning, and focussed all his effort on getting the style right. Jamie wrote steadily, word by word, line by line, and his writing matched the original perfectly.

★

Malcolm was tucked up in bed reading. Some modern jazz played loudly, and he was lost to the world; the Russell diaries were compulsive reading. He had completely forgotten that Robyn was due to visit him.

Doug hated Malcolm's choice of music. He pulled out the tiny earpiece, and watched the children play in the street. It was a slum, inhabited by Aboriginals, Greeks, Yugoslavs and Turks. The children played cricket happily together in the gutter. Malcolm's beaten-up Jag was parked outside a house with crumbling walls, covered with obscure and probably obscene graffiti in half a dozen different languages. Doug sat in a delivery van parked thirty metres up the street. From time to time he listened in to what went on in the room. He did not want to record all the rubbish music; on the other hand, he could not afford to miss something important. He took a sip from a can of beer to while away the time.

He watched Robyn's BMW pull up by Malcolm's Jag and wondered how long it would take the children to vandalise it, but they were more interested in their game of cricket than anything else. Doug switched on the tape recorder, then made a note of the time of her arrival in a small notebook.

It was the first time Robyn had visited Malcolm's flat. The place was large, and a lot more comfortable than she could imagine, judging by the exterior squalor. Malcolm stood in the doorway in his pyjamas, grinning like an idiot.

'I'm sorry. I've been reading and I'd forgotten about you.'

'That's obvious,' she said crossly.

'Do come in,' he said. 'Make yourself at home. I'm going to put some clothes on.'

He left her in the sitting room, and hurried into the bedroom. Robyn looked about the place. There were books, magazines and newspapers all over the chairs, tables and shelves. Only Malcolm's desk looked empty and tidy. His word processor was in the middle, still left on, with the desktop screen showing a tropical beach.

Robyn walked over to the desk, and was just about to open the file on JPR when Malcolm stopped her. He was wearing a pair of corduroys and an expensive cashmere sweater.

'No,' he said. 'You cannot have a look.'

'Then how about a hello, or something?'

'Hello, or something,' he said. 'Sit down, Robyn. I'm very pleased to see you. I got completely absorbed reading the Russell diaries.'

'Well, how goes it?' she asked as she sat down pushing a pile of English Sunday papers to the floor.

'I've made a good beginning, but I want to find out something more about the Russell Collection...'

'The Russell Collection?'

'Well, the missing paintings.'

'You mustn't get obsessed with that, Malcolm. I need that script yesterday, as you very well know.'

'You'll get it when I'm good and ready.'

'I need it urgently. Everybody wants it. Nobody will make a commitment without seeing the script.'

'But I thought Channel Three was going to give you the money? Ericson, or somebody—'

'Don't you worry about production matters,' she said, cutting him short. 'How can I make you finish that script?'

'You can't. We've made a deal, so stop being so bloody pushy.'

'You're a pain, Malcolm,' she said, sighing as she sat back in the armchair. 'What on earth made you choose a flat in Redfern?'

'It's handy for the university. I can walk it in five minutes.'

'Redfern is a slum. You'll probably have to walk, because they're going to pinch your car,' she said.

She realised that her own car was parked in the street, jumped up from her chair, and walked over to the window facing the street. The car was still there, untouched by the children.

'It's best that you visit me in the future. I'm not leaving my car out there again.'

'It was you who wanted to see my place.'

'And now I've seen it. Thanks,' she said, getting ready to leave.

'It's very cheap,' he added.

'No kidding?' she teased him.

Before he could say something witty, the telephone rang. Malcolm picked up the receiver.

'Yes, it's me … That's fantastic … I'll come and see you at the gallery … all right; you come to my place then. Have you got the address? … So I did … Good, see you in the morning…'

Malcolm put the receiver down and turned towards Robyn. He was smiling from ear to ear.

'That was Jamie de Selway. He's come up with something really interesting.'

'Terrific,' she said with heavy sarcasm as she started to leave.

'Don't you want a drink? Please…' His voice was pleading, with a touch of desperation. 'I went to a lot of trouble to get in the lot. Come on, Robyn, what are you drinking?'

'I must go. I'll see you, Malcolm.'

'It's your car… You're bothered about your car, aren't you?'

'I've got an early call in the morning.'

'Nobody's going to touch your bloody car. Mine's been out there all this time. They are all very nice around here…'

She did not listen as she made her way out.

'Bye, Malcolm,' she said from the door.

'Coward!' he yelled after her.

Malcolm walked over to the window and watched her run out of the house. She jumped into her car and looked up and down the street before driving off at speed. The children scattered about to avoid being run over. They cursed her and made rude signs, but she just drove on. She had not once looked back.

That hurt Malcolm. He stood by the window, and looked out into the street long after she had gone. He noticed Doug sitting in the van. Malcolm thought he had seen him somewhere before, but could not think where. He felt uncomfortable all of a sudden. There was something wrong… the air was bristling with vibrations of doom.

What the hell, he thought as he poured himself a ridiculously large drink. He gulped it down still standing at the window, looking out into the night. After a while, he went back to the bedroom, and carried on reading the diaries, trying to put Robyn out of his mind. He was falling in love with her, but decided not to think about it.

Chapter Thirteen

2nd July 1879, Southampton Docks, England.

A new diary. I have a couple of hours before we cast off; I might as well fill in a few pages. There's nothing worse than an empty diary, unless it's a new piece of canvas, wanting to be painted. Needless to say, I've done very little painting in the last four years. Nothing worth keeping, anyhow. I've left a dozen watercolours in London. The whole family is now installed there, in Acton. Father never gave in to the strikers. The affair dragged on for eighteen months. He shut down the works in Sydney, rather than lose face. The men were left out in the cold without a job. Father did very well for himself when he sold the business. A builder bought the land, and paid tenfold its book value. I had nothing to do with it. I was training to be an engineer at Roby's of Lincoln as a gentleman apprentice. It seemed like a waste of time when I began, but now it's all over, I don't mind so much. The knowledge may prove to be useful in the future, but I lost four years of my life, thanks to Father.

3rd July 1879, SS *Fremantle* at sea.

When I returned from Japan I wanted to go to art college. I enrolled at the Art School of the National Gallery in Melbourne, but Father wouldn't have it. I had to accept his plans for me in England, or leave home. That would have upset Mother. I knuckled down, and did as Father wished. He was pleased when I showed him my diploma, and threw a wonderful twenty-first birthday party for me, because I've kept my end of the bargain. I am a qualified engineer, free to do as I please, and I have the same feeling of excitement that I had before sailing to the South Seas at sixteen. So what happened since then? I can hardly remember my voyage from Sydney to London. I was so cross with Father that I spent the entire time shooting clay pigeons, one of the few luxuries that travelling first class allows you. I was surprised by the size of London. The traffic and the crowds were beyond my wildest expectations. Seeing London made me realise just how tiny Sydney is. Father suggested that I should stay with Uncle Peter, to make some moves towards reconciliation. He couldn't have chosen a worse ambassador than me. Uncle Peter has no children. His wife keeps cats and dogs to make up for it, and dotes on her horrible little pets. I couldn't have been in the building for more than ten minutes when one of her little pooches threw itself under my feet. Even then, I weighed over fourteen stone; it didn't have much chance. Pooch expired with a yelp, my aunt fainted, and I was dispatched in haste to King's Cross. Haven't been back since. Uncle Peter and Father still don't speak to each other, even though they now only live a couple of miles apart. What of Lincoln? Not a lot. Lodged with a dragon of a landlady, ate a lot of mashed potatoes and chewy mutton; got my head down to learning engineering the hard way. My memories of the place consist of the smell of boiled cabbage, mutton and cats' piss. I joined the YMCA for the boxing, but I didn't get much enjoyment beating the tar out of the puny specimens Lincoln offered as sparring partners. I also sailed on a pond in the rain under grey skies. I don't think the sun ever came out of the clouds during the three years I spent there. Not once. As for girls? No 'couplettes' in Lincoln! There were only the tarts and the mill girls. I preferred boxing. You can keep your England as far as I am concerned.

4th July 1879, SS *Fremantle* at sea.

The sun came out of the clouds as England disappeared over the horizon. It's a good omen. I am looking forward to painting again. Father gave me a generous allowance to pursue a career of my choosing, and accepted with good grace that I wish to become a painter. Before setting out I've purchased all the materials I need to paint along the way. I wish to exhibit my work at the International Exhibition. I kept nothing of my work so far. I am starting afresh. I have six months to produce something worth showing, and I shall start today.

Later. The Atlantic Ocean intervened. We had typical Bay of Biscay weather. That little bit of sun earlier today was a false dawn. I'll have to wait till we get into the Mediterranean.

6th July 1879, Gibraltar.

The weather has improved. We've put into port, but I stayed on board. I've seen the sights of Gibraltar on my first trip. Once is enough. I've been watching the men loading coal. Only five years ago I travelled almost exclusively under sail. Silent, clean and swift. Now I am on board a 25,000-tonne steam-ship, belching thick black smoke. There must have been close on two hundred men loading coal, an army of black coolies toiling away. There is no coal in Gibraltar; it has to be shipped in from England to keep the bunkers full. What price progress? In the long run we are not that much faster than under sail. I detest the constant noise of the engines.

8th July 1879, SS *Fremantle* at sea.

We bypassed Malta without putting into harbour. The weather is good; exactly what it should be in July. I set myself up on the poop deck and painted my first watercolour. I was pestered by a Dutch woman desperate for company, but perhaps it's my fault. With my silk cravat and Vandyke beard I must look like a real Bohemian. She seemed to be more interested in my body than my work. She knows nothing about art, but she is travelling alone, and I wouldn't mind exploring her body; the trouble is, I cannot think of a way of getting to her body without taking on her intellect as well. Her body is divine; her mind is non-existent; if one could only separate body from mind.

10th July 1879, Port Said.

Went ashore and visited a high-class brothel. I don't normally resort to the services of whores – well, not knowingly – but I was in need of a couplette. That Dutch woman is bothering me. She has planted some erotic thoughts in my mind. She certainly is game.

11th July 1879, SS *Fremantle* at sea.

The Dutch lady has become a constant companion. I judged her wrongly. She knows a lot about art. We talked about Renoir and

Pissarro. She did most of the talking; she was in Paris two years ago, and visited the Hôtel Druot, where the Impressionists held their famous auction. I read about the revolt against the Salon painters, but she had actually seen the paintings. She was generous enough to suggest that my work reminded her of the Impressionist school. We had dinner together, and I spent the night in her cabin. In spite of being a widow, she knows nothing about coupling. She seems willing to learn, though. It is a shame about the heat. Sailing through the Red Sea in July is like being in an oven. Not the most conducive ambience for passion.

14th July 1879, Perim Island, Aden.

A hellhole. We docked at this coaling station before the long haul across the Indian Ocean. Not exactly a pearl in the British crown; just a place to fill up with water and coal. I painted a successful watercolour using the most garish of my paints. The contrasts of colours are out of this world: the turquoise blue of the sea, the dark cobalt blue of the sky and the golden yellow sands that jump out of the seascape. I used the paints as they came out of the tube. There was no need for a wash, and the end result is like an oil painting. My affair is getting serious. She made some thinly veiled hints about marriage. I'll have to do something drastic; a couplette is one thing, a wife is something completely different.

16th July 1879, SS *Fremantle* at sea.

I am far too disturbed to do any work. How am I going to tell her to go? The affair is becoming a problem. We spend most of our time together now. She has started planning the house that we will live in, and we are already arguing about the colour of the sitting room. She has decided on crimson red for the bedroom. The colour excites her; all her undergarments are crimson silk. To take her mind off marriage, I talked about the court case of John Ruskin against the American painter, James McNeill Whistler. The ruse worked; she has met Whistler, but she takes Ruskin's side. I think Ruskin is an idiot. The British hate foreigners, whatever they say; and the damages assessed at a farthing almost ruined him financially. Honours certainly were not even. I was surprised that she felt Whistler deserved his fate, but then, all Britain screamed for Whistler's blood. Nobody could forgive him for being successful. My Dutch friend doesn't see it that way. We argued about it all night, just like a married couple, and even making up afterwards lacked excitement. I was reminded of the old Tahitian proverb: 'Sleep in anger, wake in sorrow.' She'll have to go, and the sooner the better.

18th July 1879, Bombay.

I managed to sneak ashore without her noticing. The purser was a real sport. I didn't lose much money by cutting short my voyage; he gave me a fair refund, considering the circumstances. Found a comfortable hotel not far from the port, but this town is incredibly noisy. I must find a ship out of here before I go mad. India is not my favourite country, and this climate is a killer. Bought a copy of the *Kama Sutra* and read it from cover to cover. It must have lost a lot in translation, because I found it about as erotic as cold porridge. It's a pity, because I paid a lot of money for it.

22nd July 1879, Colombo, Ceylon.

Managed to get a place on a schooner carrying machinery for a rubber plantation. Had a long talk about rubber with a fellow Australian. He believes it's the material of the future; he put his shirt on his gamble. He gave me a ball of latex as a memento. I think he is cranky putting his faith in the stuff. He told me that once they manage to stabilise rubber, it is going to be used for a million different purposes. I hope he is right, because I had a rubber impregnated raincoat in Lincoln, and a nasty, sticky thing it was in the humid weather. I preferred getting wet.

8th August 1879, Perth.

It is good to be home in Australia. To see gum trees again is like a dream coming true. I installed myself in a very comfortable hotel.

18th August 1879, Perth.

I have painted a number of successful oils and watercolours on the banks of the Avon River. I love this dry land; the desert is timeless.

Man has made no mark on this giant continent. I wish I had some formal tuition. Solving each problem takes me ages. How can I become an artist, if I am still struggling with elementary problems of craft? But my drawing has improved a lot; the four years at Roby's as a draughtsman were not entirely wasted. How far England seems now, and it is only six weeks ago that I left it.

27th August 1879, Hobart.

I visited the site of Grandfather Russell's foundry at Battery Point. A hardware store has been built over it. Though the new building is quite large, the original works couldn't have been all that big. I had a romantic notion that I would paint the old place. It is cold here after the heat of Perth. I booked myself a passage to Brisbane. It should be reasonably warm there. Coming back to an Australian winter was not such a good idea.

4th September 1879, Tweed Heads, Queensland.

I rented a small shack by the beach here. The mornings are brisk, but it gets warm in the day. I am right on the border between New South Wales and Queensland. The place is a little paradise on earth. The sea is warm, and the golden sands stretch from here to Brisbane. I can go for hours walking on the beach without seeing another person. It is so different from the South Sea Islands, where there are always people around. I like this solitude. The English never experience anything like this either; that's why they will never understand Australians. We may look like Europeans, but underneath we have the same soul as the black-fellow. Anyhow, that's how I feel; and to think that when Grandfather Russell arrived in Tasmania, the English used to hunt the black-fellow for sport. Perhaps that's why I hated the place – something of that cruelty stayed with the land. The lost souls of the black-fellow haunt the country, as Bea would say. I think of her a lot, because this stretch of beach reminds me of Tahiti.

11th September 1879, Tweed Heads.

I've been painting in the hills, in the Macpherson Range. Apart from the gum trees, the country looks a lot like Oahu in the

Sandwich Islands: the same red soil, the same lush green vegetation, and the light blue sky with little cotton-wool clouds. I am working like the proverbial beaver. I shall have to buy more canvases.

25th September 1879, *Kookaburra* at sea.

Joined a fishing party in Brisbane. I went there to buy more canvases and paint, but instead of returning to Tweed Heads, I decided to go on a cruise to Cairns and along the Great Barrier Reef. I got talking to the skipper by chance. He is an odd person. I'm not sure I'm doing the right thing, but it promises to be good sport. I'm impressed by the boat; she is a real beauty, and looks like a thoroughbred racer. There is a crew of six, all Kanakas. They are born seamen; there's nothing to worry about on that score. There are five other men on board who don't seem to know each other, yet they chartered the sloop. And are going to spend two months together at sea!

27th September 1879, *Kookaburra* at sea.

I know now what's odd about the skipper; his left leg is all wood. Lost it to a shark. It's amazing how he manages to get about without limping. There are two joints at the ankle, which allow him the most natural movement. We got drunk this afternoon and he showed me how his artificial limb works. A Chinese master carver in Port Moresby made it.

30th September 1879, *Kookaburra* at sea.

We've been eating a lot of shark meat. I don't mind it, but not every day. Complaining to the cook, I found out what unites the five passengers. They hate sharks. The purpose of this cruise is not to enjoy the scenery, but to kill as many sharks as possible. They all carry the most horrendous wounds caused by sharks, and every one of them has a missing limb: a hand, a foot, or two. The same Chinaman has fitted them all with artificial limbs. They have warmed to me, and showed me how their wooden bits work, but they are not like normal people. There is something sinister about their blind hatred for sharks. There is nothing wrong with sharks; they are only mindless fish, after all; but my companions have invested them with evil powers. They wear amulets carved from shark's tooth, have tobacco pouches made from shark's skin, and heaven knows what else. Am I dreaming all this?

4th October 1879, Cooktown, Queensland.

I left the *Kookaburra*. All that carnage made me sick. I was asked to leave, practically thrown ashore. I shouldn't have laughed when they let me into their secret that they are members of a secret Masonic Lodge dedicated to the destruction of sharks! I just couldn't keep a straight face. At least they didn't throw me to the sharks. They let me pack, so I still have everything I need for painting.

18th November 1879, Sydney.

Back at home in Darlinghurst. Odd to be alone in the house with only the servants to talk to. Visited a few aunts and uncles on Mother's side. Grandfather Nicholl died while I was away. I would have liked his opinion of my work. His studio in Woolloomooloo is exactly the way he left it. Even his unfinished sculptures are there, untouched. I had a feeling that he would walk through the door, and carry on where he left off. Whatever talent I have for art comes from Grandfather Nicholl. He was a respected artist, even though I find his work a little academic and old-fashioned; he had craft. Had my paintings framed, and hung them all over the house, seventy-two pictures. I lived with them for a week before making my final selection. The Sydney Russells visited me just to look at my work. I think they are impressed. Today, at long last, I have chosen fifteen watercolours and ten oils, and had them despatched to the hanging committee for the International Exhibition.

2nd December 1879, Sydney.

Father died of a sudden heart attack yesterday in Acton. Mother and Edith are coming home to Sydney straight after the funeral. The hanging committee refused my work. All of it.

Chapter Fourteen

Next morning, Malcolm waited in for Jamie. He sat down and tried to write, but nothing he typed pleased him. He gave up after half an hour. He tried to read Russell's diaries, but he could not settle. He was excited. If only Jamie would hurry up, he kept on thinking.

Malcolm stood by the window. The street was busy as always, but its character changed. The children were at school. Instead, women stood on the pavements chatting, fetching and carrying shopping bags, shaking rugs out of the windows; like anywhere in southern Europe, but here the Aborigines took the part of the Gypsies. It was a peaceful scene and the jabbering of the women made the place feel homely.

Doug's van was left parked where it was the night before, but there was no sign of him. Malcolm looked at the van, but made nothing of it.

He spotted Jamie walking up the street. He was hurrying along the pavement, looking over his shoulders, as if expecting to be followed, but nobody was after him.

Malcolm felt sorry for Jamie. He had no reason to, but he thought Jamie was a sad case. His face was always ashen, and his frightened eyes were deep set with constant terror of something. Jamie was a bag of nerves. What a waste, Malcolm thought.

Jamie rang the bell and Malcolm let him in.

'Hello, Jamie,' he said. 'Can I get you anything?'

Jamie said nothing, just shook his head.

'Well, sit down,' said Malcolm.

Jamie preferred to stand. He reached into his pocket, and handed Malcolm a carefully folded letter.

'No, thank you,' he said quietly. 'I haven't got much time. I've overslept. I'm in a hurry.'

Malcolm's face lit up as he started to read the letter.

'This is fantastic, Jamie.'

'It'll give you a starting point. They sent some of the archives to Canberra in 1927, for some reason; that's why we couldn't find anything. The official Opening of Parliament was in May, and I can only think they had to have something to show to the Duke of York.'

'Who?'

'He became King George the Sixth.'

'What are you talking about, Jamie?'

'They had to put on a show for his visit; that's why they sent it to Canberra. It's all there, in your missing correspondence.'

'Yes, just the break I needed,' said Malcolm. 'You're a true Brit! Sure you don't want anything?'

'No, thank you. I must be going.'

With that, Jamie turned his back on Malcolm and walked out. Malcolm stared after him. There was nothing he could do for Jamie. He was past help, and it was only a matter of time before he would give up the ghost. He walked like a zombie already.

Malcolm looked down at his watch; it was almost noon. The sun was practically overhead, and there were hardly any shadows. It was hot and bright, like any other day, but Malcolm was still surprised by the blinding light and the shimmering heat.

★

It was the Channel Three weekly barbecue. Greg Ericson enjoyed playing the host to the VIPs in show business. His lunch time get-togethers were select; being on the guest list was a sign of success.

On the roof of the office block, there was a large and well-kept garden with commanding views of the city skyline. In one corner, by a huge barbecue, a fat cook slaved over the flames. A couple of smartly dressed waiters served drinks to the glitterati of Sydney. There were around forty people present, dotted all over the roof garden. The more serious drinkers took up their position by the bar. Philippa Penders was one of them; she had a standing invitation, and very rarely missed the event. She was chatting to Terry Robinson, the obnoxious redneck of the airwaves. Philippa must have been drunk already; otherwise she would have kept away from him.

Robyn stepped out of the lift and joined the merry crowd. Ericson met her with a huge smile.

'I'm glad you could make it, Robyn. I hope you have some good news for me.'

'You took the words out of my mouth, Greg. *I* was going to say that.'

'Ah…' Ericson stalled, looking for an excuse to discontinue the conversation.

Elmer Sandak came to his rescue with perfect timing. He was a tall, overfed American; a notorious womaniser and 24-carat bore. He was heading straight for Robyn.

'Have you met Elmer?' Ericson asked her.

'I don't think so.'

'Elmer Sandak, junior,' said the American.

He held out his podgy hand and flashed a wide-open smile, revealing his perfect teeth – a masterpiece of dentistry, which must have cost at least ten thousand dollars.

'All my friends call me Elmer.'

'How are you?' said Robyn.

'Robyn Hawthorne, one of our young producers at Channel Three,' said Ericson as a waiter stopped by him. 'Black Velvet, OK?'

'Love it,' said Robyn.

Ericson handed her a glass. Sandak looked at it with suspicion.

'What on earth is that?'

'Champagne and Guinness. You should try it. It's the perfect drink on a hot day.'

Sandak took a glass from the waiter and sipped it cautiously.

'Not bad.'

'Try the king prawns,' said Ericson.

Robyn looked at Sandak pointedly before answering.

'You mean on the barbecue, Greg?'

Her little joke was lost on Sandak, who was now gulping down his drink. Ericson moved away to greet some new arrivals.

'So, you're the producer of *Palm Beach*?'

'Amongst other things,' replied Robyn. 'I've got a couple of fingers in other pies, Mr Sandak.'

'Call me Elmer, please.'

'Sure, Elmer. I've heard all about you. You're with Media International, aren't you?'

'The man himself...'

Before he could finish his sentence Philippa sauntered over to them unsteadily and butted into the conversation. She was very drunk, but managed to stay upright as she turned to Robyn.

'It didn't take our Elmer long to spot you, darling,' she said cattily. 'I hear you're an item with that good-looking Englishman. What's his name?'

'Malcolm Reid,' replied Robyn flatly. 'We are collaborating on a project, as you well know.'

'Is that what you call it?'

Sandak made an attempt to rescue Robyn. 'You're just trying to make me jealous, Philippa,' he said.

Philippa ignored him and glared at Robyn. Sandak made an attempt to lighten the atmosphere and he turned to Robyn. 'Tell me it's nothing serious,' he said.

'It's nothing serious, Elmer,' said Robyn. 'The man is writing a script for me. That's all.'

'Balls, darling.'

Philippa moved on to a different group of people. Robyn took the opportunity to get away from Sandak, and walked over to the barbecue, but he followed her closely. She looked at the food, trying to ignore him.

Ericson laid on a luxurious spread. There were steaks: rump, fillet and T-bone; pork chops, veal and lamb cutlets; pieces of chicken marinated in barbecue and curry sauce; fish of all shapes and sizes; giant king prawns; and all sorts of sausages sizzling on the hotplate. The chef constantly prodded them, and shook salt, pepper, herbs and heaven knows what over the lot. His actions were fast and furious, and he gave the impression of auditioning for a part in a movie. But he was, after all, an out-of-work actor; many of the waiters at Ericson's barbecues were trying to make an impression.

Robyn took a few prawns, and walked over with her plate to a table filled with every possible variety of salads. She chose a couple of leaves of lettuce, half a tomato and a radish.

Sandak piled his plate high with everything, and smothered ketchup all over it. He sat down at Robyn's table without being asked, and tucked into his food heartily. Then he turned to her and said, 'So, what's this new project of yours about?'

'I can't really talk about it at this stage. It wouldn't be ethical.'

'I know, but you're going to tell me all the same,' he said with his mouth full.

'No. I'm not that kind of girl,' she said. 'And besides, I'm more or less committed to Greg.'

'I'd like to have a look at the script. You know, I liked the treatment very much, but how can you write a screenplay in seven acts?'

Robyn was genuinely surprised. How did he manage to get his dirty paws on the treatment? she wondered as Sandak prattled on.

'It's a shame the painter is Australian. Now, if he was *American*... But it's still a great story.'

As he talked, he put his fleshy hand on Robyn's thigh, and left it there just that little longer than a friendly gesture would allow.

'If you need me, young lady, you know where to find me.'

'I'll remember that,' said Robyn calmly as she lifted Sandak's hand off her thigh and stood up.

She walked away from him, ignoring his smutty smile, and joined another group near the bar. She was glad to see Ericson again, but before she could give him a piece of her mind about showing the treatment to Sandak, he whispered in her ear.

'Malcolm Reid is in my office waiting for you. He wants to talk to you about something urgently.'

Ericson took Robyn's arm as he was talking, and showed her towards the lift.

'How did he find me here?'

'Obviously, he's a man of some talent,' said Ericson, as the lift gates closed on Robyn.

She found Malcolm looking at the pictures of the Australian starlets that Ericson liked to have around. They were like clones of each other, all pouting, or smiling mindlessly, and showing a lot of sunburnt flesh.

'So, what's so earth-shatteringly important, Malcolm?' she asked.

'Russell's correspondence about his paintings is in Canberra. His letters were sent there in 1927.'

'So?'

'It could be the missing link.'

'What's in the letters, then?'

'How should I know? We've got to go to Canberra to find out.'

'Why we? Go by yourself,' she said irritably, but seeing the look of disappointment on Malcolm's face she changed her mind. 'All right. Why don't you pick me up at home this evening... around seven. Now, if you'll excuse me, Malcolm. I've got a lot on.'

'I know, but I had to tell you.'

'It's a terrific piece of news, Malcolm.'

She walked out of the office smiling at him. He seemed relieved to see her smile, and there was a faithful look of admiration in his eyes. He kept on beaming for a long time after she had left the room.

I must be nice to him, she told herself. The poor bastard looks desperate. I'd better keep him sweet.

Chapter Fifteen

Penders was interrupted in the middle of some delicate negotiations, and was furious with Tony, even though it was not his fault.

'Well, what does he want?' he shouted.

'He won't tell me, Mr Penders. He wants to see you personally. He's waiting at the back.'

'All right. Is there anything I should know before I see him?'

'He's given in his notice at the gallery this morning, and bought a single ticket to London. I've got his flight details,' said Tony, and handed Penders a piece of paper.

Penders looked at it then put it into his pocket.

'I think I'd better see him.'

Tony led the way to a small room at the back of Penders' office – a room he shared with Doug. There was a long table along one wall with computers, video equipment and assorted electronic devices. There were a couple of chairs and a huge green filing cabinet.

Jamie was sitting by the table playing nervously with a brown paper folder. He looked up with a start as Penders entered the room. Tony closed the door, but stayed outside in the corridor.

'This had better be very important, Jamie.'

'It is. I've made up my mind, Mr Penders. I'm not doing anything else. I've brought along the last documents, but I've had enough. I can't take any more.'

'You have been a little edgy, Jamie, and I expected something like this. No hard feelings as far as I am concerned,' he said soothingly.

Jamie's face lit up with joy. Penders' reasonable attitude lifted a heavy weight from his shoulders. He feared Penders would not let him go so easily.

'That's very kind of you, Mr Penders.'

'I can't force you to do anything you don't want to do. Let's have a look at your work!'

Jamie handed Penders the folder. He flipped through the pages one by one without saying a word.

'It's all there,' added Jamie quietly.

'Yes, you're right,' agreed Penders. 'Very nice work.'

Penders closed the folder.

'So, what's next, Jamie? Any plans?'

'I'll take it easy for a while, Mr Penders.'

'That sounds good. I don't need to remind you to keep our business to yourself. You're not to say a word to anybody. Do you understand that?'

'Yes, Mr Penders. You can rely on me. I know how to keep a secret.'

'I hope so, Jamie, for your sake. I'm pushed for time right now, but I think a bonus is in order. Leave it with me, and I'll work out something,' said Penders as he held out his hand to Jamie. 'And thanks for everything.'

*

Malcolm was a quarter of an hour early, but Robyn was ready. She sat in the lobby waiting for him, with a small overnight bag at her feet. She was working on a revised budget for *Palm Beach*, using her laptop computer. The series had been sold to England, and some extra money was allocated to the production. It was nothing like a sudden fit of generosity from the studios, just creative accounting, and Robyn had to find a way of spending the additional cash.

She gave herself a day away from the office, and she was looking forward to a trip to Canberra. She fixed up an important business meeting there and she was quite pleased with the world. If only Malcolm would get on with the script, she thought, as she spotted him entering the lobby.

'I'm early, as always,' replied Malcolm.

He offered to carry her bag, which she accepted, but she would not let him touch her laptop. She got into Malcolm's old Jag and stretched out her legs as he set off towards the Harbour Bridge. She smiled at him, then yawned.

'Bored already?' he asked.

'No. I had a tiring day. Probably drunk too much at Greg's barbie. I don't normally drink in the middle of the day, and if I do, it always makes me feel tired.'

'How is Greg, then?' asked Malcolm.

'Not very happy, since you ask. He wants to have the script you're working on.'

'Are you trying to pressurise me, Robyn?'

'Yes. You've got it in one.'

'I'm doing my best.'

'I'll tell Greg when I see him. Seriously, I need that script. They have promised me more money, but not until I deliver your script.'

'It all depends on what we find in Canberra.'

'Don't make excuses. Just give me the script, OK?'

He said nothing. She was not in a talkative mood either. He switched on his stereo and concentrated on his driving. She was happy to listen in silence. They crossed the Harbour Bridge and made their way south along the Prince's Highway, through the most depressing suburbs of Sydney. When they reached the airport exit, Malcolm carried on along the main road.

'You missed the airport turn-off,' said Robyn.

'We're not flying. I thought I'd give the old Jag a good run.'

'As long as you don't want me to drive.'

'No. I like driving.'

'Can you make it all the way to Canberra in this thing? It's over three hundred kilometres, you know.'

'I can make it.'

Malcolm put his foot down on the accelerator. The car shot forward powerfully, leaving a cloud of black smoke behind. She looked at it in the rear mirror, but said nothing. She leaned back in her seat and yawned again. I've got to fall in with him, she thought. If he wants to be James Bond, I'll just have to admire him.

Night fell as Malcolm sped along the Federal Highway. It always caught him by surprise; Australian sunsets were sudden affairs. As they left the last of the Sydney suburbs behind, the traffic thinned out, and he was able to drive at over a hundred and fifty kilometres an hour. The speed felt nothing in his car. It just purred, and ate up the road. Malcolm was pleased with his car; it was a shame Robyn had fallen asleep, and could not appreciate his superior driving skills.

They were well past Goulburn when she opened her eyes again. She watched Malcolm for a while. He was a good driver, she had to admit, and very good-looking for his age. She wondered what he would be like in bed, but suppressed her thoughts. Not before he finishes the script, she reminded herself.

'Can I see that letter?' she asked.

'Sure.'

Malcolm shifted about as he reached over to the back seat. Then he handed a file to Robyn.

'It's in there somewhere, near the top. You'll find a map-reading light just by the glove compartment. I think it works.'

Robyn found the light, and switched it on. She flipped her fingers through the file.

'I see, you've started writing. That's more like it, Malcolm.'

'Find the letter – that's all you're allowed to read, you hear?'

Robyn ignored him, and started to read the script.

'No, Robyn!' he yelled at her. 'I mean it. I'll crash the car if you carry on.'

'That would be a smart move,' she said. 'I've stopped, OK?'

'Yes, thank you,' he replied. 'Don't worry about the script. It's all in my head, and it won't take me long to get it onto paper, I promise.'

'Right, here it is,' said Robyn. 'The letter.'

She felt the heavy vellum paper with her fingertips, then sniffed at the letter.

'You're not supposed to eat it, Robyn. Just read it!'

'I like the feel of old documents,' she said. 'Your Albert Fairburn has very neat handwriting. I suppose if you're the curator of a museum, your handwriting must be up to it.'

'People took more care in the past,' said Malcolm. 'It was a matter of good manners.'

'To the Chief Librarian,' she read, 'Thank you for your letter of the twentieth instant, and we have noted that you have filed the said correspondence under your file number WM/JPR 15 A. We are pleased to learn that our modest donation to your archives helped to explain Dr William Maloney's acrimonious letters to the Department of Education. This letter concludes our correspondence on the said subject. Remaining yours faithfully, Albert Fairburn, Curator.'

'Isn't it a wonderful letter?' asked Malcolm.

'Is it?'

'It proves that the Russell Collection exists.'

'Who is Dr Maloney?'

'One of Russell's friends. They went on a walking tour of Spain in 1883. Better known as Bill Maloney, he became a leading politician in Sydney.'

'Really,' she said dismissively.

★

Although it was late at night, Kings Cross was still full of life. An assortment of tramps, freaks and pleasure-seekers thronged the pavements. The garish neon lights of the strip joints were beacons for the insomniacs of Sydney. A white Rolls-Royce pulled up outside a nightclub, and Penders got out of it, flanked by Doug and Tony. They walked into the club. The doorman bowed, but Penders ignored him; after all, he owned the place.

Doug headed straight for the auditorium, whilst Penders waited in the foyer with Tony. They stood in the shadows, Tony keeping a respectable distance from his boss.

A strip show was in progress, but Doug was not much concerned with the fat girl on stage shedding her underwear; he was interested in the audience. He found Carlo Bellini sitting at his usual table, entertaining a couple of good-looking tarts. He wore his customary white suit, black shirt and white tie.

Doug leaned over the table, upsetting a glass of champagne as he addressed Bellini.

'Take a leak, Carlo,' he said.

Bellini was offended by Doug's ill manners and he shrieked back at him in a high-pitched voice. 'What do you want?'

'I said, take a leak. *Now!*' repeated Doug menacingly.

Bellini understood what was required of him instantly. Without saying another word, he left the table and followed Doug out of the auditorium. Doug stepped out into the foyer, and carried on walking past the waiting Penders and Tony. He headed for the men's room, and Bellini followed him obediently.

Inside the lavatory, Doug checked that there was nobody else about. Bellini stood to one side, mystified by Doug's actions. The place was empty.

'You wait here!' he said to Bellini.

'So, what's this shit, tough guy?' asked Bellini, trying to disguise his concern.

'I said, take a leak, Carlo.'

'I don't get it,' replied Bellini.

All the same, he stepped up to the urinal and tried to relieve himself, but could not.

Doug left as Penders entered the men's room, and stood next to Bellini. He used the urinal as he spoke to Bellini.

'Hello, Carlo.'

'Good evening, Mr Penders,' said Bellini with reverence. 'What can I do for you?' he asked turning away from the urinal.

'Keep on looking at the wall, Carlo.'

'Yes, Mr Penders.'

'I'd like you to do a little favour for me.'

'Sure. Anything you say.'

'You know Jamie de Selway?'

'Sure. He's one of my regulars.'

'I want you to give him uncut smack from now on!'

'But, Mr Penders, that's murder!' said Bellini, genuinely shocked by the very idea.

'Just do it, Carlo, and keep on looking at the wall.'

Penders stepped away from the urinal, and buttoned up his fly. Bellini tried to turn towards him.

'Keep on looking at the wall!'

Bellini stayed there for a long time after Penders left the lavatory, still looking at the wall. He was frightened out of his wits. It was only now that he was able to pass water. He pissed against the urinal, gushing like Niagara Falls.

★

Only the road signs indicated that Malcolm had arrived in Canberra. The town was nothing but open country and a collection of identical roundabouts, something like Milton Keynes with gum trees. He circled the biggest roundabout twice before realising that they were at their destination. The motel was just past the Houses of Parliament.

Malcolm pulled off the road into the forecourt of the motel. Robyn had her eyes shut, sleeping like an innocent angel. Malcolm collected the keys from reception, got back into his car, and stopped outside one of the bungalows. He carried Robyn in his arms, and deftly negotiated the door with his feet. He took her into the bedroom, and laid her down on one of the beds. She had not blinked an eye, but called out in her sleep.

'Are we there?'

'Yes. We are there,' said Malcolm quietly.

He fetched their luggage, then covered her up with a blanket. By the time he unpacked her pyjamas, she was fast asleep. He did not have the heart to wake her. He switched off the lights, then went into the bathroom. He was ready for bed, but his mind was wide awake. He got into the other bed, and carried on reading Russell's diaries.

Chapter Sixteen

12th June 1881, SS *Liverpool*.

At sea again. I'll have to celebrate my twenty-third birthday the best I can. There was no other ship, and we had a pre-birthday party in Sydney before I left. I am grateful for sea voyages, for I can keep my diary up to date.

Mother has not recovered from Father's death, and I had my hands full winding up his affairs in Sydney. I don't miss him, and I should feel guilty about that, but I don't. I have never been close to him. I was more upset about the rejection of my paintings I sent in for the International Exhibition. Mother talked me into reopening Grandfather Nicholl's studio in Woolloomooloo, but being a society painter didn't suit me. I didn't need the money desperately enough to make a success of the venture; and it was a financial disaster. What my clients really wanted were photographs in the Joshua Reynolds style. None of them were prepared for more than two sittings, and they kept on fidgeting, asking me how it was coming along. It gave Mother something to do for a while, but I'm London-bound. I have enrolled at the Slade School of Art. It is something I should have done a long time ago.

16th June.

I didn't spend my birthday alone. I met an interesting fellow passenger, Tom Roberts. We spent the day together, talking about art. He is from Melbourne. He won a prize at the International Exhibition, and he is using the money to pay for his passage. He is travelling second class, but being my guest, he can use the first-class decks and restaurant. He is relieved that I am paying for everything, but the price of my first-class ticket includes the lot. Perhaps he doesn't know that. He is very much concerned with money, and wants to know the price of everything in London. He has got a year's grant to study at the Royal College of Art, so we're going to see quite a bit of each other. He has done all the things I wished to have done myself, but I am not jealous. Tom was apprenticed to a Melbourne photographer, and attended night school for life drawing at the Artisans' School of Design. He used to work a sixteen-hour day, but managed to get a bursary to the National Gallery's School of Art in Melbourne. He showed me his paintings, and I was impressed by his craftsmanship. He liked my watercolours of Queensland.

18th June.

Had a talk with Tom about photography. I have never considered it a form of art, but he made me change my mind. We both hate the academic approach to painting, and agree that each generation strives for something new. Realism and naturalism opened up the stuffiness of neoclassicism and romanticism; but the ultimate form of realism must be photography. The camera never lies, they say, but I was shocked to learn how much artifice and selection goes into a realistic photograph. Tom has a collection of three hundred different skies on glass plates, and he chooses the most suitable for his backgrounds. Each of his photographs is a composite of at least three completely different pictures. I could not see the joins. We agreed that true realism is unattainable, because to paint a three-dimensional object on a two-dimensional plane can only be achieved by the use of some deliberate distortion. The artist is physically unable to paint what he sees; however, the lens of the camera manages to focus a three-dimensional world onto a two-dimensional glass plate; but even this mechanical process has a style: it reproduces the world in shades of greys. And no photograph is truly black and white.

19th June.

I am not interested in the chemical side of photography, as it cannot reproduce colour. What I detest most about bad photographs is the tinting. I tried to explain that black, and white, and greys are acceptable – like a charcoal drawing – but he defends hand tinting to the death. We agreed to differ.

20th June.

We are both interested in the nature of colour. There is a scientific way of approaching the subject, and apparently, we have both followed the same line of experimentation, and came to similar conclusions. Tom has tried using a spectroscope as an aid to painting. Newton wrote about the nature of light and colour. His theory of rays travelling in straight lines, and behaving like bullets, is clearly demonstrated by photography. I am interested in the nature of reflection, because a mirror image is on a two-dimensional plane. A reflection is the most realistic representation of a picture. Why has no artist painted canvases like that? Pictures that have been around for centuries in mirrors and in ponds. Tom thinks the answer is political. To look at the world in a realistic fashion is a revolutionary idea, and so disturbing to the established order, that nobody dared to think about it until recently. I don't know about that.

25th June.

Tom is teaching me the rudiments of photography, and I showed him some of my experiments with watercolour. We are learning from each other. What luck to have him on the same boat! He is very talented, and his dedication is frightening. I must pull my socks up if I am going to be surrounded by people like him in London. I realise now that my approach to painting was amateur-ish in the extreme. I shall have to take the Slade seriously, otherwise I'll be only wasting my time and money, but I am not sure I am ready for all that hard work.

2nd August 1881, Russell Square, London.

I have neglected my diary. I was too busy painting and drawing. Had a reunion with Tom Roberts. He installed himself in lodgings at St James Street, off the Fulham Palace Road. He'll travel to college on the District Railway. I am lucky to be just around the corner from the Slade. We had a celebratory meal at Luigi's in Frith Street, and both got very drunk. I showed him my latest work, but he was not impressed, yet I worked like a slave for the past week.

15th October 1881, London.

I am not sure what to make of the Slade. I like my fellow students, but not Alphonse Legros. He is an academician in disguise. He is meant to use the methods of the Petite École in Paris, as he was a student of the legendary Lecoq de Boisbaudron. He should be brilliant. Perhaps he is. My life drawing has improved a lot since I have been at the Slade. So why am I grumbling? I just don't like Legros. He is a noisy show-off. There was this male model with an enormous set of tools and I drew it just like that. He scribbled all over it with his red chalk, muttering in broken English to 'make 'em small, Michelangelo makes 'em small'. I think the others dislike him, too. Attending the Slade seems a pleasant way of wasting time, and a considerable amount of money. It should not be a class thing, but the Slade is certainly an upper-class establishment, whilst the Royal College is lower middle-class, if I am to believe Tom.

20th October 1881.

Half of Sydney is in London. I made a new friend – Bill Maloney, a medical student. He has been here for over a year now. He knows a couple of other Australians, and we visit a lot of Soho pubs. Tom is part of the gang. We are addicted to ale, and drink tremendous quantities of the stuff.

25th October.

Had a letter from my brother, Percy. He is coming to London to study architecture. I am looking forward to seeing him, but I don't think it's a good idea that he should move in with me. I started to box again at the YMCA. I like working off my surplus energy somehow. Whoring is not enough of an exercise, though I had a very strange experience last night. Visited a painter friend in Holborn. He was working with the two most beautiful models I have seen for ages. Identical twins, both seventeen (*they would be, wouldn't they?*), and I just had to have them. It took a little persuasion, and they insisted on sleeping with me separately at first, but they soon warmed to the idea. We had a romp. Most delightful pair of 'couplettes'.

7th November.

The terrible twins visited me again. It wasn't such fun this time. More like hard work.

28th November.

Settled down to a working pattern. Alphonse Legros may be a noisy old fart, but he helped me a lot. There is a craft to everything, and it can be learned. It hurts to think back to the struggle I had at sixteen, trying to draw a human figure. It's easy if you know how. If I only knew this when I tried to draw Bea. I still think of her a lot. I have an arrangement with the terrible twins. They come and visit me separately now. It's too tiring otherwise. Incidentally, there is no such thing as an identical twin. Each of them is unique. I know their bodies intimately, and I can tell them apart even in the dark; and as far as their personalities are concerned, you couldn't find two more different people if you tried.

2nd December.

Experimented with photography again, to Alphonse Legros's horror, but he is wrong. An artist uses what he feels is right. Photography itself could become an art if one could only control the chemical processes, but it is too much hit-and-miss for my liking. My best photographs were all accidents of one sort or another. Tom is more impressed with my photographs than my drawings. The swine.

Chapter Seventeen

It was early in the morning, but Robyn and Malcolm were camped on the doorstep of the Commonwealth Archives, waiting for the building to be opened. The reading room was almost empty. In the middle of the large circular room there were solid mahogany tables, leather chairs, and green-shaded lamps. The shelves were tightly packed with leather-bound books, embossed in gold, and the place smelt of furniture wax and old paper. Malcolm was at home instantly. He loved libraries. He thumbed through a catalogue. Robyn sat facing him, deeply lost in thought. A librarian walked over to them, carrying a bulging folder under her arm. She was a severe-looking woman in her fifties, dressed in a dark suit, her hair in a bun.

Now that's typecasting for you. I've never seen a better example, thought Robyn, but said nothing.

'It's all here, Dr Reid,' she said. 'Everything you asked for.'

'Thank you very much,' said Malcolm.

She put the folder in front of Malcolm, then sat next to him. Robyn looked at her with a raised eyebrow.

'I'm afraid I'll have to stay with you,' said the librarian.

'Oh, we don't mind,' replied Malcolm.

'Why do you have to stay with us?' asked Robyn.

'Rules are rules,' she said sternly.

'You don't know students,' said Malcolm. 'Vandals, every one of them. I would never let them loose in a library.'

The librarian smiled thankfully, then took up the stance of a disinterested observer. It annoyed Robyn, but Malcolm was used to the procedure, and got on with his reading. He worked his way through the file methodically. He had seen most of Russell's correspondence with Tom Roberts and Bill Maloney, and had photocopies of their letters. Malcolm was looking for a file marked WM/JPR 15 A. His face lit up when he found it.

'Here they are,' he said. 'Four letters.'

He read them avidly in silence.

'So?' asked Robyn impatiently.

Malcolm skipped the boring bits, and started to read the interesting parts aloud for Robyn's benefit.

'*Please find enclosed thirty-eight paintings…*'

'Thirty-eight?' asked Robyn.

'Yes, thirty-eight… *You'll find them representative of the period… it is my ardent desire to share with my fellow Australians…* et cetera… et cetera… *We thank you for your most generous bequest, but before accepting the collection we shall have to submit it to the hanging committee… Albert Fairburn, Curator…* Oh, this is the one… *Once again, we would like to thank you for your generosity… unfortunately we find the paintings are not of the high standard normally associated with the Gallery of Modern Art… We would appreciate it if you could make your own arrangements for collecting the said paintings. We are not making deliveries of this nature…*'

'The pompous turd,' interrupted Robyn.

'*Should you not claim the collection,*' Malcolm continued, '*within a calendar month, we shall presume that you do not wish to have them… we shall have to dispose of them ourselves…* blah… blah… *Yours faithfully, Albert Fairburn.*'

'Did he?' asked Robyn.

Malcolm picked up the last letter.

'He did… *Sir, I reserve the right to dispose of my own paintings, and to save you the trouble, I will personally collect them. Yours, John Peter Russell.*'

'What a gent,' said Robyn.

Malcolm handed the four letters to the librarian.

'Any chance of having these photocopied?'

'Yes. If you'd like to wait, I shall bring them to you. There is a charge, of course.'

'That's all right, thank you,' said Malcolm, smiling happily.

Robyn left Malcolm and went to her business meeting. They arranged to meet at the motel in the afternoon, which suited Malcolm. It left him time to visit the National Museum of Art.

John Peter Russell had been better appreciated in Canberra. He had a small room of his own, between Tom Roberts' and George Lambert's much grander salons. Malcolm had known about the 'Regatta in Sydney Harbour' and the 'Peasants in a field near Monte Cassino', but finding a portrait of Dr William Maloney was a definite bonus. There were about twenty paintings in the room, more than half of them watercolours. The oils impressed him, and he felt sad that Russell had abandoned painting in that medium. His works stood out a mile; they were masterpieces compared to the other paintings exhibited in the museum.

Malcolm had time on his hands, and talked to one of the attendants. Russell's paintings were valued at around a hundred and fifty thousand dollars each. Multiplied by thirty-eight, it came to five and a half million dollars; but the pictures in the museum were not insured, because the government could not afford to pay the premiums.

Malcolm had lunch in the motel. He bought a huge Chinese takeaway to celebrate a successful morning's work, and settled down to read more of the Russell diaries.

5th May 1883, Lac Cazeau.

Took the train from London to Bordeaux, and began our walking tour from there. Fell in love with the lake, and we've been here for a week. I don't think we'll ever get to Spain at this rate. The food is excellent, the wine divine, and the innkeeper's daughter has fallen in love with me. Tom approves of the place, as full board is only three shillings a week. Bill Maloney takes to the pines for day-long walks; he is trying to get himself fit for the long haul ahead. The Landes beaches are magnificent; blinding white sand, giant rolling waves of the Atlantic, pungent pine forests, and not a soul as far as the eye can see. Percy bicycles to Arcachon each day to sketch the church. He is a first-year student of architecture, and his dedication is touching. We get on surprisingly well; I never liked Percy when we were younger. Young Martine, the innkeeper's daughter, is the most unusual 'couplette'. She looks innocent, virginal, fragile, a bit like a ghost; but under that saintly exterior hides the most demanding and almost insatiable sexual appetite I have encountered. I am a little bit frightened of her. She may devour me yet.

15th May 1883, Fuenterrabia.

At long last we are in Spain. Neither Tom nor myself have painted a thing yet. Only Percy is working. Bill will never be fit, but he has enough will power to carry him to the edge of the world. Fuenterrabia hasn't got a lot to offer; cobbled streets and ancient city walls. We had fish for supper, indifferently cooked, and much overpriced.

16th May 1883, San Sebastian.

A singularly ugly town. Visited the Museo San Telmo, and looked at the pitiful Basque artefacts on display. They seem to be obsessed with death here. The only notable object is a Rubens oil, the size of a handkerchief. One of his usual fat whores. I never liked Rubens.

23rd May 1883, Burgos.

Spain has started to look Spanish. Burgos is a pilgrim town on the Camino Frances to Santiago de Compostela. The pilgrim route had been a cultural highway for a thousand years, which explains why Burgos cathedral looks German Gothic. But highways are two-way affairs, and that accounts for the Moorish influences in France. Percy is excited by all this architectural hotchpotch. The Romanesque cloisters of the Las Huelgas convent particularly impressed him. Tom and I visited the Cathedral of Santa Maria. We found some of the religious bric-à-brac very funny, and could hardly keep a straight face. I always want to laugh at these relics. It is the obsession with death; laughter must be an instinctive gesture of self-preservation. Eternal damnation is too frightening to contemplate.

19th May 1883, Segovia.

Just how I imagined Spain. There is an impressive aqueduct built by the Romans, still in good working order, bringing water to the town from the surrounding hills. No mortar was used in its construction, and it has 163 stone arches. Percy has counted them all.

11th June 1883, San Lorenzo de El Escorial.

The most depressing place on earth. The monastery, the palaces, the churches and the museums are all built from grey granite; the very stones are imbued with death. I cannot get away from a feeling of doom. There is something hostile about everything here, and the bright sun only makes the country feel even more oppressive. But Tom loves everything about Spain unquestioningly. The Escorial is packed with masterpieces: Titian, Ribera, El Greco etc. A few days' visit doesn't do the place justice, but I hate looking at fossils. Tom agreed to move on, reluctantly.

16th June 1883, Madrid.

Celebrated my 25th birthday in style. We went to a high-class brothel, and had a wonderful time. The Museo del Prado has over 5,000 canvases: Goya, El Greco, Bosch, Breughel, Botticelli, Murillo, Raphael, Tintoretto, and most of all, Velazquez. He is my hero. Having looked at his work I feel as if I am seeing the world for the first time. His paintings are the nearest to what I have been trying to achieve all my life. I would like to spend a year here.

2nd July 1883, Toledo.

The town reminds me of Segovia. The Alcazar dominates the town, and Percy has sketched it from every conceivable angle. The rest of us visited El Greco's house and a number of churches packed full of his work. I don't like his tortured portraits, but his landscapes are impressive, particularly his menacing skies. Perhaps if I were Roman Catholic I'd like his work a lot more. He is a master, without doubt.

12th July 1883, Granada.

Percy had to see the Alhambra, but I am glad we stopped here. We met a couple of painters who work here: Ramon Casas and Georges Barreau. I like their work, and it is the direction I want to follow. Talking to them I realised that, unknown to me, I have been part of the en plein air school of painting. During my travels in the South Seas I discovered that I had to work fast to capture the effects of the clouds before it all changed. They say that's what painting en plein air is all about, producing sketches that are the final works themselves. I had a long argument with Casas about perspective. I don't believe it matters all that much; colour is more important. Tom and Barreau supported me. Barreau also talked about complementary colours and negative after-images, but I didn't understand him. My French is sufficient in bed, but not good enough for a discussion about the theory of light. Met an American painter by the name of Dodge MacKnight. He studies at the Atelier Cormon in Paris. It sounds like a place I would like to work in. He offered to sponsor me, should I want to go there. Apparently, it is not an easy place to get into.

12th July 1883, Granada.

The time has come to part. Bill is going back to London, Tom is trying to live in Italy for a shilling a day, whilst Percy and I are heading for Malaga, then on to Genoa and Sydney. Even though I hardly painted a picture of note, it was a marvellous summer, and our walk made us friends for life. I shall always remember Spain, even though the country and its people scare me stiff. Well, to the future.

★

Jamie lived in a tastefully furnished room in the best part of Paddington. Some original paintings hung on the walls, and there were books everywhere. His easel was in the middle of the room, but it was obvious that he had not done much painting for a while. All his paints and brushes were put away tidily. His dead body was slumped on the floor. Next to it there was a cardboard box filled with books. A dog sat by Jamie's body, howling mournfully.

★

Robyn offered to go Dutch, but Jake Tasman insisted on picking up the tab. It was a good lunch meeting, even though little was said; all the important business was implied. The fact that Jake Tasman found time for her was more important than anything else. Robyn had made it to the top of the pile, and it was a nice feeling.

Tasman was a frontman for a Japanese merchant bank with heavy yakuza connections. Their money came from gambling, extortion and drugs. Investing in movies was a way of laundering dirty money. Tasman told Robyn that she could borrow up to fifty million dollars without collateral, payable anywhere in the world, in any currency, at two per cent less interest than the Australian Film Commission charged; but there was no provision made for failure. The investment had to be safe. It was the kind of offer that she could only afford to refuse, but she was flattered all the same.

She was more than a little tipsy when she got back to the motel. Malcolm sat on his bed, reading the Russell diaries. He looked up, and nodded to acknowledge her arrival, then carried on reading.

Robyn watched him in silence. She poured herself a large glass of Château Poolowanna, and leaned back in the comfortable armchair. She was pleased with the world. Malcolm looked very attractive. He was like a sweet little boy without pretence, innocent and vulnerable. She could hardly keep her hands off him.

Suddenly he stopped reading, and turned around.

'How was your meeting?' he asked.

'Most businesslike,' she replied. 'If Greg messes me about, I can always go elsewhere. I've been promised some money.'

'Sounds good.'

'Yeah… You'll probably think I'm a dummy, but tell me, just what happened to Russell's thirty-eight paintings?'

'Nobody knows. Isn't that wonderful?'

'If you say so,' she said uncertainly.

'It's great news, Robyn. We're going to find the Russell Collection. You and I, together.'

'Sure,' she said.

'How much would you make as a producer from the film? Go on, tell me.'

'None of your bloody business!'

'It doesn't matter. We'd make more money from the finder's fee than the movie. The Russell Collection must be worth ten million dollars. Ten per cent of that is a cool million.'

Robyn thought for a while. It took her some time before she understood what Malcolm was talking about.

'You look very masterful with greed in your eyes, Malcolm,' she said flippantly.

'You know what I'm talking about.'

'OK, OK. So, where are the pictures then?'

'He sent them back to Paris.'

'How do you know?'

'I don't know. It's a hunch, but I am getting to know my JPR.'

'Well, let's go to Paris. Why not? What the hell?' she said sarcastically, but Malcolm took her straight.

'That's right. So, you'd better come up with some cash. I've only got three weeks before term starts.'

'But what about the script?'

'I told you it was in my head. You'll have it when we get back from Europe. I promise.'

'You're a clever bastard, for a Pom.'

Malcolm stood up and hugged her. She felt soft and sensitive, and he felt a shiver going through his body. She kissed his ear. Malcolm greedily searched out her mouth, and they kissed. It seemed like a century before she broke away from him.

'No, Malcolm,' she said quietly.

'You mustn't wind me up, not unless you mean it,' he said in a husky voice.

'I mean it, Malcolm, but not yet. Not just yet.'

She walked away from him slowly. She really wanted him badly, but it was not the right time. Shit, she thought, it's not so easy being a working girl...

Chapter Eighteen

It was four in the morning when Malcolm got back home. Robyn chose to fly back from Canberra. Malcolm was physically tired, but elated otherwise. He knew Robyn wanted him, and it was only a matter of time before their affair would reach the next logical stage. The script was progressing better than he expected, still in his head, but getting it to paper would take no time at all, and with a bit of luck he just might find Russell's missing collection. He had everything to look forward to.

The first signs of dawn showed as he pulled up outside his house. The street was deserted. Everything was still. It was that dead period that only big cities have; a short interlude between the night people going to bed and the day people starting to wake up.

Malcolm noticed a police car parked across the street, but paid no attention to it as he gathered his luggage from the boot of his car.

Two uniformed policemen got out of their car and walked over to Malcolm, slowly and deliberately, as if they meant business.

'Are you Malcolm Reid?' asked the taller one.

'Yes,' said Malcolm grumpily. He just wanted to go to sleep.

'We want you to come with us.'

'What's the charge?' he demanded, in the upper-class voice he used when talking to customs officers.

'Don't make it hard for yourself, mate,' said the stockier one. 'We've been waiting for you all night, and we're not in the mood to play silly buggers.'

'Can I put my luggage inside first?'

'Sure.'

The policemen walked back to their car. Malcolm was not going to give them trouble. They sat in the car, and watched Malcolm struggle with his bags and the front door key. He piled his stuff in the front hall, and walked over to the police car.

Before getting in, he noticed Doug sitting in his delivery van some fifty metres up the road. Malcolm looked at the van thoughtfully as he got into the police car. He sat in the back with the shorter officer. The tall one started the car. They drove through the slums of Redfern without saying a word, and headed towards Paddington.

The streets were empty, but they still cruised along at forty kilometres an hour. The policemen looked bored, and gave the impression of having all the time in the world; nothing could disturb their serene mood.

'What am I supposed to have done?' asked Malcolm.

'Nothing,' said the policeman sitting next to him. 'You are what the papers call "a person helping police with their inquiries".'

'Inquiries about what?'

'You'll soon find out.'

Malcolm looked out of the window.

The grey of the sky was fast turning to orange, but before Malcolm could enjoy the full glory of the sunrise, they arrived at Paddington police station. Malcolm was shown into a small interview room. He sat down and waited. Twenty minutes passed by, but Malcolm was not bothered. A feeling of calmness came over him. He knew he had done nothing wrong; he had nothing to fear. Policemen were his paid servants.

A larger-than-life Irish plain-clothes man entered the room, carrying a mug of tea in his hand.

'I'm Detective Sergeant Costello,' he said as he sat down facing Malcolm. 'Have some tea.'

Malcolm was grateful for the tea, but after the first sip his face contorted into a grimace.

'Not enough sugar?' asked Costello. 'I've put in three spoonfuls.'

'I don't take sugar,' said Malcolm.

'Sorry,' said Costello, but Malcolm could tell he was not. He was delighted at having got under another Pommy bastard's skin. 'I'll get you another one.'

'Never mind the tea, Sergeant. What do you want from me?'

'Are you in a hurry?'

'No. I am not in a hurry, but I am very tired. I drove all night. So let's get this thing over, please.'

'Do you know a James de Selway?'

'Yes, I know him.'

'How well do you know him?'

'I've met him a couple of times. He's an acquaintance, I'd say.'

'So he wasn't a good friend of yours?'

'Wasn't?' asked Malcolm.

'Just answer the question, Mr Reid.'

'No. He isn't what I'd call a good friend,' replied Malcolm irritably.

'De Selway is dead,' said Costello brutally, 'and he's left all his books to you. Why would he do that, if he wasn't a friend?'

'I don't know. *Dead?*'

Without answering the question Costello stabbed a button on the intercom, and spoke into it.

'Bring in the effects, Ray.'

Costello looked up, and stared Malcolm in the face for a couple of seconds before speaking.

'Yes. Dead.'

'How did he die?'

'He overdosed, Mr Reid. Where did he get his heroin from?'

'I don't know,' said Malcolm, looking away.

Costello's eyes showed that he knew Malcolm was lying, and Malcolm knew he had been caught out. He had always been hopeless at telling lies.

'You don't know, or you're not saying?'

'I don't know,' lied Malcolm.

A uniformed constable came into the room with a cardboard box, and placed it on the table between Malcolm and Costello.

'Thanks, Ray.'

'Sarge,' he replied, and left the room.

Costello reached into the box, and picked up a couple of books at random, then turned to Malcolm.

'*The Pre-Raphaelites. French Symbolism. The Avant Garde in France. Salon des Refugees…*'

'*Refusés*,' interrupted Malcolm involuntarily.

'If you like,' said Costello as he dropped the books back into the box. 'So, this is what you had in common?'

'I am working on a script about an Australian painter. I met

Jamie de Selway at the Gallery of Modern Art, where I was doing some research for the script…'

'Did he take his own life?'

'I don't think so. He wasn't the type… mind you, he was a bundle of nerves the last time I saw him.'

'When was that?'

'The day before yesterday, round about eleven in the morning. He visited me in my flat. He brought me a letter I was looking for in the archives.'

'You say he was nervous. Why?'

'I don't know. Like he was missing a fix.'

'You're an expert on drug addiction?'

'Come on, Sergeant…'

'OK. Who was his pusher?'

'I don't know. You've asked me that before.'

'And I'll keep on asking you until you tell me, because you know. And I know that you know, OK?'

'I don't know his name. I only saw him once,' said Malcolm, managing to sound convincing.

'Where?'

'At a reception in the Paddington Galleries.'

'What does he look like?'

'About a metre seventy, dark hair, olive skin, and he wore a white suit. I only had a glimpse of him.'

'You don't know his name?'

'No. No idea.'

'You're not much of a help, are you?'

'I'm sorry. I really liked Jamie,' said Malcolm. 'When did he die?'

'Some time between eight and ten last night. This is the note he left,' said Costello.

He showed Malcolm a small piece of paper with an almost indecipherable scrawl all over it. Malcolm managed to work out a few words at the top. He read them aloud.

'*Dear God, Malcolm Reid… Leichhardt…* I can't make out the rest.'

'Nor could we. That's why you're here. You think these books relate to your work?'

'Oh, yes.'

'He probably wanted you to have them,' said Costello, and pushed the box over to Malcolm.

'Is that it?'

'Yeah, unless you can add something useful. If you can think of anything, don't hesitate to call me. Any time, day or night, OK?'

'Of course,' said Malcolm.

'I'll get the boys to take you home.'

Costello left the room, taking the mug of cold tea with him. Malcolm sat there for a while without moving a muscle. His brain was working in overdrive, going over the interrogation. He had described Carlo Bellini to perfection. Costello probably knew all the pushers in Paddington, anyhow. So what did he want from me? The answer came in a flash. *I didn't know Jamie was dead.* Elementary, dear Malcolm, he told himself. If I had anything to do with Jamie's death, I would have known that he was dead.

★

Penders was an early starter. Between seven and nine in the morning he ploughed through more work than most people could cope with in a whole day. Not being interrupted by telephone calls was the secret of a successful businessman. Being completely ruthless and a willingness to bend all the rules also helped.

Greg Ericson was summoned to meet him at eight. He was shown into Penders' office by a uniformed security man as Susie did not start till nine. Ericson looked dreadful, and Penders was pleased to see him at his worst.

'I hope you don't mind dropping in, Greg,' he said with a wide grin on his face.

'No sweat, Ralph,' said Ericson as he sat down.

'Help yourself to some coffee,' said Penders, pointing to the percolator on a side table.

'No, thanks.'

'So, how much does she want, Greg?'

'Forty thousand. She called me from Canberra yesterday.'

'What is she doing there?' asked Penders.

He knew that she had lunch with Jake Tasman in Canberra. He knew every move Robyn or Malcolm made. They were under constant surveillance, their telephones were bugged, and Penders received a daily report on their activities.

'Don't ask me, Ralph. She's a difficult woman to deal with. Selling *Palm Beach* to the Poms must have gone to her head. She said she needed the extra cash, because they'll have to go to Paris to complete the script.'

'We'd all love to have a holiday in Paris, Greg.'

'It's important for the story, she says. They've discovered a new angle that needs more research.'

'What did they discover?'

'She won't say.'

'All right, Greg. Give her thirty thousand dollars. She'll be happy with that.'

Penders picked up a file from his desk. It was his way of telling Ericson that he was dismissed.

'Sure, Ralph,' he said on his way out.

Penders did not even look up. I must get rid of him soon, he thought. He picked up a mobile and punched in a set of numbers.

'Yes, Mr Penders.'

'Where are you, Doug?'

'In Redfern.'

'You speak a little French, don't you?'

'*Un peu…*'

'Do you fancy a holiday in France?'

'*Mais oui, certainement,*' replied Doug.

'Come up and see me sometime.'

Penders put the mobile down, and looked out of the window. He sighed. Penders had serious problems. His financial empire was over-stretched. He needed some cash desperately. Around a hundred million dollars. It was time to cash in some of his hidden assets. He picked up the file from his desk, and carried on reading it, but his heart was not in it. I need a holiday myself, he thought. He reached for another mobile and dialled a number. Philippa answered herself.

'Do you want to have lunch with me?' he asked.

'Love to,' she said, unable to disguise her surprise.

Penders felt he had to explain. 'I need a holiday, but I can't spare the time. You know what they say, a change is as good as a holiday.'

'Shall I prepare some lunch at home?'

'No. Come to my office.'

Chapter Nineteen

2nd October 1884, Paris.

I am here at long last. Would have come earlier but for the boxing tournament I was involved in. The light-heavyweight champion of Great Britain now lives at 73 boulevard de Clichy! I've been accepted at the Atelier Cormon, and I live a hundred metres from the studio. Monsieur Felix Cormon is a real character. He is not a teacher, just a painter, who opened his doors to the students from the École des Beaux-Arts who have had a bellyful of Leon Bonnat. Alphonse Legros wrote a most persuasive letter; he is a friend of Cormon's, and Dodge MacKnight sponsored me. Cormon manages to keep five mistresses happy. He works hard, and produces a painting a day. Being the new boy, I have to pay for all the rounds in the cafés, and I am at the receiving end of every childish prank. But it is fun. My fellow students are all accomplished painters. I feel flattered to be accepted by them on equal terms. They like my landscapes, and share my belief that using primary colours is more important than perspective. They are bizarre. Henri de Toulouse-Lautrec is a malicious dwarf, and proud of it. He is only nineteen, but plans to marry the ugliest whore in Paris, and take her to Albi to the family château. He wants to settle down in the country, and concentrate on the serious work of breeding monsters. Louis Anquetin is even taller than I. It is very funny to see him standing next to Henri, but they go out whoring together on Montmartre. We think Louis is the most talented amongst us, but he is not big-headed about it. For a giant, he is a very gentle person. Emile Bernard is the baby. He is sixteen, and makes me feel old at twenty-six. He has some exciting ideas about setting up an artists' commune, where we could all pool our talents and resources together. I'm quite taken by the idea. Dodge MacKnight is here, of course. Also Julian Rabache, who always wears a bowler hat – with his bushy black beard, it is a very odd combination. I work next to Eugene Carrière, who is very popular and has already established himself as a successful painter. I find him a little intimidating. He is not the sophisticated Parisian that you'd expect. He comes from the Vosges, and he is very provincial in his ways, though Strasbourg is less of a cultural backwater than Sydney. Carrière spent some time in London, and he, too, likes Turner's paintings. His dreamy and misty portraits remind me of Turner. I have a lot to crow about. Wrote a letter to Tom Roberts and Bill Maloney to make them feel jealous.

25th October.

Went to Asnières for the day with Bernard. We painted side by side in his parents' small garden. Surprisingly warm day for late October. The sun was shining through hazy clouds with an amazingly soft light that wrapped itself around everything. No shadows.

26th October.

Went to my first open house at Cormon's. We are invited to his home on Sundays. It is the only time we can talk about work; we are far too busy during the week. Cormon encourages experimentation; according to him, there is not just one way of painting, many paths lead to the same place. That is why he is such a good master to learn from. We have the most divergent approach to painting; there is nothing dogmatic about our group. I am ignorant compared to the others. They are well read, and talk about writers and philosophers I have never heard of. I tried to hide behind my appalling French, but they all speak English. Some even read Nietzsche in the original German! I have a lot to catch up with, but when? I work a sixteen-hour day already.

2nd November.

Bernard took me to meet Père Tanguy. He is a painter's supplier who sometimes deals in pictures. Not out of choice, some of his customers pay him in kind, and he is more of a charitable institution than businessman. His shop is always full of artists arguing about money. Thank God, I have no money problems, but everybody I know in Paris seems to have. Père Tanguy agreed to sit for me. He has beautiful blue eyes and a kind face.

20th November.

We go to the Café Guerbois on Thursdays. All the talk is about politics. I am an anarchist in the real sense of the word, as I detest all form of politics. My early democratic phase in Sydney was just my way of rebelling against Father. The politics of art is fascinating. The talking point at the moment is the Grandes Boulevards against the Petit Boulevard, which splits the Impressionists into two groups. Monet, Degas and Pissarro are definitely Grandes Boulevards; they are the old and established Impressionists. Their group is named after Monet's canvas 'Impression, Sunrise', which he painted way back in 1872. The younger and more rebellious painters like Bernard and Toulouse-Lautrec and *myself* are talked about as Petit Boulevard. I got talking to Georges Seurat. He is two years younger than myself, and has been the talk of Paris all year. His *'Une Baignade, Asnières'* is a huge painting, and he must have worked on it very hard. He made twenty drawings and sixteen sketches in oil. Seurat examined colour in a scientific fashion, and he came up with a style of his own – 'pointillism'. It's all the rage now, and everybody is copying him without shame. We had a long talk about complementary colours: red/green, yellow/violet, orange/blue; and the nature of white and black, and how they are affected by their surroundings. Snow is never white and neither are shadows black. Red has a green shadow, and so on; we both use complementaries for shading. It makes sense, and can be proved scientifically. According to him, the most important rule is not to blend primary colours on a palette, but use them on the canvas in their pure state, side by side. Whatever mixing there is, it takes place in the retina of the observer. I'm going to visit Seurat in his studio next week.

24th November.

People say Seurat takes years to complete a canvas. It is not true; because his studio is stacked with paintings, and Seurat is only twenty-four. According to that logic, he must have started painting before he was born. I was impressed with his first version of the 'Baignade', but it is massive, twice the size of the one he showed in the end. He couldn't find anywhere to exhibit it, and that's why he painted the smaller canvas. The larger painting is far superior. He offered to sell it to me, but where would I keep it? I asked Seurat to keep it for me. I must write to Tom; perhaps somebody in Sydney would like to have it. It is a masterpiece.

26th November.

Went out whoring with Anquetin and Toulouse-Lautrec. We started at Le Chat Noir. It is run by one of Henri's friends, Aristide Bruant. We drank gallons of absinthe, on the house, the genuine 136° proof Pernod Fils from Pontarlier. Henri drinks a mixture of absinthe and cognac, the 'tremblement de terre' which almost killed me on the *Edithnne Louise*. It's going to be the end of him.

3rd December.

Found a good boxing club off the rue Lepic and feel a lot healthier now, having started to do some physical exercise again. The London crowd is following me to Paris, not to mention the visiting Australians. I think they are all shocked by the lack of morals in Paris. I always enjoy taking them to Le Chat Noir.

Chapter Twenty

Robyn had a soft spot for Paris. For her, it was the most romantic city in the world. Her first love was a French stuntman, whom she met while working as an interpreter on a film. They were madly in love. Their romance ended when he died in a car crash. A drunken lorry driver killed him one night, driving on the wrong side of the road. It took Robyn a long time to get over it. She never talked about it, and still woke up in fright in the middle of the night having nightmares of her lost lover.

Malcolm never got on with the French; he was suspicious of them. His mother was a cosmopolitan creature; perhaps she was to blame for his prejudices. He remembered, as a child, being dragged across the Channel for holidays. Easter was always spent in Paris, and the summer in Vence, where his mother shared a studio with a Provencal lesbian; not the bed, just working space.

Robyn and Malcolm sipped their drinks in silence, lost in their thoughts. Their table overlooked the boulevard Saint-Germain. It was midwinter in Europe. The people looked cold and miserable as they hurried along the wet pavements. The terrace was enclosed in glass; cosy and warm like a goldfish bowl in reverse. Robyn was the first to break the silence.

'What's eating you, Malcolm? You've been miserable since we landed.'

'Nothing.'

'You should be happy. We're in Paris. That's what you wanted. Everything is going your way and you're moping like an old woman.'

'Thanks a lot, Robyn.'

'Then cheer up.'

'How well did you know Jamie?'

'Oh, we're still on that? I didn't know him. I've met him once or twice. He was Mac's friend.'

'How do you know Mac?'

'Bloody hell, Malcolm! Everybody knows Mac.'

'I'm sorry, but I must know.'

'No. Forget Sydney. We're in Paris.'

'I can't forget Jamie. Just answer me a few questions. That's all I want.'

'You won't let go, will you?'

'No. I can be very single-minded.'

Robyn had to give in. He dug his heels in, and that was that. She took a deep breath.

'Ask away.'

'You said Jamie was McDonald's friend. What sort of friend?'

'They were good friends, not lovers.'

'But good friends?'

'I think so. They knew each other for a couple of years. I've always seen them together.'

'That's what I thought. Then why did Jamie leave his books to me? Was he trying to say something?'

'How should I know? What sort of books?'

'Books on art, painting, restoration; books about famous art forgers…' Malcolm stopped in mid-sentence as the idea hit him for the first time. 'That's it – he must have been forging paintings for McDonald. It all makes sense!'

'You'd have a job proving that,' said Robyn.

Malcolm cheered up considerably. He took Robyn's hand, and kissed it thankfully.

'You're an angel. I would never have thought of that myself.'

'You can't prove it,' repeated Robyn.

'I don't want to prove anything,' he said. 'I just wanted to understand Jamie. I cannot rest if something puzzles me. I've got to solve every riddle.'

'And are you solving this riddle?'

'No need to take the piss, Robyn. I know which way to look now.'

'So, no more questions?'

'No, not for the moment.'

Robyn raised her glass to Malcolm.

'Hello, Malcolm,' she said smiling. 'Welcome to the world of the living.'

'Hello, Robyn,' he said.

'Welcome to Paris, the city of love.'

'Is that what Paris is?'

'Yeah. The last romantic place left in the world.'

'If you say so.'

'I do.'

She stared deep into his eyes. He was forced to turn away, because her look aroused him so much, he wanted to tear the clothes off her; right there, in front of all Paris. Instead, he gulped his drink down to stop his throat drying out. Robyn kept her eyes on him. She was aware of her power over him as she sipped her drink. She remembered endless nights of lovemaking in Paris; her memories aroused her, and she wanted Malcolm just as much as he wanted her. There was more to life than just work.

'Let's drink up here, and go back to the hotel,' she said in a deep, sexy voice.

'Sure,' agreed Malcolm hastily.

They were staying in the Hôtel Marquant, just around the corner. Malcolm wanted to run, but forced himself to keep a leisurely pace. Robyn hooked her arm through his, and snuggled up to him as they walked along the pavement. Neither of them noticed the freezing cold and the persistent rain. They shared a two-bedroom suite on the top floor with a fantastic view of the Latin Quarter. By the time they entered the hall Malcolm's throat was completely dry. His loins ached with desire. He closed the door shut, and hugged Robyn hungrily. They kissed for a century, then Robyn broke away from him, only to hang the 'DO NOT DISTURB' notice on the door handle.

She put her arms around his neck and kissed him with all the suppressed passion of the past couple of weeks. Malcolm was surprised by her ardour. He pressed his lips against hers. He sucked in her warm tongue, and caressed it with his. She tore the shirt off his back while he fumbled with the zip of her dress. They rushed into the bedroom and fell onto the bed, and made love with uncontrolled passion. First it was Malcolm commanding, using his body to suppress her. Robyn yielded gently and passively, then little by little she took over, and played the dominant role. Hours must have passed by before they paused; for them time stood still. They ordered some food from room service, but before it arrived they were locked in passionate combat again, and did not hear the discreet knock at the door. Eventually, they fell back into the bed, silent with exhaustion.

'I'm hungry,' said Robyn after a while.

They remembered the food they had ordered. Malcolm went to fetch the silver tray with the magnum bottle of champagne and the smoked salmon sandwiches. They sat up in bed, and tucked into the food hungrily, then resumed their lovemaking, this time gently and slowly, savouring every second of it.

Malcolm woke at ten in the morning, and found himself alone. Robyn left a note: '*Gone shopping. I'll be back for lunch.*' Malcolm ordered breakfast from room service, and went into his room to unpack. He got into bed with his croissants and Russell's diary.

16th June 1885, Paris.

My twenty-seventh birthday coincided with a celebration at the studio. Felix Cormon had been awarded a silver medal at the Salon. It was a surprise party. We gave Maître Cormon a silver palm to commemorate the occasion. My friend from England, Harry Bates, sculpted it. It was a moving little ceremony. I could see tears in Maître Cormon's eyes.

22nd June.

Bates has been pestering me to model for him. He also goes on about an Italian model he met at Dalou's studio. She is meant to be the most beautiful woman on earth. He wants us to pose together. He thinks I have a beautiful body. I took it as a compliment, and went to Dalou's studio. Bates was right. She is beautiful, and I have fallen in love with her. She is twenty years old, and her name is Marianna Mattiocco. She has been in Paris since she was fifteen. She has two elder brothers, both students, whom she supports financially. She is like a goddess: blond, strong-limbed; she has high and firm breasts, and a classical Roman profile. She moves like a sensuous animal. Being naked is natural for her, and her innocent eyes look at you openly. I challenge any man to have a dirty thought in her presence.

26th June.

Bates' work is progressing very slowly. I'll be sad when he finishes, because I cannot live without Marianna. I think she likes me. I have met her brothers. They are music students. They did their best to discourage me from seeing her, but she wants to see me again. She said so. Marianna was born on 5th June 1865. Just missed her twentieth birthday. She was born in Cassino, not far from Naples. She comes from a peasant family, and we talked about spending a holiday in Cassino. She wants me to meet her family. Marianna is a devout Catholic. She was a little upset when I told her I was a fallen Protestant. She found it odd that I should be Church of England when I was born and bred in Australia.

1st July.

Marianna moved in with me, and we are lovers. She was a virgin, and gave herself to me completely, without any questions or conditions. I am honoured to be her lover. I cannot live without her, I know that. We are so happy together that it hurts. She cries sometimes and I ask her why. She tells me, because she is happy. I am the happiest man on earth.

6th July.

Found a new apartment at 1 impasse Hélène, just off the boulevard Clichy. The musician, Berlioz, lived there for some time. As we now have the space, I bought Seurat's 'Bathers'. It takes up the entire room along one wall. Marianna likes the painting, too; it will be a source of inspiration for me, I hope. I've started to learn Italian. She is teaching me, and I am teaching her English. She is very bright, and learns a lot faster than I do. We are very happy. I hardly go to the studio any more, now that I have one of my own. She has stopped modelling, and I have her all to myself. Her brothers are a pain in the butt, but she keeps them away from me. She is the most practical person I have met. We are going to have lots of children. I hope they will all have her good common sense and beauty. Everybody is jealous of me here. They tell me how lucky I am to be loved by the most beautiful woman in Paris.

12th July.

We are going for a summer holiday to Cassino. Brother Percy has come over to Paris for his summer holidays, and he'll look after the apartment. He thinks the world of Marianna, and wants to know when I am going to marry her. I have no idea. Our love is stronger than any marriage ceremony. We don't have to prove anything to anybody. Our love will outlast any contract imaginable.

Chapter Twenty-one

Robyn arrived, weighed down with parcels. She must have spent a fortune, thought Malcolm, watching her unwrapping her boxes. She was full of life, bursting with energy. Malcolm found it difficult to get out of bed. She pulled the bedclothes off him.

'Get up, lazybones,' she said. 'It's almost one o'clock!'

'Stop mucking about,' he said wearily.

Looking at her dashing about made him feel tired. He managed to pull the duvet over his head, and tried to get back to sleep. She left him alone for a few minutes, then yanked the duvet off him.

'What do you think?' she asked him as she spun around like a fashion model. 'It's a new dress, dummy.'

'Lovely,' he said grumpily.

Malcolm realised that going back to sleep was out of the question. He got up, and sat in a chair.

'You'd better get ready,' she said. 'I've booked a table in the Bistro Durak.'

'Oh, good,' he said.

He had never heard of the Bistro Durak. He went into the bathroom to get away from Robyn. As he shaved, he managed to get his thoughts together. Although he was still tired physically, his mind had started to function. Whatever else, he was in love with Robyn; head over heels in love. He was happy about that. Then somewhere at the back of his mind suspicion raised its ugly head. What if she doesn't love me? He got dressed quickly, and walked into the salon. She was waiting for him, wearing a completely different outfit.

'Do you like it?'

'Yes. You look lovely,' he said.

She kissed him on the cheek.

'OK. Let's go.'

She led the way, and he followed her obediently. She was friendly and chirpy, yet he felt let down by her. There was no love or romance about her attitude. She was exactly as before, her normal businesslike self – almost as if the night before had never happened.

The Bistro Durak was close to the hotel, on the quai de Montebello, with a good view of the Nôtre Dame. Robyn had booked the best table in the restaurant, and the Cossack waiters made a tremendous fuss over them. It was a noisy, over-friendly, tourist-packed place that no self-respecting Russian would enter.

Malcolm learned that 'bistro' was a bastardisation of the Russian word, *bjustre*, meaning 'fast'; and *Durak* meant 'fool'. They were in the Fast Fool restaurant, eating beetroot soup, drinking vodka and smashing glasses as if they had shares in Pilkingtons. He would have liked to share an intimate moment with her, but the whole world conspired against him. He was glad when lunch was over.

They took a taxi to the boulevard Clichy. The taxi driver dropped them off a hundred metres short of the impasse Hélène. They could see the Sacré Coeur on top of Montmartre. A slow drizzle fell from a grey sky, and the pavements were wet. They were only two hours late. A tall, nervous woman in her mid-forties ushered them into the apartment.

'I'm sorry, Madame Slivinsky,' said Malcolm. 'We've been held up. It couldn't be helped.'

'I don't mind,' she said in acceptable English. 'I wasn't going anywhere. Come in.'

She showed them into the studio. It was a large room, dominated by the north-light glass roof. There was a camp bed in one corner, but no other piece of furniture. Not even a chair. Scattered about the place, there were a dozen half-finished oil paintings; some Post-Conceptual rubbish without much character. Robyn and Malcolm looked about, and they were disappointed by what they saw.

'This was Mr Russell's studio from 1885 to 1914,' said Madame Slivinsky. 'An American painter uses it, but he's away.'

'I don't suppose there's anything left belonging to Mr Russell?' asked Malcolm.

'No. It was all cleared out years ago,' she said. 'There must have been a dozen different painters renting the place since him.

Nobody of importance. It's only recently that people started to ask after Mr Russell…'

'So this is where he painted?' interrupted Robyn.

It was the wrong time to butt in. Malcolm wanted to hear more about the other inquiries. He stepped in front of Robyn, and turned to Madame Slivinsky.

'Like who? Who was interested in him?'

'I don't remember their names, apart from Michel Boisset, but I told you that already.'

'What do you know about Mr Russell?'

'Nothing, really. You know more about him than I,' she said, shrugging her shoulders. 'You wanted to see his studio. Here it is.'

★

Doug took the last car ferry out of Quiberon to Belle-Ile. There was only a handful of people on board, but he kept to himself. Penders had told him to keep a low profile. To the other passengers he was just another out-of-season tourist. He stood on deck leaning on the railing as the ferry headed out into the Atlantic. Although it had rained all day, now that the sun was about to set, the clouds opened up for the last five minutes of the day. A warm, orange blaze lit up the scene, and the ocean looked like a travel poster.

Doug took a lungful of cold sea air and looked at the dramatic sky. That magical moment alone made the trip worth the twenty-hour flight. Deep down, Doug was a romantic, and he did not want to think about Penders. It turned grey and dark as soon as the sun disappeared over the horizon. Doug went into the bar, and ordered a large Calvados. That was the drink the Bellilois drank.

It was night when the ferry docked, just the way Doug wanted it. He drove straight to the Château de l'Anglais. He found the place without trouble. Belle-Ile was a small island. He parked his hired car a hundred metres short of the old Gothic building. Just like a castle in a horror movie, thought Doug, but he was not scared of his own shadow. He waited for a while to make sure there was nobody about. He could only hear the seagulls and the distant roar of the waves against the rocks. Doug walked up the drive to the front door. The house was built right on the edge of a cliff. He could see the boiling surf below. There was a small, enclosed bay with a slipway leading from the back of the house. The gardens were badly neglected and overgrown with bramble and gorse; the building itself was in a sorry state of disrepair.

Doug reached the end of the drive, and stopped at the front door. He took a plastic credit card from his wallet, and opened the door. 'That'll do nicely, thank you,' he said as he entered the building. He reached into his pocket for his small pencil torch and piece of paper. Penders had supplied him with an accurate plan of the house, and Doug knew where he had to go, and what he had to do.

*

When Robyn and Malcolm got back to the hotel, she decided to wash her hair. He was disappointed, because he wanted to make love.

'Come on, Robyn,' he protested. 'I suppose you'll have a headache next.'

'What a nasty, cynical mind you have, Malcolm!' she said playfully. 'You'll just have to wait, OK? It may be worth waiting for,' she teased him as she disappeared in the bathroom.

Malcolm got into bed and carried on with the Russell diaries.

3rd April 1886, Paris.

I am a father and Marianna is a mother. Mother and baby are doing well. She is a big, healthy girl – five kilos. Marianna comes from good peasant stock. Had a drop too much; celebrating at the atelier. I am looking forward to painting the baby. They are all out of proportion. We've decided to call her Jeanne.

6th May 1886, Paris.

Painted young Jeanne again. I am having lots of arguments with the others about my canvases of the baby. They all talk a lot of rubbish. Bernard in particular. They say I'm becoming insufferably pompous, but I don't care.

18th May 1886, Paris.

Went with Marianna to the studio of Auguste Rodin at the rue de l'Université. Marianna has been his model, and I expected a certain amount of hostility from him. He was charming. He must be getting on for fifty, and he is something of an old goat, I'm told. He must have had his eyes on Marianna. Without much success. In spite of that, we got on well, and I have an open invitation to visit him any time. Watching him modelling with clay was a revelation. His fingers move with amazing speed. I must try my hand at sculpting one of these days, but watching a master at work makes any form of art look deceptively easy.

25th May 1886, Paris.

Percy came over for a holiday. He is staying in the flat for the summer. We're planning a long painting holiday in Brittany. Marianna is keen on the idea. I thought she might not want to come with a young child, but she tells me babies are easy. Having a baby is no excuse for being housebound. It was Percy's last year in London, and he is going back to Sydney when we return from our holidays. He is going to take a few canvases of mine to Sydney. Tom is going to be pleased. He keeps on promising to come to Paris, but I think he's stuck in Australia. He should be here in France; all that's new and exciting in the arts is here.

16th June 1886, Paris.

Celebrated my 28th birthday with Percy and a few friends from the studio. We're off to Brittany tomorrow. Bernard wants me to visit Paul Gauguin; he's doing some experiments with colour. I might as well, though I agree less with Bernard each day. We are going in different directions, because I am not interested in Symbolism.

28th June 1886, Pont-Aven.

Spent the day with Paul Gauguin. I don't like him. I don't like his work; and he made a pass at Marianna. She put him in his place with a look. For somebody from a simple background, Marianna knows how to cope with the most difficult situations like a lady of aristocratic breeding. I was very proud of her. I forced myself to behave like a gentleman when I would have been quite happy to beat him senseless. I listened to his theories of painting. I pointed out, with some personal satisfaction, that he borrowed his ideas from Puvis de Chavannes. He was upset, but I only told him the truth. That's what hurt him most, but I don't care. Gauguin is a thief and a bounder. He hasn't got an original thought in his head, and he is just a self-seeking, money-grabbing boor. He'll go a long way, but I shall have nothing to do with him.

3rd July 1886, Port Louis.

Found a lovely little inn on the coast, and I've been doing a lot of work. The light has a magical softness about it, and the rugged cliffs are a joy to paint. The Bretons are friendly. I painted a group of women going to church. Marianna thinks it's my best canvas yet.

16th July 1886, Belle-Ile.

Belle-Ile is the most beautiful place on earth; a rugged little island in the Atlantic, just off Quiberon. The ocean is magnificent, particularly at the Aiguilles de Port Coton, on the south-west corner of the island. Giant granite columns stick up from the ocean, having been eroded by the relentless pounding of the waves. That's how Port Coton got its name. We rented a fisherman's cottage at Kervilhouen for the summer. Not far from here is Goulphar Creek, a picturesque little cove. Both Marianna and I have fallen in love with this place. I'll spend a couple of months painting here in complete bliss.

3rd August 1886, Belle-Ile.

We have explored the island; Goulphar is the best spot. Sometimes first impressions are right. We've been talking about living here. I wonder what the winters are like. The Bellilois are even nicer than the Bretons on the mainland. They point out that they are different, even speak a language of their own. A proud and self-reliant people, who are not afraid to take on the Atlantic Ocean. We are very happy here. I am putting on weight.

10th August.

Marianna has found a handyman and a cook. We settled in, and the islanders like us. They think we're married. I bought a sailing dinghy, and spend a couple of hours on the water each day. Goulphar bay is safe, but one has to respect the ocean; the Bellilois do. They think I'm mad to go sailing for pleasure; but being a painter, and English, they allow me a certain amount of eccentricity. I have been working hard. Being away from Paris is good for me. I can put all my theories into practice without arguments of having to justify myself to anybody.

22nd August.

Settled down to a routine. Paint from seven until eleven in the morning, and then go sailing until one. Lunch. A long siesta in the afternoon, and then start painting at four. The early morning light is soft and hazy; the evening one sharp and precise. Found my real voice. Much as I like Seurat, I am moving away from scientific principles. I still use paint straight out of the tube, pure colours, no mixing on a palette. The effect of primary colours applied next to each other gives the impression of shades. I use lines more than dots; they give direction and movement.

18th September.

I met the master today. When I went to my favourite spot at Goulphar I found another painter working there already. I watched him for a while before approaching him. He was working on three canvases, all at the same time, with extraordinary speed and energy. I knew his identity immediately, just from the style and his brush strokes. 'Are you Claude Monet?' I asked him. He was pleasantly surprised at being recognised, but at first I didn't tell him that I was a painter myself. We got talking, and I told him about myself. He prefers to be alone, and is not an easy person to get on with, but I invited him for lunch to meet Marianna. He ate like a wolf. The food must be terrible at the auberge in Bangor. Seeing how much he enjoyed the meal, we invited him to eat with us for the rest of his stay. He had to choose between having good food in the company of another painter, or eating badly alone. He followed his stomach, like any true Frenchman would.

22nd September.

I get on with him a lot better than I could have hoped for. We paint side by side, and I've noticed him watching me from the corner of his eye. Imagine, me having something to teach him, but I've learned a lot from him. He never works on a single canvas, always on a number of them, even five sometimes. It is the only way to keep in step with the changing light, he says.

23rd September.

I've lent our handyman to him as he finds it difficult to carry his paints and easel all over the cliffs. With free food and porterage provided, he is a much changed man, and we are good friends now. We discovered that we have a lot in common. He is a good friend of Rodin's, and likes his work. They are the two artists I respect most, and I feel privileged that I can consider them to be friends; but I hope I have more to offer them than just food and company.

24th September.

Took him for a sailing trip round the bay. The ocean was like a millpond when we set out, but a big swell caught me unawares, and it was a struggle to get back to Goulphar. It frightened the life out of him, and it wasn't even a storm. I got involved in an argument with him over supper. Having been trained as an engineer, proportions and size are important to me; deep down I am a naturalist, but not Monet. I wish I had kept my opinions to myself, because I upset him.

28th September.

Left the island for Paris. Said our goodbyes, and Monet picked out three of my best paintings for keepsake, and allowed me to choose three of his. He has taken the best of my work, and I feel honoured. Cannot wait to tell Bernard about Monet. He'll be green with envy.

Robyn attacked Malcolm in bed. He was surprised by her lust for him. How different she was during the day! Nothing like in bed; there were two separate Robyns: one the cool businesswoman, the other the insatiable whore who could probably win the world championship in sexual gymnastics. He had been completely exhausted on a number of occasions, but she always found a way to rouse him. Malcolm had gone from pleasure to pain, then even further, until he reached a plateau of numbness. He allowed her to do with him as she pleased, and when she satisfied her needs, Malcolm had nothing left to offer. He was empty of all sensation and emotion. They fell asleep hugging each other.

Chapter Twenty-two

Malcolm's biorhythms had been shattered. It was their second day in Paris, but he lost all sense of time; his body clock was all over the place with jet lag and excessive lovemaking. When he eventually managed to open his eyes at ten in the morning, the only form of food he could face was a cup of cocoa. Robyn had been up for hours, and she was into her second breakfast.

They wasted half the morning by the time they left the hotel. The rest of the day was equally frustrating, as they had found nothing of Russell's work at the Louvre. Although there were over twenty oils by Russell in the catalogue, the paintings were in storage somewhere near Clermont-Ferrand.

They had more luck at the Musée Rodin, where they were shown some Belle-Ile oil seascapes Russell painted in 1886, and his watercolours from his first visit to Italy. Marianna's silver bust was also there, which cheered Malcolm up considerably. Robyn was bored by it all. To make up the time lost by starting late, they had a quick lunch at the buffet of Le Magasin Moderne by the Tuileries. The food was excellent, but the place was packed with tourists, even in the middle of winter. Robyn was annoyed with Malcolm, and picked an argument with him. Ignoring the people around them, they found themselves yelling at each other.

'I thought you worked out a plan before we left, Malcolm. What are we doing here, traipsing around?'

'It's all good colour for the script.'

'We came to find the missing paintings, remember?'

'Yes, and we shall.'

'Like going to his studio yesterday? That was a complete waste of time. You talked to the woman, and she told you there was nothing in the studio. Why did we have to go there?'

'I had a feeling we'd come up with something…'

'Like what?'

'Perhaps you're right,' said Malcolm trying to placate her, 'but I know Sabatier will help us.'

'He'd better, mate, for all that money,' she said. 'Did you try to trace members of his family, Malcolm? That's where I'd start.'

'I've done all that. Now, please, don't take me for an idiot. We wouldn't be here if I had some joy with them.'

'You're like a headless chicken, running around in circles and getting nowhere fast!'

'I'll find them, don't you worry. We have to see Sabatier in person, anyhow, and Belle-Ile is an absolute must. I told you, and you agreed, remember?

'I've lost my memory. What are we doing here, right here?'

'I'm not answering that,' said Malcolm crossly.

Robyn glared at him. Malcolm went on eating his cassoulet. When he finished they left the place without saying another word to each other. They walked to Sabatier's gallery, as it was just around the corner, in the most expensive quarter of Paris. Every shop was a household name, but there were no price tags on display anywhere. There was little on show at the Galerie Sabatier; a couple of landscapes from the Barbizon school and some exquisite pieces of Louis XIV furniture. Robyn and Malcolm entered, and a dapper, middle-aged Frenchman met them.

'I'd like to talk to Monsieur Claude Sabatier,' said Malcolm.

'You are talking to him,' he replied with a superior smile. 'That is me, Claude Sabatier.'

His handshake was limp and indecisive. Malcolm was tempted to crush his hand just to be bloody-minded, but he needed the Frenchman's goodwill, and he returned the handshake in the same nonchalant way.

'Malcolm Reid.'

Robyn had taken an instant dislike to Sabatier, and wandered off looking at the paintings on display.

'Have you had any luck, Monsieur?' asked Malcolm.

'Yes. I have all the information you requested,' he said. 'It took me some time, and I am afraid I shall have to charge you for it. Time is money, as you know.'

'I didn't expect you to do it for nothing,' said Malcolm smiling. 'Paul McDonald warned me that your services don't come cheap.'

'If you pay peanuts, you get monkey answers,' replied Sabatier pompously.

Sabatier showed Malcolm into his office. There were some papers laid out neatly on top of a priceless cherry-wood secretaire decorated with mother-of-pearl and gold. Sabatier picked up the sheets of paper one by one, and handed them over to Malcolm.

'This is the complete list of John Peter Russell's oeuvre. As you know, Jean Boisset started to catalogue his work in 1931. Jeanne Russell asked him to compile a list of the paintings she offered to the Louvre. The catalogue was the basis for the retrospective exhibition in London in 1965. Quite a few Russells have come to light since, because of all the publicity associated with the show; all from private collectors. Here, we update the catalogue each time a painting is sold through a reputable art dealer...'

Sabatier seemed to know what he was talking about, and Malcolm hated to interrupt him in full flow.

'Why is that?'

'It is difficult to provide a painting with the provenance collectors require. A painting without a well-documented history is practically worthless. Now, we know that all the canvases in the 1965 catalogue were genuine, and all Russell's previous work has been authenticated by the Boissets; so if a new painting suddenly comes to the market, it is suspect until proved otherwise. We like to keep a check on all the genuine work of our artists. It is invaluable knowledge...'

'Is anybody trying to sell fake Russells?' asked Malcolm.

Sabatier looked wounded at the very mention of the word 'fake'; he stepped back from Malcolm, as if he had just discovered that he was talking to a leper.

'I wouldn't think so,' said the Frenchman defensively. 'Russell is far too obscure a painter for that. Hardly anybody collects him, but I have made a list for you of all the people who own paintings from John Peter Russell. All their contact details are included, but naturally, they are strictly confidential.'

'I understand, Monsieur,' said Malcolm as he took the list from Sabatier. 'I suppose the Australians feel guilty having ignored him.'

'Perhaps, but I think Mr Russell wanted to be ignored.'

'What makes you say that?'

'It's just an idea. I can't prove it, but I think Russell was too much of a gentleman to compete with his friends. He hardly exhibited a painting in his life; I think he hated the idea of taking a sale away from his starving friends…'

Robyn drifted into the office and interrupted the discourse.

'How is it going?' she asked Malcolm.

'All right,' said Malcolm barely suppressing his anger with her. 'Please continue, Monsieur Sabatier.'

'It's just a feeling I have about Russell, but you can never tell. Painters can be very unpredictable.'

'How about the missing thirty-eight paintings?'

'I'm sorry. Well, not unless…'

Sabatier stopped as a thought just occurred to him. He searched through the papers until he found the right page. Triumphantly, he pointed to a list, which meant nothing to Malcolm.

'In 1909 he sent some personal effects and furniture to Sydney,' explained Sabatier excitedly.

'But he didn't return to Sydney till 1921,' said Malcolm.

'Exactly,' said Sabatier as if his point was clearly demonstrated by Malcolm's remark.

'Exactly, what?' asked Malcolm.

'That's why I was looking in the wrong place,' went on Sabatier. 'Lots sixteen and seventeen on the shipping manifest were untitled paintings. These could be your missing canvases.'

'But where are they now?' asked Robyn.

'Your guess is as good as mine,' said Sabatier.

From his tone Malcolm could tell that he was not going to help him any more, probably because Robyn got up his nose. Sabatier picked up an envelope from the table and handed it to Malcolm.

'Well, thank you for all your help,' said Malcolm.

'It's my pleasure, and I thank you,' he replied, parrot fashion.

'What's that?' asked Robyn, taking the envelope from Malcolm.

'My bill, naturally,' said Sabatier.

'Don't say I won't let you do anything,' Malcolm told her. 'You can write out a cheque for that.'

Robyn was shocked to see the amount.

'This is not negotiable, is it?' she asked tamely.

'That's what we agreed,' said Sabatier stiffly.

Malcolm said nothing; he just nodded his head in agreement.

'Who else has this information?' asked Malcolm casually whilst Robyn was writing out a cheque.

'I cannot say,' said Sabatier. 'I pride myself on being discreet.'

I bet you do, thought Robyn, but said nothing.

It was three in the afternoon when they got back to the hotel. They had no chance of catching the last ferry to Belle-Ile that day and decided to leave first thing in the morning. Malcolm was glad to have a chance to sort out his thoughts and to look through the papers supplied by Sabatier. For all the money they had paid out, there was not a lot of new information contained in them. Malcolm picked up the Russell diaries instead.

5th October 1886, Paris.

I lent my studio to Vincent for the summer, and it was a mistake. Marianna doesn't like him; she thinks he is mad; but there is nothing cranky about him, he is just intense. He cares too much. We all call him Vincent; he says the French don't know how to pronounce his name properly. He has taken a liking to me, because he loves England and the English. He asked me about Isleworth and Turnham Green, and was disappointed when I told him I never heard of them. Apparently, he was a Protestant lay preacher in a number of West London parishes, but he was thrown out of his church, probably for believing in what he preached; but he'd much rather argue about art than religion. You cannot have a discussion with Vincent; he only believes in arguments. He is a regular visitor, and I like him. He truly believes in art and has a burning passion for it. He has quarrelled with everybody at the Atelier Cormon; but he still goes out whoring with Bernard, Toulouse-Lautrec and Anquetin. Unfortunately, he is getting on a bit, and he hasn't got the stamina. Recently, Vincent has taken up drinking absinthe, but it hasn't improved his temper much. He always comes to us when in need of comfort, though he has a brother, Theo, who also worries about him. Theo is grateful for our help, and both Marianna and I like Theo a lot. He offered to exhibit my work, but I didn't take him up on it. Incidentally, everybody likes my work at Belle-Ile; I had to tell, and retell, the story of meeting Monet a great number of times. They are all green with envy.

11th October.

Talking to Vincent can be very tiring. He has no shades of greys; with him everything is black or white. He likes my oils, but... then he tells me what HE believes. His French is deplorable, his English little better, and he mixes the two languages together, and adds Dutch to it. The key word is invariably Dutch, which makes his sentences double Dutch to me. He still thinks I'm an Englishman, and tells me that he likes the Englishness best about my work. If I didn't know him better, I could think he was trying to provoke me. I'd like to think there is an Australian influence in my work, but I have been away from home for so long that it could only be instinctive. I started painting a portrait of Vincent. Toulouse-Lautrec finished one of him last week. They haven't spoken to each other ever since. Marianna tells me that Vincent may do the same to me. That's unkind.

14th October.

Had an unpleasant quarrel with Vincent. It's not his portrait; he likes that. It was about naturalism – something he detests. I am trying to combine naturalism with Impressionism, and I think I've managed to make it work. Like everything else in life, truth is a paradox, but Vincent won't have that. He shouted at me, quoting Delacroix: green hatching on pink flesh. We all heard that before. He thinks he discovered something new.

19th October.

Vincent is getting me down. I've given him his portrait unfinished. Have to do some work on his hand, but not just now.

I am a coward, and have decided to go on holiday, just to get away from him. We're off to Sicily next week. I want to paint a series of related tableaux on Dante's *Divine Comedy*. Rodin's 'Gates of Hell' inspired me. Marianna started modelling again for him. I went with her to see how the work is progressing. It's an ambitious undertaking, and it is going to be fantastic, if he ever finishes it.

18th January 1887, Paris.

Didn't keep a diary in Sicily. I painted the wild almond blossom, which flowers around Christmas time. They remind me of my Japanese prints. I bought a piece of land on the cliffs over Goulphar bay, and I am going to build a house there. Vincent and Bernard have been talking a lot about a painters' commune. We'll have enough room at Goulphar to put up all our friends.

24th January 1887, Paris.

Bill Maloney came over from London for a short holiday. He has finished his medical studies, and today I began a portrait of Dr William Maloney. I am experimenting with a bitumen base. It's the latest thing amongst the Salon painters, and I'd better keep quiet about it. Vincent even sniffed at the canvas like a dog, but I chased him out of my studio. For the first time, I managed to frighten him. He even apologised for being nosy. I cannot think what came over him, as I don't remember him saying sorry before. That's his charm.

29th January 1887, Paris.

Marianna wants me to see the priest. I suppose I'll have to. I love her too much to refuse her, but no way am I going to become a Catholic.

24th February.

Bill Maloney has gone back to Sydney. I sent a couple of my Sicilian amandiers with him for Tom Roberts. They brought back memories of clear blue skies, and the brilliantly transparent light of the south.

15th March.

Vincent is in love. The lady is Agostina Segatori, who used to be Corot's model. She owns the Café Tambourin, where Vincent has been eating of late. It's his first success with a woman, and he is very pleased with himself. He talked her into an exhibition of Japanese prints. He remembered my collection, and asked me for it.

28th March.

Vincent came round again. He had some money for me; he sold every one of my Japanese prints. I never wanted to sell them, but life is full of ironies like that. I insisted that he should take his commission. We almost had an argument, but Vincent is a new person; he does not argue nowadays. Apparently, Signora Segatori agreed to another exhibition, and he wants me to show some of my work. Anquetin, Bernard, Toulouse-Lautrec and Vincent himself are the painters who have agreed so far. Gauguin is thinking about it, but if he will exhibit, then Monet won't. It seems Monet cannot abide Gauguin either. I decided not to show anything. Vincent was pleased that he could use the space allocated for me for his paintings. He talked about a commune of painters in the south. He really likes my almond blossoms, and borrowed a couple of them. He gave me half a dozen of his sketches. He wants me to go round to see Theo, and pick out any number of his paintings I like. He just wants me to have them. He made a financial agreement with Theo. Vincent gets a monthly allowance, and in return, everything he paints becomes Theo's property. It's his way of helping Vincent without hurting his pride. All Vincent wants to do is to paint. It is his mission. I wish I had the same dedication.

15th April.

The exhibition was a success, though Vincent had not managed to sell anything. What's worse, Signora Segatori's previous lover is back in favour, and she's thrown Vincent out. He is his old argumentative self again. I'd better keep out of his way.

29th April.

I signed the final contract for the land on Belle-Ile.

18th May.

Spent the weekend at Moret-sur-Loing. Dodge MacKnight is a neighbour of the Sisleys. I have always admired Alfred Sisley's work, and it was a real pleasure to paint with him side by side. I'm pleased with my canvas of Madame Sisley, though it reminds me a little of her husband's work. Perhaps it's the place that makes his pictures unique. That never occurred to me before. I wonder if Bernard or Vincent would paint her in a similar style. It could be an interesting experiment. Marianna enjoyed being in the country, and she is looking forward to moving to Belle-Ile.

25th May.

We had a revolution at the studio. It's all my fault. I told Bernard to go and talk to Seurat. He was impressed by Seurat's methods, as I was myself. As a consequence, he began an experiment of his own in the studio. Cormon did not take too kindly to it. He disapproves of the methods of Le Petit Boulevard, and will not allow them in his place. It's one of the unwritten house rules of the Atelier Cormon. We have a brown drape in the studio, and use it as a background; when Bernard painted it as alternative lines of red and green, Cormon threw Bernard out. The others were outraged, and threatened Cormon with physical violence. Nobody really meant it, apart from Vincent, who rushed off to get Theo's revolver; he was going to shoot Cormon. I was the only one who stood up for Cormon, and I wasn't popular with the others; but I believe Cormon is a good teacher, and he deserves better treatment than that from his pupils. I put all the commotion down to the unusually hot weather.

27th May.

Cormon closed down his studio for the summer vacations six weeks earlier than planned, because of the upheaval over Bernard. A couple of months away from Paris should allow tempers to cool. We're off to Belle-Ile next week.

Chapter Twenty-three

As they entered the ferry terminal at Quiberon a thick fog rolled in from the Atlantic. There was hardly any wind, and the water was calm. Visibility was down to thirty metres, and the yellow fog lamps just managed to pick out the kerb.

'So much for busting a gut to get here,' said Robyn.

'I don't know,' said Malcolm. 'The fog may lift.'

But the fog stayed. The ferry left on time, and hurtled forward into the thick fog. The engines were strangely muted, and the only sound to be heard was the splashing of the waves. Its soft rhythm was interrupted at regular intervals by the ship's foghorn, echoed by the deeper tone of the Quiberon harbour horn. They sounded like a couple of lovesick primeval monsters.

Robyn and Malcolm stood on the foredeck, and stared into the thick grey fog; the ferry was gliding over a marble sea wrapped in a cotton-wool mist. They were calm and relaxed with each other, and happy with the world. They listened to the receding harbour horn as it got fainter and fainter as they disappeared in the mysterious fog. When the sound was almost inaudible, the Le Palais foghorn could be heard from the other direction. As one faded, the other one took over.

'You've been very quiet,' said Robyn.

'I've been thinking,' he said. 'I'm happy with the progress we've made, and I'm sure that we'll find the Russell Collection.'

'How about the script?'

'Almost there, but I can't finish it until I know the end. It all depends on the collection.'

'What do you mean you're almost there?'

'It's all in my head and it shouldn't take long to get it down to paper, but I have too much on at the moment: only playing detectives and trying to find the Russell Collection stops me from writing. The only thing that still bothers me is Jamie.'

'Why?'

'I'm sure he and Mac had something going on, and Jamie's death was not an accident.'

'You mean, Mac murdered him?' she asked him facetiously.

'Perhaps.'

'What about the art forgery? How does that fit into the general scheme of things?'

'You can take the piss, but I'm not happy. I owe it to Jamie to find out what really happened.'

'You can do that later; finish the script first.'

'This is not a game, Robyn. If somebody killed Jamie, I'd better watch my step. I could be courting danger.'

'My poor, big baby,' she said, cuddling up to him. 'I think you're a lovely chunk of manhood. I'm sure you can handle the baddies, Malcolm. I have faith in you, baby.'

He smiled at her, and hugged her tighter. Robyn was his. It was all going to work out just fine.

The Hôtel Falaise had nothing memorable about it, but they were only staying for a single night. They were booked into the best suite, but Malcolm barely looked at the rooms. He could hardly wait to get into bed. By the time Robyn took her coat off, he was already under the duvet.

Robyn went to have a bath. When she returned he yelled out a wild Tarzan call, beating his chest as he threw the duvet off.

'I'm going to savage you!' he yelled, and turned the lights out.

They had a huge English breakfast before setting out for the Château de l'Anglais. Robyn drove the car along the narrow country lanes, sometimes right on the edge of the towering cliffs. The Atlantic was in a nasty mood. The waves shot thirty metres into the air as they broke over the jagged rocks. The island seemed the bleakest place on earth. 'Some place for a fairy-tale romance,' mused Malcolm.

The house loomed up in front of them all of a sudden. They were right on top of it before they realised it. It looked English, Gothic, and neglected. A red Peugeot 205 was parked by the front door.

'That must be the estate agent,' said Robyn as she got out of the car. 'And this is it, Malcolm, the Château de l'Anglais.'

'Yes. The castle he built for his princess…'

They walked up to the front door, leaning into the biting cold wind. The wet gravel crunched under their feet and the sound echoed against the solid granite walls of the building.

An estate agent's *À Vendre* sign was stuck over the front door. It was an old, weather-beaten piece of cardboard; obviously, there had not been many buyers around in the past couple of years. Before they could reach the front door, it opened and a young man stepped out of the house to meet them. He wore a dark suit, and had a little black handbag, the kind continental men carry around; he could have only been an undertaker or an estate agent.

'I am Noel Lefebvre,' he said.

His English was extremely poor, and he delivered it parrot fashion, as if he had practised it in front of the mirror before meeting his prospective clients.

'Hello there. Dr Reid?' he went on.

'Morning,' said Malcolm in the voice he used when talking to tradesmen. 'This is Miss Hawthorne. I hope we didn't keep you waiting long.'

'How do you do,' said Lefebvre stiffly. 'This is a most desirable residential property. The house needs some modernisation, as you can see for yourselves.'

Lefebvre showed the way and they followed him into the dark interior of the building. They stepped into a gloomy hall. A number of rooms opened from the baronial hall; all deserted and depressing. The house had not been used for decades, and it was completely void of furniture; but in spite of the neglect, the walls and floors were in good condition. Lefebvre was busy opening and closing doors, waving his arms about, delivering his set piece sales talk.

Robyn and Malcolm followed him around.

'The house was completed in the autumn of 1888, and the cost of building came to forty-five thousand pounds sterling. Not converted to present-day prices, naturally. That was a lot of money…'

He paused just for a split second for effect, and carried on with his speech, seeing that neither Robyn or Malcolm was impressed.

'It was built and designed by Mr Russell, a trained English

engineer, and also a famous artist. It was a big job. They blasted the terraced gardens out of granite, and used the stones for the building. There is a slipway behind the house. It leads down to the bay, with deep-sea anchorage. But you can see that later. The house was first sold in 1909 for four thousand pounds sterling then…'

'I thought buildings were supposed to appreciate in value,' said Robyn. 'What a huge drop in price!'

'Mr Russell was a gentleman, not a developer,' said Lefebvre defensively. 'When his wife died, he closed the house. He practically gave it away in the end.'

'You knew him well?' asked Robyn sarcastically, as his pompous delivery was starting to annoy her.

'Of course not. He died before I was born,' replied Lefebvre humourlessly.

Lefebvre got ahead of them, and Robyn sniggered at him behind his back. Malcolm dug her in the ribs, and whispered in her ear, 'Behave yourself!'

Lefebvre was too busy opening and shutting doors to pay too much attention to Robyn. He carried on his non-stop sales chatter.

'The house changed hands again in 1947 for thirty thousand dollars, American. The last gentleman was a keen sailor, and bought the house for its mooring facilities. Mr Russell's yacht was included in the sale of the house. And all the furniture and fittings. Mr Miller, the new owner, used to visit Europe during the summer. Otherwise, the place was not used. He died in 1978. Nobody has lived here ever since.'

They reached the first-floor rooms, which were a lot lighter and friendlier.

'Considering that the house has hardly been lived in,' carried on Lefebvre, 'the interior is in good repair, though the grounds need a certain amount of attention. There is a well in the garden; the house has its own water supply, which is an important consideration on an island. The grounds are fifteen hectares, and the water frontage is part of the estate—'

'Yes, very interesting,' interrupted Malcolm. 'Would you know if anything was left of the original furniture or anything else?'

'I don't think so, but I've never been up on the second floor…' The agent stopped talking and looked down at his watch. 'Have you seen all you wanted to see?'

'No, not really,' said Malcolm. 'I could spend a day here just wandering about. Are you in a hurry?'

'Well, I've got another appointment…'

'Why don't you just leave us here? We'll be all right,' said Robyn helpfully.

'I am not sure,' said Lefebvre.

'We'll close the door, don't you worry, and drop the keys into your office,' said Malcolm.

'It is a little irregular,' said Lefebvre unhappily. 'I suppose that will be all right. I might see you again.'

'Thanks a lot,' said Robyn.

'Goodbye then, Dr Reid, Miss Hawthorne.'

'Bye,' said Malcolm. 'We'll probably see you back at your office with the keys.'

'I hope so,' said Lefebvre, then he ran down the stairs with a smile on his face, waving to Robyn and Malcolm. 'I will see you in my office later.'

'What an idiot!' said Robyn.

Malcolm and Robyn carried on exploring the first-floor rooms. They heard Lefebvre's car start up and drive away. The house was almost silent, but the constant murmur of the sea could be heard in every room. They made their way up to the second floor, where the children's bedrooms were. The original furniture was still in place, all under dust sheets, which must have been placed over them in 1978. Robyn lifted up some of the covers, then let them fall back in place. She looked out one of the windows directly over the ocean. It was a breathtaking sight.

'What a view! This is a fantastic house, Malcolm. I hope my Prince Charming will build something like this for me.'

'Not for forty-five thousand quid.'

He walked out of the room, and made his way up to the attic. Robyn followed him.

'Where are you off to?' she asked him.

'To the attic – where else? You always find secrets in the attic, don't you know that?'

She followed him up the narrow staircase. It was dry and warm in the attic, though the wind was quite strong outside.

'It's not as creepy as I expected,' she said.

'Exciting, though,' said Malcolm as he set about to explore the huge, dusty attic.

There were broken bits of furniture lying around, covered in thick dust: a flower pot here, a hatstand there; the kind of rubbish people keep for ever. In a corner there was an old broken desk. Malcolm pulled out the drawers, one by one. They were empty, but in the top drawer there were some shipping-line brochures, all dated 1909. Malcolm blew the dust off, and showed them to Robyn.

'Look at these! Fascinating, isn't it?'

She studied the brochures, but found them dull and boring.

'Terrific,' she said.

Malcolm had not noticed her sarcasm, and carried on browsing through the old leaflets. They showed the sailing times, ports of call and freight rates of 'The Oriental & Occidental Steamship Company'. Malcolm also found a Manila paper envelope. He opened it. Inside, there was a shipping manifest written in beautiful copperplate. Malcolm recognised Russell's handwriting instantly. He read the document to Robyn excitedly.

'Lot eight: item one, set of naval charts of the Channel Islands. Item two, ship's compass. Item three, sextant.'

Malcolm turned the pages quickly until he got to lot sixteen. Malcolm was practically shouting as he read the list aloud.

'Lot sixteen, item one: "The Terrace" by Edouard Manet, 1882. Item two, "*Une Baignade à Asnières*" by Georges Seurat, 1883. Item three, "Boating Party" by Georges Seurat, 1888. Item four, "The Baker's Wife" by Pierre Renoir, 1892. Item five, "Sunset" by Claude Monet, 1897. Item six, "Sunflowers" by Vincent, 1888. Item seven, "Lilies" by Vincent, 1889.'

Malcolm could not contain his joy. He lifted Robyn off her feet as he hugged her.

'It's not Russell's work. He was collecting his friends' paintings. Imagine that, Robyn! Thirty-eight paintings by the most famous painters in the world.'

'What kind of money are we talking about?' she asked calmly.

'Don't talk to me about money, Robyn, at a time like this. This is the find of the century.'

'It will be, when you find the paintings. All you have at the moment is just a piece of paper.'

'I love your positive attitude.'

'Come on, Malcolm. What kind of money?'

'The last van Gogh "Sunflowers" went for eighty million dollars. You work it out for yourself, but they're probably worth four, five hundred million dollars…'

'Half a billion?'

'Yes, dear. Half an American billion.'

'Perhaps I'm thick or something, but I seem to remember that Seurat's most famous painting, "*Une Baignade à Asnières*", was at the Tate Gallery.'

'Yes, that's correct, but Seurat painted a much larger version of it. It was so big that he couldn't find a place to show it. So the painting at the Tate is probably a smaller – and tattier – version of the same thing. Russell managed to get the original into his studio. He bought it from Seurat in 1885. It was kept in the studio Madame Slivinsky showed us two days ago. It must have been along the wall facing south. This is too much, Robyn!'

He read through the list of the other paintings, shaking his head in disbelief and delight. They searched the house before they left, but there was nothing of interest.

As Robyn was driving back to the estate agent's office, Malcolm had an idea. He took out Sabatier's list of owners and read through the names again.

'*Eureka!*' he cried out.

'What have you found?' asked Robyn.

'A connection. There is a Miller-Fenton on this list. He seems to be a keen collector of JPR's work.'

'Sounds like a long shot to me,' said Robyn.

'Maybe,' agreed Malcolm, 'but worth checking out.'

They dropped the keys in at the estate agent's, and found Lefebvre waiting for them.

'So, how do you like the house?' he asked.

'It's lovely,' said Robyn, 'but we'll have to think it over.'

'I understand.'

'Who is the vendor?' asked Malcolm in a flat voice.

Sabatier had to look up the file before he could answer.

'Here it is – a Mr William Miller-Fenton.'

'I suppose he's a relative of the last owner?' said Malcolm.

'I suppose so, too,' agreed Lefebvre. 'He lives in London.'

'Would you let us have his contact details?' asked Malcolm.

'That's not possible. I can contact him on your behalf.'

'We're on our way to London,' lied Malcolm. 'We could save you a lot of trouble.'

Robyn looked at him questioningly, but said nothing.

'It's against the estate agents' code,' said Lefebvre. 'I could lose my job over that, Monsieur.'

'Would you rather lose a possible sale?' smiled Malcolm. 'Especially as you've had the house on the market for thirty years.'

'You are twisting my arm,' said Lefebvre, as he wrote down the contact details of William Miller-Fenton.

They drove back to the hotel and checked out in time to get on the 11.10 ferry to the mainland. Malcolm managed to contact William Miller-Fenton on his mobile and made an appointment. Robyn was unhappy about the extra expense, but agreed reluctantly.

'If going to London is a waste of time and money, I shall deduct it from your fee, Malcolm.'

'It won't be,' he said. 'Mark my words.'

From Quiberon they headed for another car ferry port – Cherbourg. Robyn was driving the car, because she wanted to catch the seven o'clock ferry that evening. Malcolm carried on reading the Russell diaries.

Chapter Twenty-four

19th February 1888, Paris.

Went to the Gare de Lyon to see Vincent off. He is going to Marseille. He had been seeing a lot of Seurat, and I think he talked Vincent into going south. I hope it will work for him, but any change could only be for the good. Vincent is not well – it must be the absinthe; must have got to his brain. According to Bill Maloney, absinthe is a killer. Its main ingredient, wormwood, is a poison; it can cause fits like epilepsy. I hope the sun will do Vincent some good. Marianna is expecting. It's time we got married, she told me.

21st February 1888, Paris.

Married Marianna today at the Hôtel de Ville in a civil ceremony. A handful of friends came to witness the affair: Julian Rabache, Dodge McKnight, Henri Bisbing and Achille Cesbron. Shame Vincent is not here. We had the reception at Le Chat Noir. Toulouse-Lautrec was the life and soul of the party. Theo made it to the reception, and even Felix Cormon. Everybody was there – Marianna's brothers, and Rodin with Rose Beurat. That's something of a miracle, because he never takes her anywhere socially. Marianna was very pleased.

25th February 1888, Paris.

Postcard from Vincent. He never got to Marseille. Left the train at Arles, and decided to stay there. He is mad, because he wants me to join him, when he knows I am going to Belle-Ile. I discussed my plans for the house there with him; how could he forget it? He must be mad. He is staying at the Hôtel Carrel. It should mean something to me, but it doesn't. Most confusing card. Could hardly read the writing.

2nd March 1888, Paris.

Visited Rodin at his studio with Marianna. We went to say goodbye, as we are going to Brittany next week. Met an interesting young man there. Had a long talk with him about the South Seas. Apparently, he also met Gauguin, who mentioned my name in connection with Tahiti. I was surprised; I don't remember saying a word to Gauguin about my holiday in Tahiti. I told young Bernard, and I suppose he must have said something to Gauguin. It's a small world. I'll be glad to get away from Paris gossip. Anyhow, it seems young Robert Louis Stevenson will go a long way. He impressed me.

5th March 1888, Paris.

Bernard came to talk about a commune of painters. He wants to set it up at Pont-Aven, with Gauguin. I told him that Vincent has the same idea, but in Arles. He rented a house there, a yellow house. He asked me to visit him there, and paint with him, but I'm off to Belle-Ile to build myself a house there. I shall have room for them all, with the exception of Gauguin. Bernard rather likes him, though. I bought a couple of paintings from Bernard. I told him about my idea of a collection for Australia. I have already assembled a collection to represent all the Impressionists. I showed them to Bernard. He was pleased that I included what he considers to be his best work. I am not going to collect rubbish; I want nothing but the best. Bernard thought I should carry on painting, but I am not really a painter. Not like my friends are. They paint because they have a burning passion. I paint for pleasure, like an amateur, and that is using the word in its proper sense. Recently people refer to amateur as inferior. They are ignorant people who murder the English language. I am as proud to be an amateur painter as an amateur boxer; after all, I am the champion of Great Britain at light-heavyweight.

15th March 1888, Belle-Ile.

Laid the foundation stone to the studio on the Ides of March, but I don't believe in superstition. The natives were terrified, but I don't see what the killing of Julius Caesar has to do with me building a house. I picked the best possible view from the cliff. I shall see all of Goulphar bay from my studio window. It will be a joy to work surrounded by the Atlantic. I shall never get bored with the picture right at my feet. The plan is that we move into the studio as soon as it is built, then get on with the house. I am having a slipway blasted out of the granite, as I have plans to build a yacht. After the house is finished, I'll build a workshop. With all this activity I still manage to find time for painting. Odd how the more one does, the more time one manages to find to fit everything in. I paint Marianna a lot. I am fascinated how her body changes from day to day. The pregnant female shape is the most beautiful thing on earth. I love her now more than ever.

8th April 1888, Belle-Ile.

The studio is completed. Started on the main building today. The Bellilois are the most wonderful people. They are independent, hardy, proud; and good at everything. All the labour is local, and they have taken to building as if they had built nothing but cathedrals all their lives. For fishermen, they are the greatest craftsmen you could find. They are all enthusiastic about the house. They have christened it the Château de l'Anglais, and the name has stuck. Even Marianna and I refer to it as such.

16th June 1888, Belle-Ile.

Celebrated my thirtieth birthday in style. The building is coming along splendidly. We shall get it finished by the end of the month. We are about three weeks ahead of schedule due to the exceptionally good weather. Marianna is well and happy. I must have painted at least a hundred oils of her during the last couple of months. I am very happy, and I don't miss Paris. What a joy it is just to be alive!

It was half past eleven at night when Robyn and Malcolm got off the ferry at Portsmouth. They booked into the first motel they came to. They were both excited by the Russell Collection. Mentally they were in overdrive, but their bodies were tired. They fell into bed, made love as a matter of routine, and went to sleep.

They both woke early, just after six. Breakfast was not served till seven thirty. They made a cup of coffee; the room was provided with an electric kettle and individual sachets of instant coffee and powdered milk. It was only slightly better than nothing.

Robyn stayed in bed, reading the Russell diaries; Malcolm went through the shipping manifest for the hundredth time. They were like a married couple, who knew each other well and could spend hours on end without saying a word, and yet be close to each other.

At half past seven Malcolm put the documents away. He looked at Robyn, who was still in bed, reading. He kissed her gently on her lips. She put her arms around his neck, and pulled him into the bed. They made love.

They set out for London at half past nine. Malcolm was driving; Robyn looked out of the window. A little mist hung about, but it was a sunny winter morning. There was hardly any traffic on the A3, and the countryside between Petersfield and Liphook was still relatively unspoilt.

'I always forget how green England is,' said Robyn.

'It's on account of the rain,' he replied.

'There's one thing that bothers me about the Russell paintings,' she said.

'What's that?'

'The dates don't tally. The shipping manifest is dated 1909, but he did not offer the collection to the Australians until 1921. That's a twelve-year discrepancy. How do you explain that?'

'That's a good question.'

'I know. Why don't you answer it?'

'I can't, but it's very encouraging. It only goes to show we're on the right track.'

'Come again?'

'It sounds Irish, but when you've done a lot of research, you get a sixth sense about things. A little bit of discrepancy, some inexplicable piece of mystery, is always a hopeful sign. All truth is paradox; when looking for it, beware of logic.'

'You're right,' said Robyn, 'it sounds very Irish, but I take your word for it.'

They fell silent again. It became busier after Milford, but the road was virtually a motorway all the way to London, and Malcolm could allow his mind to wander. Driving was pure routine.

'You know,' he said to Robyn, 'nobody talks about Mary Cassatt or Berthe Morisot nowadays, yet they were Impressionists, both respected by their contemporaries. Russell has a painting from each of them – probably their best. I find that very exciting.'

'How fascinating,' said Robyn with a touch of sarcasm.

'I thought you'd be more interested.'

'I'm not a feminist, Malcolm.'

'I know that. All the same...'

'All the same, what? Those two bring the value of the collection down a couple of million dollars.'

'To hell with the money, Robyn! This is the most exciting thing that's happened to me so far.'

'Oh?'

'Russell got together an incredible collection to represent that magical decade. That's how long Impressionism lasted, and think of the paintings produced during that short period. What a collection!'

'I can't wait to see them, Malcolm.'

'Same here. You could base a television series on the thirty-eight paintings. Each painting has its own story. That would be fantastic. They were wonderful people, every one an eccentric. That's the kind of project I wouldn't mind getting involved in.'

'How about finishing the script on Russell first?'

'That's practically in the bag. Don't fret yourself over that.'

'But I do. Will you ever write it down?'

'Yes, you know I shall... even better, I *will*. I still have to have a couple of questions answered. It's all in my head, and I shall write around what I don't know. All I need is a brilliant ending. It will come, don't you worry. I start lecturing a fortnight today, and I'll have to get it finished by then.'

'How can you write around the missing bits? What kind of script are you working on?'

'A brilliant one. I've always wanted to work on a complex

structure. This is as complex as you can get. A seven-act structure accommodating pure impressions of reality. One giant Impressionist jigsaw puzzle in vibrant primary colours.'

'I see what you mean,' said Robyn.

'The act of living is a complex event,' continued Malcolm. 'That's how it should be portrayed in any form of art, including the cinema. It has to be stylised. You'll love the script.'

Robyn was concerned. Shit, I hope he's not an art movie buff, she thought, but said nothing.

'Dreams are the nearest thing to film,' he went on. 'I have the most fantastic dreams. They are like films; unfortunately, I can never remember them when I wake up. Once I tried an experiment. I had a notepad by my bedside and I jotted down everything in my dream, whilst still asleep. I could hardly wait to wake up in the morning. The alarm clock went and I read my notes. Guess what?'

Malcolm paused for dramatic effect.

'Go on. What happened?'

'I couldn't read my notes. I filled a complete notebook with squiggles and dots like a bird's footsteps in the snow. I've still got that notebook somewhere. It was very important to me at the time, because I was going to create a new literary form, something beyond a stream of consciousness; a new form of reality in which past, present and future are simultaneously expressed subjectively. To a one-eyed man the physical world is two-dimensional, and a blind man sees an entirely different world...'

'Sure,' interrupted Robyn. 'The blind man who sees... Come on, Malcolm!'

'It sounds like a contradiction, but I met a blind man in Norfolk, in a pub; he never had sight, not even as a child, but he described the saloon bar accurately. He told me what the landlord looked like, what the regulars wore, got all the colours right, even though he had no concept of colour as such. The most amazing thing is that he had got it right in every detail, but one: he never saw the dirt.'

'Most profound,' she said.

'Yes. The world I write about you can't express by using words and language.'

'Bit like a fur-lined teacup, if you ask me. Not much bloody use.'

'Only music allows you the freedom of abstraction to express yourself freely. Even now, while I am talking to you, I am also driving a car, but glimpses of the past also intrude my present: the smell of freshly baked bread, when I was five and went shopping with my mother; or sitting on a beach when I was three, looking at the hairs on my legs; or a street corner in Istanbul when I was eighteen. All these elements make up just one second of my existence in the here and now, like a multilayered chocolate cake, layer upon layer.'

Malcolm ran out of words. He smiled at Robyn triumphantly. He was quite pleased with his eloquence.

'The only trouble with that,' she said, 'is that all the references are personal to you. They won't mean a thing to anybody else. If I saw a movie where you cut from a bakery to a beach, then to a street corner in Istanbul, I'd probably walk out, and ask the manager for my money back.'

Malcolm said nothing. He had to concentrate on his driving. They were in London. Robyn looked out at the busy street scene. Malcolm's intellectual gymnastics worried her, but before she could ask him how all that theory related to the script, they arrived at their destination. Malcolm turned off the Brompton Road to Knightsbridge Square. There was nowhere to park, though he drove round the neat little square twice. In the end he put the car in a residents' parking spot. It was a hire car from Paris; he was not bothered about collecting a parking fine.

They soon found William Miller-Fenton's house. It was a part of London where house prices began at around the £4 million mark. Robyn was impressed.

'He's a right proper gent, ain't he?' she said in her best cockney.

'Being rich doesn't make you a gentleman, you know.'

'Don't be so bloody pompous, Malcolm.'

A Spanish maid met them. She showed them into the library. The walls were covered with oak panelling, the bookcases filled with leather-bound first editions, and the antique furniture was exquisite. There were even a couple of John Peter Russell watercolours on one wall. Malcolm pointed one of them out.

'Portofino, in Italy,' he said.

William Miller-Fenton joined them silently. He overheard Malcolm. 'Santa Margherita, actually. The next village up the coast. I am William; what can I do for you?'

He was a tall, lean man with an engaging smile. His dark suit was well cut, hand tailored, perhaps a little severe, but it matched his looks perfectly. He was in his early sixties, and wore the much-coveted tie of the Solent Yacht Club.

'Robyn Hawthorne,' said Malcolm introducing her. 'And I am Malcolm Reid. I see you're a yachting man?'

William was pleased that Malcolm recognised the tie. He held out his hand to Robyn and Malcolm.

'Haven't missed a Cowes Week yet,' he said with some pride. 'A little bit like Grandfather Miller. Sit down, won't you. You've come a long way. I hope I can help you.'

He had a slight speech impediment and a nervous hesitancy to his delivery, which made him seem more vulnerable than he really was. Behind the facade of an upper-class incompetent, he was one of the toughest merchant bankers in the city.

'To cut a long story short,' said Malcolm, 'we are trying to find thirty-eight paintings by J P Russell.'

'I see... Do you mean the ones he offered to the Gallery of Modern Art in Sydney in 1921?' he asked.

'Yes,' said Malcolm.

He was surprised to find that William knew about the paintings. Malcolm said the paintings were by Russell on purpose, as so far everybody believed them to be. He was pleased that William did not know better. That was good news.

'Nobody knows where they are,' said William. 'I have had a number of enquiries about them. I can tell you they are not in Europe. They must be in Australia somewhere.'

'How do you know they are in Australia?'

'I looked for them myself, and I found nothing; I can only surmise that they are in Australia. I am very fond of John Peter Russell's paintings. My grandfather bought his house on Belle-Ile, as you know. Hence my interest in JPR. I bought some of his paintings from his daughter, Jeanne.'

'So, you met her?'

'No, I'm afraid not. I bought them from a gallery in Paris.'

'Really,' said Malcolm. He was not going to say anything about the confidential list he obtained from Sabatier. 'How did you find out about the missing paintings?'

'I had a letter from a gallery owner in Sydney.'

'Paul McDonald?'

'Yes. That's the gentleman. Apparently, JPR's work is in demand, and those paintings could be worth a few bob. Paul McDonald was hoping that I'd know something about them.'

'So, you have no idea what happened to them?' asked Robyn.

'Heaven only knows,' said William, smiling. 'JPR is likely to have given them away, or burnt them.'

'Don't say that, please,' said Malcolm.

'Well, he burnt three hundred paintings of his wife, Marianna, in a fit of remorse… Can I get you a drink?'

'No thank you,' said Robyn.

'Perhaps you'd like to know that I have JPR's yacht.'

'His yacht?' asked Robyn.

'Yes, the very same yacht JPR built over a hundred years ago. It's a real joy to handle.'

'I didn't realise he was that keen on sailing,' said Malcolm.

'JPR hadn't missed a Cowes Week while he was in Europe. He thought about giving it up in 1908, when his wife Marianna died, but his children talked him into carrying on. In 1909 he sold the house on Belle-Ile, and shipped everything to Sydney, apart from his paintings in his Paris studio. He was going to go back to Australia even then.'

'Why did he change his mind?' asked Robyn.

'He got married again. He and Caroline lived out of suitcases for twelve years, but he never missed Cowes in all that time. He came back for that every August. He carried on sailing in Sydney, though, and built another yacht. Some green and blue monstrosity with a primitive eye to ward off evil spirits. Russell got quite eccentric in his old age; perhaps he planned to sail into the sunset, all ablaze like some Viking warrior.'

'How did you get hold of his yacht from Belle-Ile?' asked Malcolm.

'Well, that's a long story.'

'I'd like to know.'

'Well, JPR sold his house to a local fisherman in 1909, and the yacht went with the purchase. It was used as a fishing boat until my Grandfather Miller bought the house and the boat in 1947.'

'And he was a keen yachtsman, I suppose?' asked Malcolm.

'Very much so. He bought the house in the first place because of the boating facilities. He used JPR's yacht at Cowes, and then my father took over the tradition from Grandfather Miller. I am only following the family tradition.'

Chapter Twenty-five

3rd August 1888, Belle-Ile.

Completed the building of the house. Just as the last slate went on the roof Marianna gave birth to a baby boy. We're going to call him John Sandro. We had good weather all summer, when it mattered. While the roof was going up I laid the keel of my yacht. The hull is designed like a Norse ship, but she will ride a lot higher. I'll have sloop rigging with an adapted forestay sail in the kanaka style. Everything I've learned about boats is incorporated in the design; the best of everything. She looks good on paper, and I can only hope she'll manage to stay afloat.

12th August.

Had a letter from Vincent. I liked his drawings in the letter. It seems Gauguin is going to join him in Arles, and Vincent is excited by the prospect. He decorated a room for Gauguin already. He wants me to buy some of Gauguin's work. I would love to oblige, but I shall not help Gauguin as a matter of principle. I have often bought paintings to help my friends in need, but Vincent misunderstands me. I am not a charitable institution, and I have to like the work I buy, because I only want to send the best to Australia. I must sort them out one of these days.

13th August.

Theo's letter came in the following post. He, too, urges me to buy from Gauguin. He has even offered to arrange a visit, as Gauguin is in Pont-Aven for the summer. Comparing the two letters, I can see that some of his sentences are identical to his brother's. No doubt, Vincent wrote to Theo pleading with him to write to me. It is touching how hard Vincent tries to help Gauguin. I am sorry, but I shall never change my mind about Gauguin. I am not going to help him, whoever asks me, however touchingly.

11th September.

Another letter from Vincent about the financial affairs of Gauguin. My letter rejecting the idea was completely misunderstood. I must make my point a lot firmer. Dodge MacKnight visited Vincent in Arles, but they did not get on. He moved out of the yellow house after a week. I only have Vincent's version of the story; I am reserving judgement until I hear from MacKnight.

14th September.

Letter from Theo offering to come over with Gauguin's work. Vincent must have put him up to that. Theo sold some of Gauguin's ceramic works. His visit to Arles is definitely going ahead.

26th September.

Theo turned up with a dozen canvases from Gauguin. He'll just have to take them back again, I'm afraid. This time I stood my ground, and was very firm in my refusal. He has also brought with him half a dozen paintings from Vincent and a portfolio of his drawings. They are very good. I particularly like the oil sketches of his friend in Arles, postman Roulin. He reminds me of Père Tanguy; it's the beard, I suppose. Vincent's work has improved considerably. His loneliness must help him to concentrate his mind, but his health is deteriorating, according to Theo. That's very sad, and I wish there were something I could do to help Vincent.

18th October.

Bernard came to visit us. He and his sister spent the summer at Pont-Aven with Gauguin, but they fell out with each other. He is very upset. Bernard has been experimenting with using flat, bold colours enclosed by solid black lines; something like working in stained glass, or a technique used in enamelling they call cloisonné.

He painted a group of women in that style, '*Les Bretonnes dans la Prairie*'. Gauguin was impressed, and painted an almost identical picture, '*La Vision après le Sermon; La Lutte de Jacob avec l'Ange*'. He even borrowed Bernard's leftover paints. Bernard discovered something exciting, and Gauguin is claiming the credit for it. That doesn't surprise me. I asked Bernard to show me the painting, but he gave it to Gauguin to take to Arles. Gauguin's financial problems have been sorted out at last, and he is going to stay in Vincent's yellow house. I hope Gauguin doesn't steal all his ideas as well. There must be more to Bernard's story than he told me. His sister is a very beautiful woman, and I know what Gauguin is like in that respect. I wouldn't be surprised if he upset her too. It was good to see young Bernard again, in spite of all his problems.

3rd November.

The weather turned very nasty suddenly. We decided to return to Paris for the winter.

17th November 1888, Paris.

Gave a dinner party for some Australians, a newly-wed couple on their honeymoon – Tom Roberts' friends. They were dreadful people. I hope that my Paris address won't be on the itinerary of every social climber in Sydney. I was suitably rude, and I think they understood me. One good thing about the evening: Rodin agreed to sculpt a bust of Marianna. He is the best sculptor in Paris, though still far from being recognised as such. I consider it an honour that he accepted the commission from me.

25th December 1888, Paris.

Had a family Christmas. Marianna's brothers came over for Christmas lunch. I made a fool of myself trying to help with the turkey, but Marianna didn't mind.

26th December 1888, Paris.

Vincent fell out with Gauguin on the 23rd of December. They had a violent quarrel. Gauguin left the yellow house, and stayed at a hotel for the night. When he went back on Christmas Eve he found the police there. During the night Vincent cut off his ear, and gave it to a prostitute in a brothel, then went back home to bed. He was found half dead in the morning. He was taken to hospital, and Theo spent Christmas by his bed. Gauguin and Theo returned from Arles today. Vincent is still in a critical condition. Sent him a telegram, offering to go down to Arles.

30th December 1888, Paris.

Vincent is getting better, and sent me a telegram. He wants me to stay in Paris. He prefers to sort out his problems himself and doesn't think my presence would help matters much.

1st January 1889, Paris.

Marianna is expecting again.

5th January 1889, Paris.

Went to see Theo. Vincent has been discharged from the hospital. He visited his yellow house, but he is staying in a hotel for the time being. He is getting better, and wants us to leave him alone.

8th January 1889, Paris.

Theo tells me that Vincent is back at home at the yellow house, working again. He wrote to Gauguin, and asked him to return. He is not going to. I should visit Vincent, but Theo is advising me against it. He says his brother is a completely different man. Seeing me may upset him far too much. I shall have to take Theo's word for that.

22nd February 1889, Paris.

Visited Rodin. He showed me a model of Marianna's bust. It is a wonderful piece of work. I have three hundred portraits of her, yet not one of them captures her classical beauty as much as Rodin's lump of clay. We decided to cast it in silver, life size.

25th February 1889, Paris.

Letter from Vincent. He has fully recovered, and paints three canvases each day. He misses Gauguin. Asked me to persuade him to return to Arles. How can I tell Vincent that I don't even talk to the man? Reading between the lines, I feel Vincent is working against time. He knows he is not going to live much longer, and he is cramming in as much work as his body can bear. Dear Vincent, I wish I could help him.

10th March 1889, Belle-Ile.

The yacht is almost ready. The islanders got on with it during the winter, but there is little else they can do in the rough weather. With a bit of luck we could launch her next week.

16th March.

The yacht is beautiful. The Bellilois are genuinely impressed. They had never thought she would float. She is a magnificent creature, graceful, sturdy and responds to every command like a thoroughbred horse. I'll name her *Woolloomooloo*. Walked around my little fiefdom in the afternoon, and felt very smug. How dare I be so happy when my friends have nothing but problems?

28th April 1889, Paris.

Rodin finished Marianna's bust. He is showing it at the Galerie Georges Petit, where he is sharing an exhibition with Claude Monet. Went to the opening. It was good to talk to Monet. Marianna created a stir; people wouldn't let her move away from her silver image. Rodin was pleased. That's the way to get good commissions, he told me. Monet is also pleased with the exhibition. He sold fifteen of his seventy paintings on the opening day. I find it hard to equate success with selling, but I'm sure the fault is all mine. The bust of Marianna was so popular that Rodin wants to show it at the Palais du Champ de Mars as part of the Société des Beaux-Arts exhibition.

19th May 1889, Belle-Ile.

Marianna gave birth to a little boy. We'll call him Cedric. The islanders turned up to pay their respects. Everybody brought something: flowers, fruit, cakes etc. Marianna is very popular with the Bellilois, and they call me 'Seigneur'. I have to accept my role, and live up to their expectations.

16th June.

Celebrated my birthday in style. Rodin came over for a visit. Took him for a trip round the island in my brand new yacht, the *Woolloomooloo*. We were caught by a big swell on the west, but she rode it well. Rodin is glad to get away from Paris. He has too many personal problems there, but I am not interested in his romantic entanglements. I hope he keeps his affairs private, and leaves me out of them. I've become a father figure to my friends, even to Rodin, who is old enough to be my father. I think he wants my advice, but I am not encouraging him to confide in me. Much as I admire him as an artist, his morals I find a little strange, to say the least.

18th June.

Moret Cesbron is here for the summer. He's taken over my workshop, and locked himself in. He is working on a monster of a painting, six metres by four. Rodin and I went to visit him, but Cesbron had gone out for a walk. In the privacy of the workshop, Rodin told me that he is in love with Camille Claudel, his secretary, assistant and mistress for the past three years. His dilemma is that Camille wants him to leave Rose Beurat, who is his housekeeper, mistress and wife... for all it matters. Although both women are prepared to put up with his philandering, and don't mind him working off excess energy, they will not tolerate another permanent relationship. They both want Rodin's love, but from what I hear, Rodin has no understanding of the meaning of love. He is confusing copulation with love. I tried to explain the difference. Camille has given him an ultimatum: either he leaves

Rose, or Camille will leave him. He asked me what he should do. How can I answer a question like that? Camille's brother, Paul, went to see him and called him names. He won't tell me what names, but apparently, Paul referred to his sculptures as a 'banquet of buttocks'. Come to think of it, Rodin's work is not far removed from pornography. I wish he never confided in me. It's a miracle Marianna managed to keep him at arm's length, but one look from her is enough to put any man in his place. Why is it that great artists have to destroy people while they create something memorable? Rodin is destroying the lives of two women at the moment, and who knows how many others were driven to madness or suicide because of him! Then Vincent, he is creating something beautiful on his canvases, and destroying himself in the process. Look at me, I stopped painting, creating a happy family, but that is destroying my work as an artist. It's a shame you can't have your cake and eat it. I tried to put that into French, but it lost a lot in translation; and Rodin seems more confused than before.

Malcolm put down the diaries. He looked at Robyn, who sat next to him in the aircraft. She was stretched out, sleeping like an angel. Malcolm was glad she booked them first class; the twenty-hour flight was anything but comfortable. He watched her for a while. She was the most beautiful woman in the world, and he loved her so much that it hurt; yet she did not love him. They had sex, but that was not love. Malcolm recalled their week of romance minute by minute, but not once had they said, 'I love you.' He counted the number of times he wanted to tell her those three words, but she always found a way of diverting the conversation to safer ground. They never talked about the future, not a mention of their relationship; it was almost as if they never had an affair. Perhaps it was all just a dream. He tried to imagine sharing his life with Robyn. Who would go shopping, do the washing up, take the children to school? He couldn't see her having children, or being married. Not Robyn. That thought depressed him, but he managed to banish it for a while by trying to reassess his position. He would start lecturing in six days' time, and he wanted to have two clear days to prepare for that, which left him four days to finish the script. That was more than enough, he thought. Finding the Russell Collection was going to be more difficult, though he prepared a plan of action. Russell had nineteen surviving relatives. Malcolm had to contact them again, and try a little harder.

As for Jamie's death and McDonald, that was even trickier. There was no obvious connection – nothing that he could prove. He had a gut feeling that Jamie had been forging paintings for McDonald. But why should McDonald want to kill Jamie? There was no question of suicide. Jamie overdosing could have been an accident. And why did McDonald lie about the Russell Collection? Malcolm remembered that McDonald pretended not to have heard of them, yet he wrote to William Russell-Fenton about the missing thirty-eight paintings. Why lie, when he would probably be found out in the long run?

There was one thing Malcolm was pleased about; so far, nobody else knew the real nature of the missing paintings. The Russell Collection was going to be the sensation of the century; he only had to find it first.

Malcolm wished the aircraft would hurry up. He had a busy time ahead in Sydney, and could hardly wait to begin. He picked up the diaries again. The entries became shorter each year. They announced the arrival of three more sons. There were items about German measles, broken limbs, and an ever-changing list of governesses and tutors. There were reports of cricket matches with the Bellilois, trips to the mainland, and lots of birthday parties. Malcolm flipped through the pages until the name Matisse caught his eye.

11th August 1897, Goulphar.

Met a young man, Henri Matisse. I was painting on the very spot where I met Claude Monet in 1886. He asked for my permission to watch in a polite fashion; obviously, a young man of breeding. I was working on a watercolour, and used the colours straight out of their tubes. He was fascinated by the simplicity of my method. I found out that he was trained by Adolphe Bouguereau and Gustave Moreau, two painters I detest. 'Old Buggery', as Vincent and I called Bouguereau, was a pornographer, who sold smut dressed in academic garb. His big-tittied nudes were popular with the nouveau riche. Moreau was another academic without much talent, the last surviving relic of the Romantic school. He took over at the École des Beaux-Arts when Leon Bonnat retired. I felt sorry for the young man on account of his poor masters, and told him so. He was plucky enough to defend Moreau, but said nothing about 'Old Buggery'; naturally, nobody could say a word in his defence. I liked his loyalty, and decided to help him. He was keen to learn about Impressionism. I told him that its founders have already abandoned Impressionism; and they all moved on in other directions, yet its basic principles have not yet reached the academic world. I felt it my duty to teach the young man how to use colour properly. He recognised a good thing when he was shown one. Young Henri Matisse has seen the light, and he is not going back to his old ways again. I know that, just as I changed my style after painting with Monet. The young man has helped me to regain some of my enthusiasm for painting. There have been too many other things interfering with my work lately.

30th August, 1897, Goulphar.

Young Henri Matisse has gone back to the mainland. Before he went, I gave him a couple of sketches from Bernard and Vincent as a parting gift. He was deeply touched. He asked for something of mine, and I let him choose a watercolour. Matisse has the same natural talent as Vincent had, but he is more disciplined.

28th September, 1897, Goulphar.

Had a postcard from Henri Matisse. He tells me his friends observed that he has acquired a passion for the colours of the rainbow. What a thoughtful gesture. Left the island for the winter. We're off to Cannes and hope to spend Christmas there.

That was the last entry in the penultimate diary. The last one started on 20th August 1921. The most important event in Russell's life was the loss of Marianna. It was just like the man to keep his grief to himself. Malcolm knew she died of cancer on 30th March 1908. Russell's children also kept diaries, and every one of them recalled how their father, demented with grief, gathered up his paintings of Marianna, and built a giant bonfire on the beach. It was the same story, only the number of paintings changed in each account, anything from a hundred and fifty to four hundred.

As the aircraft started to make its final descent for Sydney Airport, Malcolm knew exactly how to end his script.

'*Eureka!*' he yelled happily and woke Robyn.

She smiled at him and he kissed her on her cheek.

'So what have you found now, Malcolm?' she asked.

'I know how to end the script.'

'I'm glad our trip wasn't a total waste,' she said sarcastically.

'You took the words out of my mouth. And I'll tell you something else – I am going to find those paintings if it's the last thing I do.'

'Finish the script first.'

Chapter Twenty-six

They landed at Sydney Airport at eight thirty in the morning. As they stepped out of the aircraft the hot air hit them like a wall. It was like walking into a giant oven. The sky was cobalt blue, changing to hazy white over the runway. The light was blinding; Malcolm screwed up his eyes and blinked as he reached for his sunglasses. He was glad to be in Sydney again; even though going through immigration was a pain. It was meant to be an ordeal, but Robyn was subjected to the same offhand treatment; rudeness was an Australian welcome, dished out to allcomers.

Malcolm's body clock stopped. Travelling east was a lot worse than the other way. He resigned himself to a couple of weeks of complete disorientation, and sleepless nights. Who needed sleep, anyway? He had too much to do.

They struggled with their luggage to a taxi rank and joined the fight to get a cab. Queuing was not a strong tradition in Sydney. They managed to get into the cab of the rudest taxi driver in the city. The driver offered no help as Malcolm packed their luggage in the boot. Robyn sat in the back seat waiting for Malcolm to get in. As he closed the door, the taxi moved out of the terminal lethargically.

'Where to, mate?' asked the driver.

'To Neutral Bay, but first to Jacaranda Crescent in Redfern, just off Parramatta Road.'

'I know where it is, mate.'

Malcolm shot a filthy look at the driver.

'Good. If you get a move on, we might even get there today…'

'I'm not breaking no speed limits, mate,' said the driver.

He was used to having the last word, and so was Malcolm. Robyn watched the verbal battle with a wry smile. Like a pair of school kids, she thought as she leaned back in her seat. She was wondering if they would eventually come to blows.

'I didn't ask you to,' snapped Malcolm.

'It sounded like it to me, mate.'

'I am not going to have an argument with you,' said Malcolm. 'Just drive us to Redfern, there's a good man.'

'Whatever you say, mate.'

Malcolm took a deep breath, leant back in the seat, and made a show of ignoring the driver, who was watching Malcolm in his mirror. Having succeeded in upsetting another fare made him a happy man.

The taxi crawled through Marrickville and Newtown. It was going to be another scorching hot day. A welcome change from winter, as far as Malcolm was concerned, though he looked miserable in the back of the cab.

'You're a bit down, Malcolm,' said Robyn.

'Aren't you?'

'It's end-of-holiday blues, but I'm glad to be back. I have a lot of work to catch up with. I always like coming home to Sydney.'

Malcolm looked out of the window. They were in the middle of the ugliest slums in the world. He shook his head in disbelief as he turned to Robyn.

'I see what you mean,' he said cuttingly.

'Bollocks to you,' she replied.

The driver pricked up his ears, but said nothing. He always enjoyed an argument, even if he was not one of the participants. But there was no argument at the back, just a prolonged silence. Robyn started talking again after a while.

'I know this isn't the time and place to ask you, but when do you think you'll be ready with the script?'

'You're right.'

'What?'

'It isn't the time and place,' said Malcolm.

'Be like that – and double bollocks to you with brass knobs on!' she said, turning away from him.

Malcolm said nothing. He picked up a newspaper left behind by a previous passenger, and pretended to read it. It was a useful prop to hide behind. Why am I being nasty to her? he asked himself as he turned the pages absent-mindedly. She has done nothing wrong.

On an inside page he saw a photograph of Carlo Bellini

smiling at him. The headline read: MYSTERY DROWNING OF DRUG DEALER. He read the article with interest, but all it said was that Carlo Bellini's dead body was found floating in the sea off Ben Buckler point. He lived in a unit on Bondi Beach.

'Do you remember this guy?' asked Malcolm, showing her the picture in the paper.

'No, I don't think so,' she said. 'Why?'

'That's Jamie's pusher, Carlo Bellini. I pointed him out to you at the reception, when we first met.'

'I don't remember him.'

'I find that hard to believe.'

'You believe what you like.'

Malcolm decided to leave it at that on the least-said-soonest-mended principle. They had both been on edge since they got into the cab. Malcolm put it down to bad vibes from the taxi driver, and he was glad to get out. He took his luggage out of the boot, and kissed Robyn goodbye.

'I'll call you as soon as I've finished the script,' he said. 'Could be tomorrow, if I'm lucky.'

'Terrific,' she said as the taxi drove off.

Malcolm watched the cab going down the street, quite fast now, certainly breaking the speed limit. As it turned the corner, Malcolm picked up his cases and crossed the road.

His beaten-up old Jag was where he had left it, untouched. Right behind it, Malcolm noticed a delivery van with Tony sitting at the wheel. Malcolm looked at him, and tried to recall where he'd seen him before; he was absolutely sure that he knew him from somewhere, but he could not remember.

Malcolm opened the front door and walked into the building.

Tony picked up his mobile, and dialled a number. 'Our male friend is back at home. Hang on... he's coming out again. He's getting in his car. I'd better follow him. Call you later...'

Malcolm threw the newspaper on the seat and turned the ignition key. The car started at the first try. He was pleased about that. He had been away for a week, and expected to find the battery flat. He drove down the street. In his rear mirror he noticed the delivery van following him, but did not make much of it. His mind was in overdrive thinking about Jamie.

Malcolm parked his car outside Paddington police station in a bay reserved for detectives. As he walked into the building he noticed the delivery van passing him and heading towards Centennial Park.

Costello did not keep him waiting long. He seemed to be pleased to see Malcolm, even shook his hand.

'Sit down, Mr Reid. What can I do for you?'

'Do you remember Jamie de Selway?' said Malcolm as he sat down. 'I couldn't tell you the name of his pusher. I've got a name for you. Carlo Bellini. There he is.'

Malcolm handed Costello the paper. He looked at the photograph for a while, then put the paper down.

'Oh, him?'

'That's the man,' said Malcolm. 'I am absolutely positive about that. He was Jamie's pusher.'

'Thanks for letting me know.'

'Well, is that it?' asked Malcolm.

'Yeah. Thanks for your help.'

'Don't you want me to make a statement? Shouldn't I sign an affidavit, or something? Surely, you'll want me to testify in court.'

'That won't be necessary.'

'And why is that?'

'Jamie de Selway's case is closed. The coroner brought in a verdict of misadventure.'

'But this Carlo Bellini could have murdered Jamie de Selway, or as good as damn it,' said Malcolm excitedly.

'You don't know that. You can't prove it, not now that Carlo Bellini has drowned. His inquest also resulted in an open verdict. Bellini is dead. De Selway is dead. The case is closed.'

Malcolm was lost for words. He just glared at Costello.

'Thanks for your help, Mr Reid. It was too little, and too late. But thanks all the same.'

★

McDonald was in his office when Penders walked into the gallery. There were a handful of tourists looking at the paintings as Penders made his way towards the back. McDonald watched him through the two-way mirror and opened the door for him.

'Come into the office, Mr Penders,' he said. 'Nice to see you again, and what can I do for you?'

'Nothing. I've popped in to say hello,' said Penders.

'I know you better than that, Mr Penders.'

'All right. You could help me with some background information. You may be aware that Robyn is working on a film project for me about JPR. She hired a new writer…'

'Malcolm Reid?' offered McDonald.

'He came to see you some time ago.'

'Yes, he did.'

'What did he want?'

'He was looking for Russell's missing paintings.'

'And what did you tell him?'

'Not a lot. We've all been looking for them without much success. I told him as much as I knew, and Sabatier's contact details. I think he and Robyn went to Paris to see him. They should be back by now.'

'They are back,' said Penders. 'Can I use your loo?'

'Please… Up the stairs, second door on the left.'

'Thanks, Mac.'

Penders walked up to the first floor, and entered the bathroom. He put on a pair of surgical gloves, then opened the medicine cabinet. There was a hypodermic needle kit on one shelf, and a couple of bottles of insulin. Penders poured the insulin down the pan, produced a plastic container from his pocket, and filled up the bottles with some liquid of roughly the same colour. He put the container and gloves back into his pocket, and flushed the lavatory pan.

*

Malcolm drove home fuming. He was cross with Costello, with Robyn, with the taxi driver from the airport; he was furious with the whole world.

'What am I doing here?' he asked himself as he went to bed and tried to sleep. He tossed and turned, but could not get to sleep.

He got up, made himself a jug of sweet cocoa, and sat down by the telephone. He took the list of John Peter Russell's surviving relatives, and called them, one by one, all nineteen of them. It took him the rest of the day, but he talked to them all, even the one who lived in Canada.

As he suspected, none of them had a clue where the missing thirty-eight paintings were; however, they had confirmed that Malcolm was not the only one looking for them. The other person was Paul McDonald, but Malcolm knew that already.

Malcolm pored over his notes, then on a clean sheet of paper made a list of all the oils owned by Russell's relatives. On a separate piece, he made a list of Russell's watercolours they had sold recently, and the art galleries acting for them. He compared his list to Sabatier's and jotted down a few names. It was a long shot, but worth pursuing, he reckoned.

It was getting late in the evening when he telephoned Philippa Penders. She was pleased to hear from Malcolm, and spent some time chatting to him. She was in good form, and sounded very happy. Penders had agreed to her starting a family, she confided to Malcolm. He wondered if all Sydney knew about it, but was too much of a gentleman to ask. He was pleased for her. She invited him to a party later in the week, and he accepted. Philippa also obliged him by telling him about all the Russell watercolours she bought from the Paddington Galleries.

Malcolm's head was buzzing with ideas, but it was well past ten in the evening, too late to follow up his hunch. Instead, he opened his computer, and began his last marathon session on the script. He was hell-bent on finishing it that night.

Chapter Twenty-seven

It was seven in the morning when Malcolm finished the script. The life and times of John Peter Russell, told in the Impressionist style. Malcolm had succeeded in producing a feature film script according to the literary equivalent of Impressionism. It was the best thing he ever wrote, and felt very good about it. He was glad Robyn had twisted his arm into writing it.

He had a shower, and his body clock started to work again as normal. He fancied a proper cooked breakfast: bacon, scrambled eggs, sausages, grilled tomatoes, toast and tea. He went round the corner to Giorgiou's Caff, and ordered his fry-up breakfast with great expectations. The bacon was undercooked and greasy, 'scrambled eggs' meant 'omelette' in Greek, the sausages were deep-fried in batter, the tomatoes came out of a tin, the toast was soggy, and the tea tasted of disinfectant. Malcolm wolfed it all up hungrily, and enjoyed every mouthful of it. He went back to his flat, telephoned McDonald at the Paddington Galleries and made an appointment to see him. Then he packed up the script and walked to Leichhardt University.

It was another glorious morning, and Malcolm enjoyed his walk, though it took him through the worst slums in the Western Suburbs. He ordered ten copies of the script in the duplicating room, and wandered over to the common room. He killed an hour or so in there, chatting to his fellow lecturers. Malcolm was looking forward to lecturing. An academic career had a lot going for it. It was cosy and protected in comparison with the real world. There was bitchiness amongst academics, but that only made it more interesting. It was going to be a change from editing a magazine.

He spent the rest of the morning nosing about in the state archives, going through the annual returns of the Paddington Galleries for the past ten years. They were not as detailed as Malcolm would have liked them to be, but they told him most of what he wanted to know.

He tried to call Robyn at home, but she was out. He tried her at the studios, but she was in conference. He resigned himself to eating alone, and drove to their favourite fish restaurant in Rose Bay. They gave him a small table next to the lavatories and overcharged him. The John Dory was good, however, and he drank a bottle of vintage Dom Pérignon with it. Malcolm was feeling pleased with the world; if only he could find the Russell Collection…

After lunch Malcolm drove to 22 Pacific Street in Watson's Bay – Russell's last address. There was a 22 Pacific Street, but it was a new one. The old fisherman's cottage had long since been pulled down, and a block of flats built in its place. The marina Russell cut into the rock was still there, but it was turned into a rock pool. He talked to the caretaker and a couple of the residents, but found no clues. He gave up and went home for a little siesta. It was hot enough for it.

He woke at four. He felt fresh and full of energy. He collected his notes and drove over to Paddington. The gallery was almost empty, as usual, but Philippa was entertaining a couple of tourists at the far end of the room. She smiled and waved at Malcolm, but carried on talking to the visitors.

Malcolm was greeted by an ashen-faced and miserable-looking McDonald. He came out of the office and offered Malcolm a limp handshake. He tried to sound cheerful, but his voice was weak.

'How nice to see you,' he said. 'How was Paris?'

'So-so,' said Malcolm, 'but I've never liked the place.'

'Was Claude Sabatier any help?'

'Not to his knowledge, but yes. He was certainly very expensive.'

'Running an art gallery costs a lot of money. It's not a social service, as I've been telling you…'

'Amongst all the lies,' interrupted Malcolm.

'We'd better go into the office,' said McDonald. 'I don't want to embarrass Philippa with any unpleasantness.'

'What is she doing here, anyway?'

'I haven't been well recently, and she is helping me out.'

They walked into the office and McDonald closed the door.

'Before we go any further, Malcolm, let's agree to behave as gentlemen. I am allergic to any form of unpleasantness.'

'Sure, let's behave like gentlemen.'

'I drink to that. A drop of malt?' he asked.

'Please,' said Malcolm.

'Anything with it?'

'No, thank you, I'll have it straight,' said Malcolm.

McDonald poured him half a glass of his best Isla Malt, and fixed himself a gin and sugar-free tonic.

'How can you drink that shit?' asked Malcolm.

'Sugar-free tonic?'

'Yes,' said Malcolm.

'It's simple – I want to live,' replied McDonald without elaborating any further. 'Now, what about these lies?'

'Just the one,' said Malcolm. 'When I told you that Russell offered thirty-eight paintings to the Gallery of Modern Art, you pretended not to have heard of it. In fact, you've been looking for those paintings yourself. William Miller-Fenton told me in London. Why did you lie to me?'

'I wasn't lying, Malcolm,' he said with good humour. 'I was only being economical with the truth. Being an Englishman, you must be used to that by now.'

'But why?'

'I wanted to get there first, and I've tried even harder since you've started poking your nose about.'

'I know,' said Malcolm.

'Russell's paintings are worth a lot of money.'

Malcolm sipped his whisky in silence. Good, he thought, McDonald thinks the paintings are Russell's, and I am not going to tell him otherwise.

'A drop more?' asked McDonald.

'Yes please,' said Malcolm as he held out his glass. 'Jamie de Selway was a friend of yours, wasn't he?'

'Yes. What about him?'

'You know he died under suspicious circumstances?'

'Took an overdose. Nothing suspicious about that,' he said defensively.

'Do you remember Carlo Bellini? You knew him, too, didn't you?'

'Malcolm, I know everybody in Sydney. Of course I knew Carlo, and I miss him a lot. It's not easy to get good quality… What are you after, Malcolm? You're going about it in a very obscure fashion.'

'Does it bother you?'

'I wish you'd come out with it straight.'

'That's not my style,' said Malcolm. 'How about playing a "suppose" game?'

'Fine, as long as you understand that I may not play it to your rules,' he said threateningly. 'I win at games, dear boy.'

'Now, let's suppose I am a picture restorer, and I am short of money.'

'Go on,' said McDonald.

'I have an expensive habit, and I need money to support it. What if I forged the odd old master and wanted to flog it. How would I set about it?'

'You can stop right there. I am not playing those kind of silly bugger games with you.'

'Why not?'

'I want to live, Malcolm. In Sydney people get murdered for ten bucks in their wallet.'

'So, Jamie was murdered?'

'I am not saying that, and you are abusing my hospitality, Malcolm. I'd like you to go now.'

'Not until I've had my say.'

'Go ahead,' said McDonald with a desperate sigh.

'I'm not bothered about abusing your hospitality,' said Malcolm. 'This is far too important. I made a list of the Russell watercolours you sold during the last ten years. I also made another list of the Russell watercolours sold by the nineteen surviving relatives of Russell. There is a discrepancy of twenty-three. You sold twenty-three watercolours Russell never painted.'

'You'll have a job proving that in court.'

'Jamie painted them for you, and you sold them. Fifteen of them to Philippa Penders.'

McDonald looked at Malcolm without saying a word. He was trying to think of a way out of this particular tight corner. He decided to use charm.

'OK, Malcolm. Now it's my turn to play my "suppose" card. Suppose a forger came to me, a respectable art dealer, and offered me forgeries. Why should I buy them?'

'Greed. That's a good motive.'

'Sure, I like money like the next man, but I could not afford to get involved with a forger for any amount of money. You must see that.'

'Suppose somebody came in with a Russell pencil drawing,' said Malcolm. 'Nothing very exciting, just a simple little sketch. Let's say he asked for fifty bucks; you know you could sell it for two hundred and fifty. What would you do?'

'Give him thirty, and sell it for three hundred.'

'It wouldn't bother you if it was genuine or not?'

'Not for that kind of money, no. If it looked like a Russell drawing, that would be enough for me.'

'What about a small watercolour?'

'Perhaps, perhaps not. Where does that get you, Malcolm? You'd have to prove that in court.'

'Jamie was murdered by Carlo,' said Malcolm in a low voice. It was not a 'suppose' game for him any more. 'Carlo gave Jamie uncut shit, which killed him. And Carlo was killed to keep it all quiet.'

'No way, Malcolm. If I killed Carlo and Jamie, what makes you think that I won't kill you?'

'You didn't do it, but you know who did, and you're going to tell me one way or another.'

'No, Malcolm,' he said smiling. 'The only thing I'm going to tell you is to forget about Jamie. Forget about Carlo. They are both dead, and you won't bring them back. As to your theory about phoney Russells, forget that too – you'll never be able to prove it, and after I've dragged you through the courts, you'll be a very poor man.'

'I'm not so sure about that,' said Malcolm tamely.

'I am,' said McDonald. 'And that's not a promise, it's a threat.'

'Are you threatening me?'

'What do you think? Just what did you expect me to do, Malcolm? Fall to pieces, and confess to murder? It's just as well that you're barking up the wrong tree,' said McDonald as he filled

Malcolm's glass again. 'We all liked Jamie. It is very noble of you to try to find his killer…'

'So you agree with me? Jamie was killed, wasn't he?'

'I don't think Jamie was killed, no. He was an addict, and you could say Jamie killed himself. As to that other thing; suppose I took a few dodgy paintings off Jamie – and I'm not saying that I did – the amount of money involved is peanuts. Not enough to go into an elaborate scheme with his pusher. You've been watching too many crime stories on the telly. You think about it, Malcolm. It doesn't make sense.'

Malcolm thought about it. He sat in McDonald's office, and went through all the permutations possible in his head. McDonald was right – it made no sense. All of a sudden he felt very stupid. What if Jamie forged the Russell watercolours, and what if McDonald sold them? There were no scientific tests available to tell an Impressionist forgery from the genuine article. It was all a matter of opinion. On reflection, McDonald was not capable of killing anybody. Being a crooked art dealer was one thing, but a murderer was something completely different.

'I'm sorry, Mac. I feel a bit of a fool.'

'Don't worry about it, Malcolm. Forget it. And just one other thing: promise me not to bother Philippa with your theories.'

'As if I would?'

'You can leave by the back,' said McDonald, opening a door leading to the back yard.

Chapter Twenty-eight

It was nine in the evening when Malcolm left Redfern, and drove across the Harbour Bridge to Neutral Bay. His stereo played a Sonny Rollins tape at full volume. The street lights shone through the windscreen and created colourful patterns, shifting and shimmering to the rhythm of the music. He was wearing a dinner jacket. Next to him, on the passenger seat, there was a gift-wrapped package and an enormous bunch of flowers. Malcolm sang with the music as he turned into Robyn's road. He was happy and full of expectations for the night. He parked the car and hurried into the building, still singing as he got into the lift.

Robyn opened the door and let him in. She, too, was dressed for an evening out. They looked at each other, and they were both surprised. She kissed him on the cheeks, and took the flowers and the parcel from him.

'What lovely flowers. You shouldn't have…'

She led him into the flat. He stood in the middle of the room as she ripped open the parcel.

'Is this what I think it is?'

'The finest piece of writing in the English language yet,' he said.

'So, you're quite pleased with it?'

He just nodded his head, smiling from ear to ear. He looked like an upper-class twit, but Robyn kept her observation to herself.

'Shit, Malcolm. You should have phoned me.'

'I thought it would be a surprise for you.'

'It is, believe me. A big surprise.'

She put the flowers in a vase, and placed the script on her desk.

'I'd like to offer you a drink,' she said with a certain amount of embarrassment, 'but I'm on my way out. I've got a dinner date.'

'*Cancel it*,' said Malcolm masterfully.

'I can't.'

'Don't tell me it's business…'

'It isn't,' she said. 'It's strictly pleasure.'

Malcolm looked at her, utterly dejected. He refused to believe that the woman he loved could be so callous.

'And don't give me that hurt spaniel look,' she added. 'You don't own me, Malcolm.'

'I thought we were in love.'

'We were, but that was in France. This is Sydney, Australia. Do you understand?'

'Only too well,' he said.

He turned away from her and walked out of the flat without another word. Robyn followed him angrily, and banged the door shut with some force.

Men…

★

Penders was seated by his desk watching the bank of television monitors in front of him. He kept on changing channels with his remote control, and spooling fast forward and backward. He was interested in the output of Channel Three and always managed to find some time to keep himself up to date.

Tony walked into the room and coughed respectfully.

'You wanted me, Mr Penders,' he said.

Penders picked up a piece of paper and handed it over.

'Yes, Tony. I'd like you to set up a meeting with Sergeant Costello from the Paddington Police Station CID.'

'Yes, Mr Penders.'

'As soon as you can. Any time. Any place. I don't mind, I'll make time for him.'

★

Malcolm stopped at the all-night liquor store and bought a large bottle of Château Poolowanna brandy. He was going to get very drunk. He'd always known that she would ditch him when it suited her, but didn't expect it to happen so soon. He was not prepared for the shock. He drove home in a foul temper and looked out for taxis to push off the road. Malcolm was fighting mad, and ramming up the backside of a cab was the kind of action he was after. The taxis he met all took evasive action, and he made it back to Redfern in one piece.

As he turned into the Parramatta Road he hit a large pothole. It had always been there, and Malcolm managed to avoid it; but in his state of mind he drove right into it. His beaten-up old Jag took it badly. The engine came off its mounting, and shifted forward. Jaguar engines are delicate instruments, and the slightest misalignment can make a difference. In Malcolm's case the fan blades moved forward at an angle, and punctured the radiator. The fan belt also slipped to one side, and the alternator stopped recharging the already suspect battery. Not that Malcolm was aware of any of that.

Then it all happened at once. As Malcolm turned into Jacaranda Crescent, the ignition failed, and the radiator boiled over. Malcolm coasted down to the bottom of the road and pulled into the Indian garage, just as they were about to close. After ten minutes of haggling over the cost of repairs they agreed on a hundred and eighty dollars.

'That's more than the car cost me.'

'Then take my advice,' said the mechanic chirpily. 'Walk away from it. Don't bother repairing the Jag; buy another one.'

It was sound advice, but Malcolm ignored it.

'Just get it ready as soon as you can.'

Malcolm walked home, and fixed himself a drink. He sat in front of the television set and watched a local programme, but did not take any of it in. It was noisy wallpaper to look at. He finished the bottle in under an hour. Suddenly, he felt very tired. He crawled into the bedroom, and threw himself on the bed. He was too tired to undress. He buried his face in the pillow and cried himself to sleep. It was three thirty in the afternoon when he woke. He had a dreadful hangover, and even a cold shower failed to revive him.

Malcolm fetched his car from the garage. The Jag was running as well as before, he noticed to his satisfaction. When he got back home, he read his mail. There was a notice from the post office to collect a registered letter. He just managed to get there ten minutes before the sorting office was to close.

He tore open the large brown paper envelope, and read the official-looking covering letter. It was from his mother's solicitor. Malcolm's mother was dead. She had died in her sleep.

Malcolm was too tired to have any reaction to the news. When he got home, he took a hot bath, and sat in the steaming water for a good half-hour. He sweated out the poison from his body, and although he still felt tired, his brain started to function again.

'Mother is dead,' he said to himself aloud.

The statement failed to produce a reaction. He was neither sad, nor happy; he just accepted that his mother was dead. It was an incidental detail of history, and it would go unnoticed by the rest of the world.

Malcolm put on some clothes, sat by his desk, and opened the envelope. He read the letter again informing him about the death of his mother, the funeral arrangements, and the reading of her will; which was a joke, considering that he was the sole beneficiary. Looking at the dates, he realised that he was not going to make them. He was relieved not to have to attend her funeral. Being stuck in Sydney seemed a good enough excuse. Malcolm looked at his watch, then figured that it was eight in the morning in Llangollen. Too early to telephone the solicitor. There was a separate letter in the envelope. Malcolm recognised his mother's handwriting:

Dear Malcolm,

I shall be dead when you read this letter. You'll find my gesture ridiculous and theatrical, but I shall not mind. I tried to be a good mother to you, but I know I failed you. It is the nature of parenthood, perhaps you will discover the same one day. But I shall not bore you with my shortcomings.

I promised that I'd tell you who your father was. I waited for the right opportunity, but it never came. I should have told you, face to face, but I could not go through with it. You'll see why.

Your father is Commandant Pierre Bousquet, a major in the French Foreign Legion (now retired). I knew him briefly, and only realised who he was after the event. Naturally, I loved him.

Considering what he stood for, and my own political commitment, I could not marry him. He is unaware of your existence. It is up to you to decide whether to contact him. His address is: 16 bis, avenue de Pierre-Paul Riquet, Naurouze, Haute Corse, France.

I recall once we talked about the existence of a life after death, and we made a pact that the one who goes there first will let the other one know. I changed my mind about that, and I shall not haunt you. Please don't expect any signs from me. I loved you, and still do, and I shall love you for ever.

Your loving M.

Malcolm used to have fantasies about his father. They were all shattered. A military action man was the last thing he thought of. He had no desire to contact Commandant Bousquet. He telephoned the solicitor's office, and told the senior partner that he could not leave Sydney for the foreseeable future. He gave his go-ahead to the funeral arrangements. Malcolm's mother left him some stocks and shares, her collection of Celtic icons and all her paintings. The solicitor asked for instructions for the transfer of the shares, and wanted to know what to do with the paintings.

'Sell them,' said Malcolm without hesitation. 'Just send me the money. They may fetch a few bob.'

*

Robyn sat in Greg Ericson's office. Malcolm's script lay on the top of the desk. Ericson was on the telephone to Penders. Though she was pushed for time, Robyn waited patiently for Ericson to finish sucking up to Penders. This was the meeting, the big one.

Ericson put the telephone down and looked at her. He said nothing; he just glared at her, then stared at the script. He picked it up with obvious disgust, and thumbed through the pages. He threw it down and turned on Robyn.

'It's just a pile of shit, Robyn,' he yelled.

'It's different,' she said quietly.

'It's not even in English.'

'It's in good English, Greg. You read so much rubbish that you don't recognise a masterpiece when it bites your balls.'

'Oh, it's a masterpiece? That's what it is?' he kept on shouting at the top of his voice. 'You've got to change it, Robyn. I'm not going with this piece of shit.'

Robyn had nothing to fight Ericson with. She knew he was right, but she could never concede that. She got up from the chair in the most dignified fashion she could muster.

'So that's it then, Greg?'

'Yeah, that's it, Robyn. Surely, you didn't think I'd buy this—'

Robyn got up and made her way out.

'And take your pile of crap with you!' he said, sneering at her. 'You should know better than to give me that.'

'You hang onto it, Greg. You've paid for it.'

'Thanks for reminding me,' he said.

Robyn opened the door, and waited for Ericson to cool down. He walked over to her, and put his hand on her shoulder in a lame effort to comfort her.

'I'm sorry, Robyn. It's just not on.'

Robyn lifted Ericson's hand off her shoulder, and looked him straight in the eye.

'Thanks for being you, Greg,' she said.

Robyn walked out of the room, and closed the door quietly. Before Ericson could have thrown a fit, the telephone rang. It was Penders again.

'Greg, I forgot to ask you to send over a copy of Malcolm's script.'

'No sweat, Ralph,' he said.

'Right away, Greg.'

'Sure, Ralph, no sweat. I'll send it by a despatch rider straight away. I hope you like it a lot better than I do.'

'I take it you had a bad reader's report?'

'I read it myself, Ralph, and it stinks.'

'Just send me a copy, Greg. Don't tell me how bad it is.'

Chapter Twenty-nine

Penders was at Philippa's cocktail party, which was almost unheard of, but he took more interest in her than before, and she was a changed woman. She had stopped drinking, and looked better for it.

It was an intimate affair; there were only a dozen people in the huge sitting room, and it looked almost empty. Robyn and Malcolm were having a private argument in one corner, trying to keep their voices down.

'Listen, Malcolm, I don't want to go into all the details, and I'm not going to teach you how to write. You should know all about that, but I'll have to get that script changed.'

'It's the best thing I've ever written.'

'You've got to change it.'

'You can't be serious.'

'Come on, Malcolm. Grow up.'

'I am not changing a word, not one single word. I won't even shift a comma. I've worked very hard to produce it. Why can't you just accept it as is?'

'Because it is just an unfilmable pile of shit, Malcolm. OK, OK, don't change a word of your masterpiece, but it's your funeral,' she said, moving on to another group.

Malcolm tried to think what Robyn was so concerned about. He was happy with the script, and that was that. It was Thursday evening, and he was to start lecturing on Monday. Even if he agreed to change the script, he had no time to do it. But why change a masterpiece?

Philippa joined him.

'Nice to see you again, Malcolm,' she said.

'You look fantastic. You must be a happy lady.'

'I've heard about your trip to Paris. Robyn tells me you had a wonderful time.'

'We did. There was nothing wrong with Europe.'

'Is Robyn giving you a hard time?'

'Do you really want to know?' asked Malcolm.

'Yes, if you want to tell me.'

'I do.'

While Malcolm poured his heart out to Philippa, Robyn was talking to Penders. She was surprised to find that Penders knew all about Malcolm's script.

'Did you really read it, Mr Penders?'

'No, not all of it. Only the first and last two pages. That's all you ever need to read of any script.'

'Do you think so?'

'I know so. If there's a good opening and a good ending, your audience will forgive you whatever happens in between. Take my word for that.'

'Well, it's a good ending, Mr Penders. In fact, a brilliant ending, isn't it?' asked Robyn.

'Yes, completely unpredictable, but very good.'

Robyn tried to think how Penders could tell what was predictable or not, if he had only read four pages of the script.

'But I spotted a mistake,' added Penders.

'What mistake?'

'That blue and pink boat in the end sequence. It was never burnt. It is still around. I've seen it in a boatyard on Pittwater Road. Bayview Marina, I think. I'm sure that's where it was.'

Robyn was keen to find out more about the boat, but Philippa took her husband away to meet somebody.

'Excuse me, Robyn,' she said. 'Somebody wants to have a word with Ralph. It's business, I think.'

Malcolm was talking to McDonald by the bar. He was still drinking gin and sugar-free tonics, but looked very ill on them. Malcolm was going to ask him what was wrong with him, but Penders' leaving the party distracted him. From where they stood Malcolm could see into the hall. Doug and Tony were waiting at the front door. Detective Sergeant Costello was with them. Malcolm watched Penders join the three men. Malcolm remembered that he had seen Tony outside his house in Redfern. Penders exchanged a few words with the men, then showed them out of the hall.

Malcolm turned to McDonald.

'Who are those men?'

'I know two of them,' said McDonald. 'Tony and Doug. They are Ralph's minders – well, two of his many minders. There's a whole security firm dedicated to minding Ralph, but I haven't seen much of those two lately. They must have been away.'

Malcolm could not think what business Sergeant Costello had with Penders. He decided to say nothing about Costello to McDonald.

'You seem to know most people in Sydney, Mac.'

'It's the rule of the three-keeps.'

'What?'

'Keep your head down, keep your ears close to the ground, and keep your nose clean. And keep your mouth shut, but that makes it four,' smiled McDonald. 'The four-keeps. They're essential if you want to make a living in Sydney.'

'I was going to ask you a favour,' said Malcolm.

'But you're not going to,' quipped McDonald.

'I am, I am – hear me out!'

'I was in a good mood today, don't ruin it for me, please.'

'Would you know somebody to advise me on a film script?'

'I've heard you've got problems there.'

'No, Mac. I haven't got a problem,' said Malcolm. 'Robyn has, but I can't understand why. I've given her a fantastic script.'

'Have you heard of David Swaab?'

'He'd be just perfect,' lied Malcolm.

Malcolm knew of him. Nobody carries off the Hirondelle d'Or without making a name for himself. He also suspected that Swaab was Robyn's lover, and hated his guts for that. All the same, he was flattered that somebody as famous as that would give an opinion on his script.

'He's the kind of person I was hoping you'd suggest, but will he read it?'

'He'll read it. I'm seeing David later tonight.'

'That's brilliant. I have a spare copy in my car; I'll get it for you even as we speak. Any chance of me seeing him in the morning?'

'I'll ask him,' said McDonald. 'David owes me a favour or two. I'll call you in the morning.'

'That's very kind,' said Malcolm, and went to get his script.

Malcolm walked over to his Jag parked at the far end. As he opened the car door, he noticed three men inside a nearby Volvo: Tony, Doug and Sergeant Costello. They were having a heated argument about something, but Malcolm was too far away to hear. There was no sign of Penders. Malcolm picked up his script and went back into the house. By the time he got back, the party had started to break up. Everybody seemed to have somewhere to go to. Malcolm gave the script to McDonald, then walked over to Robyn.

'Are you doing anything tonight?' he asked her.

'I'm washing my hair,' she said. 'I'll see you tomorrow, Malcolm, and please, think about what I said, won't you?'

'Yes. I'll think about it,' he said dejectedly.

As Robyn walked away from Malcolm, Penders approached him with a broad smile. He noticed that Malcolm was in a bad mood and tried to make light of it.

'A lovers' tiff?' he asked.

'Yes, as it happens, Mr Penders. You could say that. I shall never understand women.'

'Join the club. I was hoping to have a word with you.'

'Oh, yes?'

'I don't normally get involved in scripts, but I must declare an interest when it comes to JPR. Philippa has been collecting his work for some time.'

'Indeed. I have seen some of the watercolours she has.'

'I've seen your script. Greg Ericson sent me a copy of it. I flipped through it and found it very interesting.'

'Thank you,' said Malcolm.

'Mind you, the ending is all wrong. Russell never set fire to that boat of his. I've seen that pink and blue boat. It's still around, and I can vouch for that…'

'Where?' asked Malcolm excitedly.

'In a boatyard on Pittwater. In the Bayview Marina. Ugly thing, too, with an eye painted on the bow. Some pagan sign to ward off the evil eye, I was told.'

★

Robyn had a date with Elmer Sandak. She was convinced Channel Three was a lost cause. Penders may have liked the first and last couple of pages, but she did not think he would part with any money. He may have tried to wind her up about Malcolm's script. The project needed some real money, and in any case, the Russell story was the kind of film that only the Americans could afford to make. She arranged to meet Sandak at the bar of the Wynyard Hotel. Robyn was two minutes early, but Sandak was already waiting for her in a secluded corner.

'Sit down, Robyn,' he said, smiling at her. 'You're on time.'

'No, Elmer,' she corrected him jokingly, 'I am early. In my dictionary there's no such thing as being on time. Either you're early, or you're late.'

'Whatever you say,' he beamed at her. 'I'm sure there's a debating point there, somewhere.'

He was interrupted by the arrival of a waiter. Robyn asked for a large gin and tonic, and Elmer had his customary bourbon with branch water. Robyn took a copy of the script, and handed it to Sandak. He held it in his hand, weighing it for some time.

Robyn had no idea what he was up to, and thought it was best not to ask, but Sandak provided her with an explanation.

'I met this driver in London,' he said. 'He worked for Twentieth Century Fox, and was notorious for his accuracy in timing a script. He was just an ordinary guy, but if you gave him a script he could tell exactly how long the finished movie would run. Just by feeling its weight. You don't believe me.'

'I do,' protested Robyn as the drinks arrived. 'So, what do you think, Elmer? What's the running time of this one?'

'Oh, I'm not very good at guessing, but I'd say around a hundred and eighteen minutes.'

'I'm speechless,' said Robyn.

She sipped her drink slowly. Sandak opened the script, and flipped through the pages without reading any of it.

'It's very neat,' he said.

Robyn just nodded without saying anything.

'And you want me to read all this?' asked Sandak.

'Why not?'

'I don't read scripts. I have other people who do that for me.'

'You said you wanted to see the script when it was ready, right?'

'That's right. I did, I did. To see it, but not to read it,' he said, laughing at his own joke. 'It's a pity this Russell character wasn't an American.'

'One of his friends is. Dodge MacKnight is American, and he's got a very good part. You'll find out when you read it,' she said, trying to persuade him.

'You really want me to read it?'

'Yeah, I do.'

Sandak leant forward and put his hand on Robyn's thigh and left it there. 'You read it to me. Tuck me up in bed and read it to me.'

Sandak squeezed Robyn's flesh and looked into her eyes. His meaning was clear.

'I mean it,' he said.

'I know you do, Elmer,' she said.

She lifted his hand off her, not so much as a gesture of rejection, but more for doing the right thing at the wrong time.

'I thought you had Channel Three tied up.'

'So did I,' she replied. 'But I don't like them, and I'd like to buy the project back.'

That was not what Sandak had heard on the grapevine, but he said nothing. He just smiled at her.

'It's over to you, Robyn,' he said. 'Read it to me, in bed.'

Chapter Thirty

It was ten past eight in the morning when Ericson arrived in Penders' office. He was ten minutes late. He was out of breath and looked dreadful. Hurrying to get there at eight had put him out considerably.

'Sit down, Greg,' said Penders. 'You normally do without being asked; why not today?'

'Sure,' replied Ericson.

He sat in the chair facing Penders. He was aware of the unfriendly atmosphere. In spite of all his failings, Ericson was aware of moods. He knew instinctively that he was about to receive bad news.

'You must be wondering why I called you over.'

Penders drank his coffee slowly, but he did not offer any clues to Ericson. It was a childish game, and Ericson knew that there was worse to come.

'You'll tell me, Ralph, I'm sure,' said Ericson.

'I wanted to talk to you about Malcolm Reid's script. I read it yesterday, and I think it's good. It's the kind of movie we should be making at Channel Three.'

'Can I have some coffee?' asked Ericson.

He was only stalling for time. He tried to decide whether to speak his mind, or do what Penders wanted. Should he resign before being fired? That was the big question.

'Help yourself, Greg.'

Penders watched Ericson pouring himself a cup of coffee. He said nothing. He waited till Ericson sat down again.

'What do you think, Greg?'

'I think that script stinks,' he replied.

Ericson decided to defend his opinion, come what may. That made him feel a lot better. He knew there was no profit in being rude to Penders – he was notoriously vindictive – but he was not going to take any rubbish from him. Ericson had his pride.

'You told me,' said Penders calmly. 'And I am telling you, I want that film made as scripted.'

'I shall have nothing to do with it, I am sorry.'

'Then you're fired.'

Ericson sipped his coffee. When he finished it, he put the cup down, and looked Penders in the eye.

'OK, but tell me why. What's the real reason?' he asked. 'I'd like to know, just for the record.'

'You're a rude little jerk,' said Penders, 'and I don't like you. Good enough reason for me.'

'Sure, Ralph, no sweat.'

'And you said "no sweat, Ralph" once too often,' added Penders, as the door shut behind Ericson. He felt a lot better for that.

★

McDonald telephoned just after eleven, and told Malcolm that Swaab read the script. He wanted to meet Malcolm and Robyn together. He was pressed for time, and could only manage lunch. Malcolm suggested that they should meet in the Greedy Pig.

It was the tackiest pub in Paddington, but it had a nice beer garden. It offered an 'eat as much as a pig' lunch for fifteen dollars, and it was always crowded with media folk. The pub was a landmark, and still had the original furnishings and decor from 1923. The price of the set lunch changed from time to time to keep up with inflation. The advertising business regulars drank Perrier, and ate a few leaves of lettuce. The Greedy Pig was a profitable business.

Robyn, Malcolm and Swaab sat at a corner table, out of the way of the general mayhem. The noise was deafening, but they could just about hear each other. Robyn and Malcolm were doing all the talking as Swaab picked at his half tomato and quarter of beetroot. He was serene as a Buddha, unmoved by the fact that Robyn and Malcolm were arguing about his presence at the table.

'You had no right to bring him in!' she yelled.

'But do you know who he is?' asked Malcolm.

'Don't you teach me my business, Malcolm. David's been involved with the first draft. It's unethical, unprofessional and probably illegal to ask him for an opinion.'

'I didn't know that,' said Malcolm. 'You should value his judgement all the more for that.'

'His judgement is worth bugger all if he can't come up with the money.'

Swaab raised his hand as if he were asking for permission to go to the loo.

'I can get you a deal, Robyn.'

'You keep out of this, David.'

'But the money is no problem,' went on Swaab.

'You can talk about the money later,' interjected Malcolm. 'Tell her what you think of the script.'

'I like it a lot. It stands on its own as literature, it's a profound poem, an ingenious jigsaw puzzle. It works, Robyn. Great stuff.'

'There you are,' said Malcolm. 'Straight from the horse's mouth.'

'The characters are credible,' said Swaab. 'The dialogue is good, but it's not a movie script.'

'*What?*' shouted Malcolm angrily.

'Not the way it is,' said Swaab soothingly. 'I'll have to work on it a little.'

Malcolm took a deep breath. He was pale with anger, but tried to keep civil.

'Work on it a little? On my script?'

'Yeah. All my movies are credited as "a film by David Swaab". There is a reason for that.'

Robyn looked at Malcolm's face, and could not help smiling. She positively enjoyed his discomfort. And you haven't heard the bottom line yet, Malcolm, she thought. You don't know our David, mate.

'You told me you loved it!' shouted Malcolm.

'I do, very much,' said Swaab, and he patted Malcolm's arm reassuringly, 'I love it. It's the kind of script I've always wanted to write. I wish I had time to write, but I'm under tremendous pressure. We are going to do this picture, Marvin, and I'll find the time from somewhere to do a rewrite.'

Malcolm exploded. He snatched the script out of Swaab's hand, stood up, and snarled at Swaab.

'Nobody is doing a rewrite on my script. Screw you, Donald.'

Malcolm was about to storm out of the garden, but Robyn grabbed his arm.

'I've got to talk to you, you stupid bastard,' she said.

'I've heard all I want to hear.'

'It's about Russell's pink and blue boat.'

'What about it?'

'It exists. It's at the Bayview Marina, up Pittwater Road.'

'I know. Ralph Penders told me about it.'

'I was going to tell you last night,' said Robyn.

'Well, thanks for telling me at all.'

Malcolm pushed his way through the crowd, taking his script with him. He was in a fighting mood, and the people in his way sensed it: they opened a way for him. Malcolm felt like Moses crossing the Red Sea.

'What's the matter with him?' asked Swaab.

'Artistic bloody temperament,' said Robyn. 'You should know about that, David.'

'I'll give him a credit, but you know how it is.'

'Yeah, I know how it is. He's done all the work, and you'll take all the credit for it.'

★

The Paddington Gallery was closed. Philippa opened the door with her key, and walked across the empty floor. The silence unnerved her; she had a strange feeling that there was something wrong.

'Mac?' she called out.

There was no answer as she headed for the office. She opened the door, but there was nobody in the office.

'Mac? Where are you?'

The silence was deafening as she mounted the stairs. Philippa opened the door to the master bedroom, and walked inside. McDonald's body lay on the floor beside the bed. He was dead.

'My God…'

Philippa sat down beside the body and lifted up McDonald's right hand. It was cold and stiff.

As she walked away from the body, she started to cry.

★

Malcolm made up his mind not to touch the script. It was all finished and done with, never to be discussed again, and not even to be thought about. The script was one thing; however, the Russell Collection was something else. Now he was keener than ever to find it. As for Robyn, he still loved her, he could not alter that, but he knew that their love affair was over. That is, if they ever had an affair...

Malcolm looked up Pittwater Road on his Sydney street map before he set out. He had never been that far up the North Shore. He drove through a string of sprawling little suburbs, one after another, a single continuous strip of air-conditioned shopping malls wedged in between the ocean and the bush: Mosman, Manly, Harbord, Deewhy, Collaroy, Narrabeen and Mona Vale. Before reaching Bungan Head, he took a left-hand fork of the road, and drove along the south shore of Pittwater towards the Ku-Ring-Gai Chase.

He calmed down considerably by the time he got to the Bayview Marina. The sun was high in the sky still. It was a scorching hot day, and the light was dazzling. 'Marina' was a pretentious name for the derelict boatyard. The paint was peeling off the timber sheds, weeds grew through the broken tarmac, and there were potholes everywhere.

Malcolm left his car outside on the main road, and walked through the open gates. He noticed a Holden station wagon parked across the way with Penders' two minders sitting in the car. He recognised them, and was wondering what they were doing there.

He walked over to a small wooden hut with 'Office' painted on the door. The door was open, but there was nobody inside. He walked on. The place was a graveyard for boats. There were hundreds, some fallen on their sides, some propped up, others on ramps; all wrecks in various stages of decomposition.

Malcolm wandered about the yard looking for some sign of life, but only the flies buzzed about in the heat, trying to eat him alive. As he turned a corner, Malcolm met a tall, lean man with sharp, sunburnt features. He looked ageless and could have been anything between fifty and a hundred. His clothes were tattered, he sported a five-day-old beard, and wore a wide-brimmed hat. The only thing missing were the dangling corks. He even had a set of second-hand dentures.

'How are you, mate?' he said.

'I'm Malcolm Reid. I teach at the university. I've been doing some research on John Peter Russell, the painter. I believe his yacht is here somewhere.'

'I'm William Jones – they call me Willie,' he said as he held out his hand.

'Do you own this place?' asked Malcolm.

'I only look after it now, mate. I sold it, back in the Sixties.'

'What an incredible place.'

'My father was a boat builder, but when he died the business's gone crook. I'm no good with business, and I had to sell it. I look after the place now.'

'As you said.'

'How can I help you, mate?'

'Do you know anything about John Peter Russell?'

'Don't think so… But I know you. I've heard you on the Terry Robinson Show.'

'There's fame for you,' said Malcolm.

'Didn't understand a word you said, mate, but you sure made a fool of him. Can't stand the bastard.'

'Russell was a painter.'

'A painter, you say. House painter?'

'No, artist painter. A gentleman. He used to live in Watson's Bay. He built a boat in the early Twenties. A pink and blue boat.'

'With a queer fish eye?'

'I think so, painted on the bow.'

A flicker of recognition showed in the old man's eyes as he smiled at Malcolm, revealing his ill-fitting false teeth.

'Your friend was a mate of my father. I remember that boat; it's got that evil eye. Ugly thing it is.'

'Where is it?'

'It's here somewhere,' he said.

'Could I see it?'

'Sure. No harm in that, I suppose.'

Jones led the way. He knew all the short cuts through the avenues of derelict boats, and they were soon staring at a huge pink and blue yacht propped up by stocks. It was in a good condition, considering that it had been left there for over seventy years. On the bow there was a pair of bizarre-looking eyes.

'Pagan-looking thing,' said Jones. 'Ugly. Real ugly. Used to frighten me when I was a kid.'

'Would you mind if I took a look inside?'

'You help yourself, mate. See if I can find a ladder somewhere.'

Jones left Malcolm alone as he went looking for a ladder.

Tony was standing on the roof of the Holden station wagon. He was looking at the boatyard through a pair of binoculars and, holding his mobile in one hand, he was also talking to Penders.

'Yes, Mr Penders, he is inside the yard.'

'What is he doing?'

'He's been talking to old Willy Jones, but we're not wired up to know what they've said.'

'That's all right.'

'Now he's sniffing around that blue and pink boat.'

'So, he's found the boat?'

'He is still walking around it. What do you want us to do?'

'Nothing. You don't need to keep an eye on him. Call it a day, Tony. I'll see you both tomorrow.'

Malcolm walked around the boat excitedly. He was communing with Russell's spirit. The yacht was an impressive structure. It was large, and dwarfed the other boats around it.

Jones came back with a ladder and leant it against the side of the boat. 'Up you go, mate,' he said. 'I'm not climbing up there. Watch how you go. I'm not insured, so don't go breaking your neck.'

'I'll be careful,' said Malcolm. 'Don't you worry about me.'

Jones walked back to the office, a timber shed by the main entrance. Malcolm climbed up the ladder carefully. Standing on the deck he realised that the yacht was even bigger than he thought. It was built to be an ocean-going craft, and every detail showed craftsmanship of the highest order.

Malcolm looked towards the sea. The sun was lower in the sky now, and its rays glittered like quicksilver on the dark blue water. An armada of sailing boats crossed the bay from Church Point towards Newport, racing each other. It was a lovely sight, and Malcolm thought about taking up sailing as a hobby.

He walked around the deck cautiously, then opened the hatch leading into the cabin. He was excited as he climbed down. He clambered over fifty years of dust. The interior was a lot bigger than it looked from the outside. It was an eight-berth affair, with a galley and two bathrooms, designed to accommodate a large party in comfort. Malcolm found it difficult to move about, as all the available space was crammed full of junk. The boat was used as a storage place. There were packing cases, sacks and suitcases. Some of the faded labels could still be deciphered through the thick layer of dust. Malcolm wiped one clear, and examined it closely. It read: *Oriental & Occidental Steamship Co. J.P.R. Lot 7 of 24.*

Malcolm could not believe his eyes. He was gripped by a fever, and his throat went dry. It was like discovering a gold mine. He searched excitedly for lots sixteen and seventeen. They were in the middle berths. The canvases were in rectangular crates, and Malcolm wondered how they were brought on board, because they completely filled the available space.

Malcolm's hands started to shake, but he managed to loosen one of the planks. The paintings inside were wrapped in waxed paper for protection. He tore away the paper to reveal the corner of a large painting inside. The colours were bright and fresh, and the picture was painted in the unmistakable style of Vincent van Gogh.

Malcolm almost fainted. He sat down on a crate, shaking with spent nervous energy. It took him a long time to recover his strength. He checked the other crate.

All the thirty-eight paintings were there, apart from Seurat's extra-large canvas. That could not have fitted into the hold of the boat; all the same, Malcolm spent some time looking for it. He was rewarded in the end. He found the painting rolled up amongst the sails of the yacht. He could not tell whether it was damaged or not.

Malcolm was crying with joy as he climbed down the ladder.

The sun was setting over Pittwater. He had spent the whole afternoon inside the boat. When he got back to the boatyard office he found it shut. Jones had gone, and the gates were padlocked. Malcolm had to climb over the fence.

There was no sign of the Holden station wagon. There was not a soul to be seen anywhere as Malcolm got into his car and headed back to Sydney. He kept on looking in his rear mirror. There were lots of Holdens about, but he could not see the station wagon anywhere.

By the time he got to Collaroy he gave up looking; he was sure that nobody was following him. As the sun set, the pale blue city lights were switched on. It was a glorious evening.

Chapter Thirty-one

Robyn and Sandak had finished making love. Sandak lit up a huge cigar as she slipped out of the bed. Her clothes were thrown all over the floor. She collected them, and went into the bathroom. Sandak's penthouse overlooked Circular Quay and the Harbour Bridge. The huge steel structure was bathed in violent shades of orange and red by the setting sun. The city lights flickered like fireflies, but the beauty of the evening was wasted on Sandak. He was cocooned in a thick cloud of smoke as he got out of bed.

He slipped on his underpants, then poured out two glasses of champagne, and placed them on the coffee table. He took an official-looking document from his Gucci briefcase, and placed it on the table next to the drinks. Robyn returned to the room fully dressed, and sat on the sofa. She picked up a glass of champagne, and drank it without a word. Sandak pushed the document in front of her with a theatrical gesture.

'You've got yourself a contract.'

Robyn picked up the papers, and started giggling.

'What's the matter?' asked Sandak with concern.

'You're too much, Elmer! You're pure Hollywood.'

He took her remark as a compliment.

'Truth is stranger than fiction,' he said pompously. Sitting there in his underpants he looked comical.

Robyn managed to keep a straight face by looking at the contract. She read it carefully, line by line, while Sandak walked over to the window leading to the balcony. His cigar smoke followed him like a cloud.

'Why just associate producer?' asked Robyn. 'I want to produce the movie myself.'

'You'll produce the next one, OK?'

'Then I want to be script editor on this one.'

'That's fine,' he said. 'What about the rest?'

'I don't suppose I'll get better anywhere else.'

'You won't. I think we'll make the American... what's his name?'

'Dodge MacKnight.'

'We'll make Dodge MacKnight the central character, and keep all the action on the island. That makes it nice and tidy. An island is an island is an island, you know what I mean?'

'It's easy, when you know how.'

Robyn's voice was loaded with all the sarcasm she could muster. It was lost on Sandak. He strutted about the place like a proud turkey on his own dung heap, telling Robyn what a magnificent movie they were going to make together.

★

Tony was driving the Holden station wagon towards the city. Doug sat next to him looking out of the window. They were both silent, and busy with their thoughts. They had worked together for a long time, and did not feel the need for idle chatter.

They were descending the steep hill towards The Spit when their car exploded. It careered across the busy highway, and it was a miracle it missed all the other cars. The wreck came to a halt as it hit a telegraph pole. As the station wagon burned, a fractured water hydrant shot a geyser of water high into the air. Some passing cars stopped. Their occupants ran over to help, but Doug and Tony were incinerated instantly. There was nothing anybody could do for them.

★

Robyn took another shower when she got home. She felt dirty. The thought of Sandak's touch made her flesh creep. She was angry with herself, but above all with Malcolm. He made her do it by refusing to change the script. 'The stupid bastard,' she said to herself.

She was falling in love with him, and that only made it worse. She'd hoped to carry on as before, but she could not forget France. Malcolm was different from other men. Why him? she asked herself. Why did I fall for him?

She'd expected Malcolm to call on her, and when he turned up with a huge bunch of flowers on her doorstep, she was not in the least surprised. She was glad to see him, and hated his guts at the same time, not that it showed. Behind a cool facade she managed to keep her emotions secret.

'You and your flowers, Malcolm,' she said. 'You might as well come in, now that you're here.'

Malcolm was dying to tell her about the Russell Collection. She took the flowers off him, and showed him into the living room.

'You'd better sit down, Malcolm,' she said, 'because I have something important to tell you.'

Malcolm did not like the tone of her voice.

'All right, your news first,' he said.

'I made a deal with Media International, and the Russell project has gone into production...'

'Media International?' he interrupted her. 'I thought you had a deal with Channel Three.'

'Hear me out, Malcolm. I am trying to explain what happened. Stop interrupting me.'

'I have a feeling I'm not going to like this.'

'You can't say I didn't warn you. I'm sorry, but you wouldn't listen to me. You wouldn't change a single word, remember? It's your own bloody fault...'

'Go on. Don't stop now!'

'I bought myself out of the Channel Three contract. We are going ahead with the movie, but not with your script. Dodge MacKnight is the central character now; it makes the project more accessible to the American market...'

'I'm sorry to interrupt, but who is this *we*?'

'Elmer Sandak of Media International. I am developing a new script with one of their writers. Sorry, Malcolm,' she said.

She was genuinely sorry, and Malcolm could tell. All the same, he worked hard for her. That script had taken a lot out of him. He glared at her angrily.

'I wish I could pay for your time, but we used up the development money on the European trip.'

Malcolm was searching for the right words to insult her

properly, but his mind went blank. He just glared at her, then stood up, and Robyn stepped back involuntarily. He frightened her.

'You used me,' he said slowly and quietly.

'It wasn't like that. I tried to tell you.'

'You used me in every possible sense of the word,' he said, turning away from her.

'What about your news?' she asked.

'It doesn't matter now.'

Malcolm walked out of the room without looking at her. He let the door shut behind him with a gentle click of the latch. Robyn started to cry inwardly. There were no tears in her eyes, but the pain was almost unbearable. She knew she had lost him for ever.

Malcolm felt emotionally drained as he got in his car. He was at a loss what to do next. He drove across the Harbour Bridge without thinking about where he was going. His stereo was playing a Shelly Manne tape, and the music calmed him down.

He had to tell somebody his news about the Russell Collection, but he was glad he'd said nothing to Robyn. She did not deserve to be the first to hear about it.

Malcolm called Paul McDonald on his mobile, but there was no answer. The telephone kept on ringing on the end of the line; the answerphone was not switched on.

Malcolm remembered a short cut from Woolloomooloo to Redfern, and turned into the narrow side street. The sharp movement of the car shifted the engine off its mounting, and it fell out, literally, right onto the road – the whole engine.

Malcolm looked at it in disbelief, then took all his tapes and personal things out of the car. He looked through his pockets for the Indian mechanic's business card. He found it, and called the garage on his mobile.

'Patel's Garage. How can I help you?'

'You'll probably remember the Mark 2 you fixed for me?'

'Oh, yes, Mr Reid,' chirped the Indian voice. 'How is it going?'

'It's not going at all. The engine fell out.'

'Oh dear…'

'Completely. It's sitting in the middle of the road.'

'That's bad.'

'I paid you a hundred and eighty dollars to fix it.'

'That's no problem. I'll fix it. Where are you?'

Malcolm looked at the nearest house. 'Outside twenty-seven Lachlan Crescent in Woolloomooloo.'

'I know where you are. I can't come right away. Just leave the car where it is and I'll come and collect it.'

'What do you mean, leave it there? The engine fell out, and it's sitting in the middle of the road. How the hell can I do anything else but leave it where it is?'

'Now, don't get excited. Just take the ignition out and put it under the clutch pedal. I'll be there in less than an hour.'

'All right. Call me when it's ready.'

'Yes, Mr Reid.'

Malcolm switched off his mobile, and stopped the first taxi passing by. He was lucky that the road was popular with taxi drivers as a short cut to Redfern.

Chapter Thirty-two

The first thing Malcolm had to do was to find out who owned the paintings. He called Paul McDonald a number of times, but there was still no answer. He got on the Web to do some research and after a while, he found out that Bayview Marina Pty was owned by Palm Beach Properties, part of the Woollahra Real Estate Investment Pty. They were a subsidiary of City Finance, which belonged to the Amalgamated Industries Group, one of Ralph Penders' better-known companies. That was as far as he got; there was nothing else on the Web that interested him.

He called Philippa next. The houseboy answered the telephone and told him that she was at the Paddington Galleries.

The telephone rang. His car was ready for collection. He took a taxi to Patel's Garage, just off Parramatta Road.

The Jag was ready and looked as good as ever. There was no sign of any damage. Malcolm walked around his car pretending to know what he was doing. He kicked the tyres for good measure; he had often seen second-hand car dealers doing that.

'The tyres are fine,' said the Indian mechanic. 'No problem there, Mr Reid.'

'Is it going to cost me any more?'

'No. Just the standard call-out charge.'

'And how much is that?'

'Seventy dollars. That's all. The rest is on the house.'

'Thanks a lot. I've given you a hundred and eighty dollars already. I thought you'd fixed the problem.'

'Yes, I fixed the problem. I got you a new set of rockers.'

'If you say so,' said Malcolm.

The mechanic picked up a small square box from a nearby work bench and handed it over to Malcolm.

'I've found this under your battery. It must have been there before, but I didn't spot it.'

'What on earth is that?'

'I think it's a radio transmitter. It was wired up to your battery.'

'Why?'

'For the power, for the electric power.'

'And what is a transmitter doing in my engine?'

'What, indeed?'

'I didn't put it there,' said Malcolm.

'Well, somebody did, Mr Reid.'

'And why would anybody want to do that?'

'To track your movements.'

'Well, thank you, Mr Patel,' said Malcolm.

'I'm not Patel. That's my father-in-law. I am Gopal.'

'Well, thank you, Mr Gopal,' said Malcolm.

He got into the Jag, and looked for the ignition key. The mechanic was dangling it in front of him.

'You're forgetting something,' he said.

'The seventy dollars,' said Malcolm, and handed over the money.

★

Robyn sat facing Penders in his office. It was the first time she had been invited into the inner sanctum of the business empire. She was wondering why she'd been summoned. She did not have to wait for long, because Penders wasted no time on preliminaries.

'I'm really disappointed with you, Robyn,' he said. 'You shouldn't have done that deal with Sandak, considering that I paid for all the development.'

'But he paid you back with a fifty per cent premium. You've done well out of it, Mr Penders.'

'It's the principle of the thing.'

'So? What do you want me to do?'

'Just don't do it again,' said Penders smiling. 'How would you fancy running Media International?'

'Media International? That's Elmer Sandak's outfit…'

'No, it's mine… I bought it this morning. So, how about it?'

'What's the catch?'

'There's no catch, but I'd like you to make it up with Malcolm.'

'I can't refuse, Mr Penders. It would certainly solve my money problems. I'm close to losing my glorious home…'

'What about Malcolm?'

'And I've grown fond of Malcolm, in a maternal sort of way.'

'Really?'

'Really. I know he is much older than I am.'

'There's just one other thing,' interrupted Penders. 'I don't know what Malcolm really thinks about the Russell Collection. Find out, and let me know. I'm sure I can rely on you being discreet.'

'Absolutely.'

★

Malcolm parked his Jag outside the Paddington Gallery. The place was locked up; a 'Closed' sign hung on the door. He looked inside to see if there was anybody about, but the gallery was empty. Malcolm rang the bell and knocked on the door.

Philippa let him in. She looked upset.

'Isn't it terrible, about Mac?'

'What is terrible?' asked Malcolm.

'He's dead. I thought you knew.'

'No. I tried to telephone him… When did he die?'

'I found the body yesterday morning.'

'That must have been awful for you,' Malcolm sympathised.

'He was a diabetic, you know. I'm told he's taken the wrong dose of insulin. I can't understand how.'

Philippa fell silent. Malcolm wanted to comfort her, but did not know what to do.

'What did you want, Malcolm, anyhow?'

'This is not the time…'

'Life must go on. You said you wanted to talk to Mac. What about? Perhaps I can help.'

'I've found the Russell Collection,' said Malcolm.

'Which Russell Collection?' asked Philippa, but she was not in the least interested.

'The thirty-eight missing paintings, but they are not Russell's work. He had been collecting canvases from his friends. Every Impressionist is represented.'

Malcolm reached into his pocket and handed Philippa a list of the paintings. She read it with mounting excitement.

'Mac would have been thrilled,' she said. 'Where did you find them, Malcolm?'

'In a boatyard on Pittwater Road. Bayview Marina. They were inside the hull of the yacht that Russell built.'

'Bayview Marina? I think that's one of Ralph's companies.'

'I know,' said Malcolm. 'A subsidiary of City Finance, which belongs to your husband.'

'What a pity that Mac isn't here. He would have been pleased. This is the find of the century, Malcolm! Does Ralph know?'

'You are the first person who knows, Philippa. I had to tell somebody – that's why I wanted to see Mac. I suppose you're in charge of the gallery now.'

'I suppose so,' she agreed. 'Mac and Ralph are partners – I mean, were. It would be great to show the collection here, don't you think?'

'Indeed. As a memorial tribute to Paul McDonald.'

'Exactly,' said Philippa. 'I was so miserable all morning, but this cheers me up, Malcolm. What wonderful news!'

'I suppose the paintings belong to your husband now.'

'Perhaps, but it doesn't matter whom they belong to. Just imagine, thirty-eight paintings from the Impressionist masters…'

'Perhaps you should tell the media about it,' said Malcolm.

'I'd be delighted,' she said and hugged him.

'I'll let you get on with it,' said Malcolm. 'I shall start lecturing tomorrow, and I have to get on with my preparations.'

'See you later,' said Philippa, walking him to the door.

'Yes, see you later.'

Malcolm walked out of the gallery, got back in his car and set off towards Redfern. He hoped that the paintings would not belong to Ralph Penders, but to the Russell family. It would be the ultimate irony of fate if the collection should belong to the man in Australia who needed the money least. However, Malcolm agreed with Philippa that the Russell Collection should be shown at the Paddington Galleries.

He parked the Jag outside his home in its usual spot. He settled down to work with the television on, but without the sound. He put a Cannonball Adderly CD on his stereo full blast.

Malcolm did not want to think of Robyn, Jamie, Ralph Penders, or John Peter Russell and his friends. He had to prepare some papers for a lecture on Structuralist literary criticism. That was something he should have done weeks ago.

He was well into his notes when an item on the television caught his attention. He turned up the sound as the images of Doug and Tony flashed onto the screen. They were both wearing uniforms.

Malcolm turned down the jazz on the stereo and increased the volume on the television. He listened to the reporter's voice with interest.

'The bodies of the two men involved in the accident at The Spit last night have now been identified. They were Douglas Hutchinson and Anthony Moreno. Both men worked for Intercity Security Pty. They were married with young families.'

Then the pictures on the television screen changed to a film of the accident. Not a lot was to be seen; only the burnt-out shell of a Holden station wagon.

'They were off duty,' continued the reporter, 'when their car caught fire and crashed. No other motorists were involved. It is believed they died instantaneously. Early police reports indicate brakes failure, and a further investigation of the cause of the accident is under way.'

The television changed to a different news item, and Malcolm switched it off. He had to think clearly. Seeing both men in those uniforms had sparked off an idea.

'Elementary, dear Malcolm,' he yelled at the top of his voice. 'I couldn't see the tree from the woods!'

It was a blinding revelation. Malcolm had discovered the most daring act of forgery and deception yet. Just by thinking laterally. The who and the why was no problem. It was Ralph Penders, because he was greedy. Rich people are greedy, and to be as rich as Penders, they also had to be criminals. All great fortunes have always been based on some act of criminality, morally at least, he reflected.

The 'how' was a little more complex. Malcolm's scenario was that Penders must have discovered that some of the watercolours Philippa was buying from Paul McDonald were fakes. Penders said nothing to Philippa, but contacted the forger, and commissioned the Russell Collection for himself. Jamie de Selway was the forger, and once his work was done he was murdered by Carlo Bellini.

To cover his tracks, Penders murdered Bellini, or had him murdered. Paul McDonald was not involved in the scheme, because he had been looking for the missing thirty-eight paintings in the belief that they were Russell's own work. Penders might have frightened him about the fake watercolours, but that was a side issue now, because McDonald was also dead – probably murdered.

He wondered if Robyn and Philippa were accomplices, but Malcolm doubted that Penders could trust anybody, even his own wife. If they had a part to play in the scheme, they were used without them realising it.

The person used to best advantage was Malcolm himself. He had discovered the paintings. Stumbling over them accidentally would provide the perfect proof to their authenticity.

Even the most ingenious scriptwriter could not have dreamed up a better way. When Penders learned that Malcolm was working on the Russell script, he decided to use him. Russell's diaries were given to him to encourage him to look for the missing paintings, and the shipping manifest was carefully planted for him to find in the Château de l'Anglais. It was an inspired act of improvisation by Penders, because Jamie must have been forging the paintings for years. The Russell diaries were also fakes. Malcolm had underestimated Jamie, for he was a great literary talent to write so convincingly of the period. Some of Russell's correspondence and even the shipping manifest were forged. It was a well-planned and elaborate swindle. But it had to be. The key ingredients must have been in place for a long time, waiting for the right opportunity to break the news. Malcolm's arrival in Sydney was an unexpected bonus, and Penders made good use of it.

The only miscalculation was Sergeant Costello giving him Jamie's books on art forgery, but Penders could not foresee that. It did not make much difference to the overall plan. Malcolm realised that Penders' minders must have followed him and Robyn everywhere, and knew their every move, providing Penders with the information required for manipulating him. It was all fiendishly clever.

Knowing it was one thing; proving it was something else. With Jamie de Selway, Carlo Bellini, Douglas Hutchinson, Tony Moreno and Paul McDonald all dead, there was not a shred of evidence to support Malcolm's theory. He poured himself a large glass of Château Poolowanna brandy to help him think.

Chapter Thirty-three

Malcolm decided that a desperate situation needed a desperate solution, and picked up the telephone. He dialled a number he had never thought that he would use.

'Paddington Police Station,' said a male voice.

'Sergeant Costello, please,' said Malcolm.

'He's not available…'

'Where is he?'

'Sergeant Costello is dead. Died of a heart attack last night. I'll put you through to Sergeant Farrell.'

Malcolm put the telephone down. At least one of the questions he was pondering over was answered. Trying to prove his conspiracy theory was not a very good idea. Not if he wanted to live. He remembered Mac telling him that he wanted to live.

Penders must have invested a considerable amount of time and money in his scheme; he was going to protect his investment. He had murdered the five key witnesses already; six, counting Sergeant Costello. He may be the killer himself, or he may have had them murdered; either way, he would not hesitate to kill again if he had to.

Malcolm's best plan for survival would be to play the innocent. He had to believe in the authenticity of the Russell Collection, and had to support Penders in every possible way. His life depended on acting the part allocated to him by Penders; and above all, he must not let on to anybody that he had any doubts about the authenticity of the thirty-eight paintings.

Malcolm sat quietly, sweating. He felt cold all of a sudden in the middle of a hot summer's day. It was not a game, but a matter of life and death: his life. He could not help admiring the nerve of the man. It was the perfect crime, and he was going to get away with it. And Malcolm would help him, though every atom in his body wanted to fight Penders. Malcolm was sad that the diaries were forgeries, because through them he'd come to love John Peter Russell.

Jamie was a good writer... or was it Penders? he asked himself.

He was never going to find out. Even the choice of the thirty-eight paintings had a touch of genius about it. Every one was on the painter's favourite theme, well documented with drawings, sketches and studies. Another version of a popular painting made it credible. It was the perfect way to establish the collection's provenance.

A thought struck Malcolm. Jamie's books were full of these references. He got up from his chair to check the shipping manifest against the books. Only they were not there any more. All the books Jamie left to Malcolm were gone. Nothing else was missing from the flat, only the books. That's why Sergeant Costello went to see Penders, Malcolm realised. It all fitted together like a jigsaw puzzle.

His thoughts raced about in his head like a Chinese dragon chasing its tail, but there was no way out, other than playing the role Penders had chosen for him. 'And you'd better give an Oscar-winning performance, Malcolm,' he said to himself. 'Because your life depends on it.'

He was interrupted by the telephone ringing.

'Yes?' asked Malcolm.

'It's Robyn. How are you?'

'Don't tell me you care.'

'I care very much. I feel bad about last night, and I'd like to make it up to you. Why don't you come over?'

Malcolm hesitated for a while before answering. Was Robyn in the know? he asked himself. Perhaps that was just another thing he would never find out.

'Sure, I'll see you this evening. What time?'

'Why not now?'

'I'm busy. I'm starting lecturing tomorrow. I'll see you this evening, if that's all right?'

'Come at eight,' said Robyn.

★

The dining table was laid for two. A couple of lit candles flickered in the dark. Robyn was pottering about in the kitchen when Malcolm arrived with a bunch of roses in his hand.

'Honestly, you and your flowers…'

Robyn threw the flowers into a vase, and embraced Malcolm hungrily. He was surprised, but responded to her advances. They rushed into the bedroom, shedding their clothes on the way. There were no explanations, there was nothing spoken; they just made love like there was no tomorrow.

They both lay in bed, physically exhausted. Malcolm was the first one to speak.

'I shall never understand women.'

'Just like I shall never understand men,' replied Robyn.

'Why? I'm easy to understand.'

'That's what you think, Malcolm. Why didn't you tell me last night that you'd found the paintings?'

'I was going to.'

'But you didn't. I found out about it listening to the radio. It was our baby, remember?'

'It was for a while,' said Malcolm. 'It's not our baby any more.'

'Whose baby is it, then?'

'Philippa thinks the paintings belong to Ralph Penders. She is probably right. We shall soon find out. Not that he needs the money, but as the Bible says, to those who have shall be given.'

'So, what are they worth?' asked Robyn.

'Are you buying or selling?'

'Stop farting around; how much?'

'You can't put a price on them. This is the art find of the century. It's priceless. It could bankrupt even the Getty Museum.'

'Come on, how much?'

'Five hundred million dollars at least.'

'A cool half a billion dollars! I wonder what our percentage is going to be?'

'Our percentage?' asked Malcolm. 'What for?'

'For finding them. You know, the finder's fee.'

'Nobody asked us to find them. And I'm sorry to point out, Robyn, but you had nothing to do with the finding. If anybody is entitled to a finder's fee, that's me, but I am not expecting anything.'

'You'll get something,' she said.

'But why? Perhaps if they were stolen, and I were an insurance investigator, only then.'

'All right – how much would you get then?'

'Ten per cent is the going rate, I believe. Some people steal to order, to collect just that, but I don't see how this relates to me.'

'So, you're not entitled to anything?'

'Exactly.'

'Half a billion dollars,' said Robyn. 'But are they for real?'

'I think so. They looked genuine to me. They're not forgeries, if that's what you're driving at.'

'They could be.'

'Nobody would have the nerve to forge a collection like this, Robyn. It's just not on.'

'Why not?'

'It's a gut feeling, Robyn,' said Malcolm, as convincingly as he could manage. 'I'm sure art experts will agree.'

'But you can't prove a thing with an Impressionist painting,' said Robyn, trying to tempt Malcolm into an indiscretion. 'I thought it was a matter of expert opinion. There are no scientific tests available for such recent works.'

'That's not strictly true,' replied Malcolm. 'There's a lot you can do. Though most of the mass-produced paints used today were also available then, the Prussian blue, zinc white and sepia were made by a different chemical process. You can test for those, and you can test the canvas itself. There are lots of little things you can test for.'

'You seem to know a lot about all this.'

'Absolutely. I did a lot of research for your script, remember?'

'Yes, of course you did.'

'The work of these painters is so well documented that once the preparatory work is allocated to each painting, there won't be any question about their authenticity.'

'And what's that in English?'

'Painters make drawings, sketches and smaller versions of their paintings before they start on a larger canvas.'

'So, if you were a master forger, this is the kind of collection you'd come up with?' asked Robyn provocatively.

'Yes, if you had the bloody nerve, yes. But don't talk to me about forgery. It's bad form, Robyn.'

Penders was in bed when the telephone rang on his confidential line. Only a few knew the number. Philippa was washing her face in the adjoining bathroom. She stopped and listened to the conversation. It was not her nature to spy on her husband, but she was curious who the late caller was. She could only hear Penders' voice, and she soon gave up on finding out.

'Ralph Penders…'

'I hope I'm not disturbing you calling you so late,' said Robyn.

'You're not disturbing me. What is it?'

'I've just seen Malcolm.'

'Good. What does he think about the paintings?'

'He thinks they are genuine.'

'Good. Anything else?'

'No, but I'm worried about him.'

'You're worried about what?'

'Malcolm thinks he's a great lateral thinker,' said Robyn. 'But I think he is barking mad. I can't trust him as far as I can throw him.'

Philippa was about to enter the room, but she stopped by the half-open door and listened to what Penders said.

'I'm glad you called me, Robyn. Don't worry about Malcolm. Leave it to me, I'll take care of him. There's nothing you need to do. I'll talk to you later.'

Philippa joined her husband in bed.

'Who was that?' she asked.

'Business. Nothing to concern yourself with.'

★

Dozens of armed security guards and an army of workmen descended on the quiet street in the heart of Paddington. Malcolm had to wait until they found his name on a list of people invited to the press conference before they allowed him to park his Jag in the car park at the back of the gallery. He left the car by one of the windows; he intended to keep an eye on it.

He fought his way through a thronging crowd of journalists,

photographers, television crews and security guards, and walked inside. The gallery was packed to the rafters with the media. All the paintings of the Russell Collection had been hung on the walls. It was an impressive show.

Philippa met Malcolm, and guided him through the crowd.

'Ralph wants to have a word before you go on,' she said, then added in a quieter voice, 'and I must talk to you. It's important. Come and see me as soon as you've finished with Ralph.'

Philippa showed Malcolm into the office, and went back into the gallery. Somebody else wanted her.

'There you are, Malcolm,' said Penders.

'Hello, Mr Penders. I keep on pinching myself to make sure I'm not dreaming.'

'I know the feeling... Now, I talked to my lawyers. They tell me I owe you nothing, but my heartfelt thanks... However, you deserve more than that,' said Penders, handing Malcolm a cheque for one million dollars.

'One million dollars!' said Malcolm excitedly.

'Anything more would have been silly on my part, and anything less an insult to you.'

'I don't know what to say,' said Malcolm.

'How about, thank you?'

'Thank you, Mr Penders.'

'The television people want to talk to you,' said Penders as he showed Malcolm out of the office. 'You're the star attraction.'

'I think the paintings are,' said Malcolm.

'Well, they want an interview with you, anyway.'

Malcolm went back to the gallery and stood near the television crew who wanted to interview him. Standing directly in front of a van Gogh canvas, a young reporter was in full flood.

'This is the most exciting art story since the Mona Lisa was stolen from the Louvre. These paintings will force a re-evaluation of the entire art market. Art experts all around the world are still debating just how important the Russell Collection is...'

The mews was almost deserted as Penders opened the side door and stepped into the car park. There was a security guard at the entrance to the mews. He saluted Penders as a form of recognition. Penders waved back, then turned his back on the guard as he approached Malcolm's Jag in the car park.

Penders was wearing a pair of surgical rubber gloves. In one hand, he carried a small, brick-shaped object wrapped in a black plastic bag. He opened the Jag with a key, placed the plastic bag under the driver's seat, and then closed the door gently.

Penders smiled at the guard at the top of the mews, and then walked back inside the building.

Malcolm had noticed Penders in the car park, but made nothing of it. He was busy helping himself to a drink at the bar. Philippa grabbed him by the arm, and led him towards the main entrance.

'I've got to talk to you, Malcolm. Let's go outside…'

'What about the interview?'

'Sod the interview. This is really important,' she said.

They left the gallery and walked along the pavement towards the mews car park. Apart from a couple of security guards who knew who Philippa was, there was nobody about.

'So, what's so earth-shatteringly important then, Philippa?'

'I've overheard Ralph talking about you last night. Somebody called him quite late.'

'Robyn?'

'Yes.'

'The bitch,' said Malcolm. 'The 24-carat bitch.'

'Ralph said that he'd take care of you. I know he meant it, and I'm worried about you.'

'And I'm worried about me.'

They reached Malcolm's Jag. He was about to get in, but Philippa held him back and took the ignition key out of his hand.

'I'm coming with you. Let me drive. I've always wanted to drive a Mark 2 like this.'

'Why? It's a pile of junk, but you're welcome to try.'

Philippa got into the car, still talking.

'We must get away from him… Ralph is evil… I have so much to tell you about him, but we must get away… Ralph is dangerous…'

Philippa turned the ignition key. The car exploded instantly. The blast threw Malcolm in the air and to one side. The peace of the suburban street was shattered by the explosion. Malcolm picked himself up. He was badly bruised and cut, but still alive.

He looked at the remains of the car, then he remembered Penders standing next to the Jag. He must have planted the bomb that was meant to kill him. Why on earth would he have parted with a cheque for a million dollars? Malcolm was not meant to be alive to cash it in.

'*Why Philippa?*' he screamed out loud.

He moved towards the wreckage, but she was dead and there was nothing anybody could do to help her.

The fire from the explosion blew backwards with an unexpected force, and broke open the windows of the gallery overlooking the car park. The flames were sucked inside the building, and within seconds the paintings were engulfed in a raging inferno.

All the guards, reporters, and members of the television crews tumbled over each other trying to vacate the gallery through the front door. Amazingly, they all managed to get away safely.

Malcolm stepped back from the wreckage. He was still dazed by the explosion.

'Why Philippa?' he cried out again.

Penders was the only person left inside the room. Holding a fire extinguisher in his hand, he was trying to fight the inferno, but he lost the battle against the flames.

All the canvases were on fire. The oil paint flaked off them as the paintings burnt. Swirling shapes and forms were created by the raging fire and the loose paint fell on the floor, collecting in turbulent pools of impressionistic colours.

Penders looked demented as he got deeper and deeper into the flames. He was completely surrounded by impenetrable walls of fire on all sides. Soon he was consumed in a raging ball of fire.

Printed in the United Kingdom
by Lightning Source UK Ltd.
110673UKS00001B/7-21